A Day in the (Revised Edition)

Written by: Thomas G. Arndt

Chapter 1

The past isn't all its cracked up to be.

<u>Day 1</u>

There are things that always set us apart, even the smallest of thing. Like the beginning of a journey always starts with the first step, so can a life time that might have been. It is a shame when you are just another being that exists day to day, with the same rules and law that guide us all. They say it's a shame to live in the light, and yet be perfectly at peace to just sleep.

I am just a no body that lives to exist, and yet has an important part in the demise of many. That isn't entirely true though, I am a somebody, even though many wish I didn't exist. My name is Jonathan Edward Williamson, pretty fancy name for a dutch dock worker isn't it?

But that was a very long time ago now, plus as long as I've lived here I have primarily became and American. If you listen very closely you can still hear just a hint of an accent, but as they say, when in Rome do as the Romans would have you do. I guess that's whats the problem with my kind, they like to do what they like to do. Well I guess if they didn't though, I would be out of a job, even though that's about to change.

You see there are a group of these guys called enforcers, but we aren't like the comic book hero's. I guess you could say though we could inhabit the pages of a comic book though. What do they say again, we are that which nightmares are made of, and all that isn't known usually comes from the likes of us. Sounds spooky doesn't it, but if you met one of us, you'd be very disappointed.

I won't tell you something stupid like we rule the world, or we are what is the richest of the world. Well because we aren't. You see when it comes to vampires there is really nothing that can rule them. Well except maybe other supers, oh that's what we call all that's supernatural. Supers or some of the younger just call ourselves Sups. Then again like I have said we are those that nightmares are made of, I've seen it first hand.

Being a vampire though is a very lonely life, even though some paint us as almost normal. Maybe in some respects we are, even though I don't really see it. Let me show you what our world is like though. You see you are born into this world threw the blood, or as you can imagine the transfer of said liquid. After this it permeates your life forever, with the constant need to get and have it.

Even though it isn't true that you have to have a drink everyday, or that you must kill to obtain it. I won't lie to you though and tell you we don't kill for it, but we now have so many ways to get it we really don't have to. With all that is good though usually also comes with the bad, and even though they existed when I was born into this life or unlife as it maybe. There are thing that have also made our existence harder in the long run.

You see I wasn't made into what I am yesterday, it has been well over three centuries now. I wasn't brought into this world on my own accord thought either, I was forced into this existence. The man that made me wasn't a good man, as he just used me to escape the vampire authorities. To make good his escape he took me from my young family as he had no care of anything that existed around me. I think that may have been the last time I truly loved anyone, well except that that's part of the reason why I started this story.

With knowledge comes power, and my new master wanted to keep me as ignorant as possible. So I had no idea there were any other vampires until they caught up to him for his crimes. Even the creation of me was a crime, and in a sense that would have been the end of me to, if this hadn't been such a new land. I did return to the old world to find my family gone, and in this not only did he rob me of my life, he robbed me of what I cared for the most.

They say to everyone in our existence, that we are nothing if not civilized. That maybe true, but I've seen the most barbaric side of our unlives. I am nothing if not a plain man though, so like a plain man I want to see that which is right set right. This is how I got my job in a technical sense. I could explain this better, but in the simplest sense my job is to set right which isn't. So I destroy that which I am so as to set things right. I kill vampires.

Some might look at this as a hero, yet I have never felt heroic in my endeavors. Some may even say that I am truly evil, because I destroy that which is more evil then I am. In truth though if you think about it, we do what we must do to keep existing. That doesn't set us very far from just being another human, well that is if a human could do what a vampire could do. Then again I also think that makes us as neutral in our own psyche as a mere human is though.

You have to realize though, not all vampires are created the same. You see there are many kinds of vampire, breeds or species so to speak, even though I'm not sure that's even correct. It is said though there were thirteen original vampires, and that because of this there are also thirteen families, houses, or more like warring clans. I mean we aren't really warring so to speak, I guess it would be better to say we just don't get along that well.

Here's the real rub though. You have all these old guys from the old world, trying to control the unlives of every vampire. They use the titles of the old world to enforce these rules, then they bring their old game to the new world, where we really don't want to have anything to do with them. This cause a real void, and in this void things seem to grow out of that, which all existed in the old world first. Which means that us in the new world have to deal with it, along with the new in this free world.

Sounds like fun doesn't it, and now you know kind of whats going on in the new world. Then again I could talk politics for hours, and I don't want to bore you to death. Plus they lied to all of us, I mean I've counted and there has to be at least twenty two families. Of course my experience is tempered by the fact that I've lived almost my entire vampire unlife in the new world. Then again they do, do a few good things, like they've helped permeate the world with vampire false hoods so it makes it real hard to believe in vampires.

I think this is usually where we should start discussing the differences between reality and fantasy. The problem is I have to cover a lot of that in my story, so don't mind me if I don't do that. Plus if you think of all the differences, there is a fact that we are all the same in a way. The problem is when you are a young vampire its very hard to really see this truly, so it's easy to separate everyone in accordance to their family group.

Now I can tell you of one that I have, it's sort of a kind of insight, even though my family group aren't know for insight. You see I go places as I feel that it's the right thing to do, then I arrive and find out its usually worse then I even thought. It isn't always an easy thing, but many times I have left a city, and the vampire population is significantly lesser. So to say that anyone welcomes my entrance to a city would be truly stretching the truth.

Now I can tell you where I was coming from as it has no importance to the story until later. I had been in New Orleans and was on my way back to Los Angeles. Around Houston I felt the pull, so I made a turn toward Dallas, thinking that I would get a good contract there. To my surprised I felt the pull dragging me even past this city, I wasn't so sure about going to Kansas City. But that may have been wishful thinking, as I entered the next major city and felt I had been drawn there.

I can tell you that I was truly surprised as I passed threw Norman to Moore and it got heavier. This isn't an exact science as you can imagine, but I got close to the tall building of this small city. I knew the sun was coming up, so I set to find a place for the day. We in this world don't have much, but I had learned to use a band debit card just like everyone else. So I found a hole in the wall motel to sleep the day away in, and I moved in with the chair to lock the door.

Then as was the best way to do this, I removed all my clothes as I lay in the tub in the locked bathroom. I also place my weapons so as not to easily be disturbed. I'm sure the house maid would of screamed to see this dead man lying in the shower with a knife and gun across his body. For me though, when I was on the road it was the simplest way not to be disturbed.

Oh about the sun light, we can take limited amounts of direct sun light, even though we can't stay out there. Indirect sun light was much easier to take, even though it makes your skin crawl as well. The less sun you get the better off you are, but there's another reason for the tub though. The easiest time to injure us is when we are first getting up, so if you aren't where they think you should be. Well lets just say that makes you less dead.

I never could sleep long though, and after eight I was sure to be up, even if the sun were up. That just gave me extra time to do what needed to be done, like place my weapons on the toilet, and just turn on the water. In my time in the wilderness though I learned to enjoy cold bathes, and so that's how I normally washed myself up even now a days. I can tell you though I'm so happy that these modern places offer towels, it's bad enough to put anything wet in my bedroll.

They say vampires don't know the concept of money, well I sure do, as I looked at my three new shirts I had recently bought. I had bough a pale green one and had wore it already, so now I was looking at my yellow, red, and blue ones I had left. Finally I made my mind to go with the blue one, so I slipped it out of the wrapper and put it on. I undid my leather trousers so I could push the tails down into them. I did them back up and looked at my long hair, then grabbed my leather thong to tie it in a pony tail.

I sat on the toilet to put my boots on, I always like the feel of new tube socks. Once I had them on so far I liked to kick them on the rest of the way. Then I grabbed my pistol belts and placed them on, I had them set for two weapons, even though I usually only carried my Glock. With that I placed my Kukri knife in the back on my trousers, of course I would take it out when I drove. You don't know how uncomfortable it is to drive with a knife shoved up your butt.

    I then place everything else in my bedroll and rolled it up, well except for my coat. It was never wise to advertise what kind of weapons you were carrying. I place my little cooler and bedroll on the counter, I think they call my cooler a six pack cooler. Then I put on my leather coat, and looked at myself to see if anyone could easily see my weapons.

    Once I was satisfied no one could, I took my bedroll in one hand and my cooler in the other. Then I would make my way to the office and hand in my key, once this was done I went back to my car. I had to wonder where exactly would I actually look for this cities ruling council. Well there was no place better then starting with down town, I had to wonder if they would be receptive to the likes of me.

    So I opened my trunk and started to put my stuff away for the drive to the down town area. The whole time I moved to my car I couldn't help but feel like I was being watched. Now that's something that my family are very good at, it almost like perceiving when something isn't right. I guess you could call it like a sixth sense. I won't go there though, and many times its really nothing.

    You can imagine that I was already on a level of alert as I started what needed to be done. So I placed my bedroll down as I went to work on securing my cooler. With that I suddenly felt every hair on my body stand up on end. With inhuman speed that even the best vampires would be hard pressed to see. I moved in a blur as I pulled my knife out of it's place, and I was twirling around as the silver of my blade flashed against the last of the sun. I knew this would place me off balance and any vampire with an ounce of experience could defend against this move. This was the first sign of the inexperience of what I was trying to deal with. As I moved to my intended target, and within an instant the face registered in my mind.

I suddenly saw the face of an angelic choir boy, and with the sudden horror of what could be. I then used the strength I had, which could only be described as a herculean effort. As I tried to pull my blow as it passed dangerously close to the angelic creatures neck. I saw his eyes get huge as it registered in his mind what was happening. With an involuntary movement of his hands as they moved upwards. I saw my blade pass his neck as I followed threw, and the tip seemed to just barely hit his neck. I just knew that I had just killed an innocent as I moved to the final out come of my blow.

When I was able to finally recover from my move, I came back around to see exactly what I had done. With the speed I knew I had, I saw his hands completing the journey to his neck as I looked. This was the first sign that he wasn't what he seemed to be, as I saw only a slight weeping of blood on his neck. The second clear sign was with the power his hands hit his throat it should of caused more bleeding, but nothing. I knew though he was clearly the lucky one here, as my swing would of even separated a vampires head from his body. You have to know that it isn't easy to take a head off, but when your business is just that you become an expert.

I could see he had been traumatized by my action, as I moved close to look at what I had done to him. I could also see how inexperienced he was, when he didn't stop me at looking at the damage I had just done. Most normal people would have at least tried to resist a little bit, but this was also my first sure sign that he was a vampire. I saw that his wound was already healing, even though not as fast as a normal vampire. A human by at least this time would have been becoming faint from blood lose also. We all have good hearing though also, so I listened for his heartbeat. A humans heart is easy to hear, whereas a vampires heartbeat can barely be heard.

I then stated the obvious, "Good thing you're a vampire, That blow would of killed any human."

I really didn't have much time to really make small talk, as I was surprised by another voice. This one that was next to me said,

"Good thing too..." I cut off what was said to explain what I did next as he spoke. You see I had put my knife away already, and I had my hands up away from my body, so I didn't have the time to retrieve it again. But I was already moving at speed to attack whatever just spoke. So instead I went for a hard punch, and I'm sure it would have really hurt anyone else. First though, he was a little to far away for a normal punch, so that was in his favor. Secondly he moved with an uncanny agility that only certain vampires have. And finally his statement kind of helped me pull my blow. As he went on, "he's one of our oldest members. It woo, what the hell!"

The ending of his statement though also told me I had completely taken him by surprise. I looked him straight in the eyes as he moved easily to a battle stance. I then caught the slight glint of a yellow flash in his eyes, as a certain kind of anger seemed to flash over him. I spoke scolding to him then as I said, "You should never sneak up on an elder kid! That could of gotten you killed!"

"Hey ass whip you tried to hit me! I should kick your ass, you ass hole!"

I have to give it to this kid, he's got balls. Plus he really showed a good aptitude for the fight. That narrowed down my selection of what family he came from, with the eyes that even narrowed it down even more. So I thought about just how far I could actually push him. I then said what I did with the special additive at the end to see what it would bring. As I said, "You might find that very difficult, Son."

Man he was really one of his family as his anger mounted, as he spit out, "Son! I got your son, right..."

But his friend then cut him off with, "Billy we aren't here for that! We need to talk to him. We need his help dude. You aren't helping are cause if you go to killing him now."

He was so hot under his collar, but his friend had done it. So the kid that was obviously called Billy said, "But Arty? He tried to hurt me dude?"

I really wanted to laugh or chuckle, something. I did know though it was probably better not with these two. I then took in the two of them as I said, "Damn you two really are green, aren't you? One of our most basic rules when meeting a new one of our kind, is never, and I mean never ever tell them your name until you know them."

The one I know knew as Arty then said, "That's what I mean mister. We don't know shit about what it means to be a vampire."

I couldn't believe these two. So I knew I had to school them on this, "Ok that wasn't the first rule. The first actual rule is to never talk about being what we are, at all, especially in public. I mean what do you really want? Would you want an elder to just put you down? Where in the heck are your elder's in fact?"

Arty replied, "We don't know where they are. All we know is they went out to check something and never came back. There's a long story behind that, and it might take too long to explain it right now. So do you have time to talk somewhere else?"

I had to look the two of them in disbelief, as I couldn't believe what they were asking of me. I turned to the trunk of my car as I said, "You have until I get this cooler strapped down."

I don't know why I did what I did next though. I decided to take my time as I was strapping down my cooler. Arty started off with, "Well the plain and simple truth is we need your help. Our elders turned most of us recently for some unknown reason. Even though I'm the oldest I barely know how to be what we are, or should be at least. Billy is just a little younger than me. So in a sense we are the best of our kind we actually know, well until we met you. I can tell you that the only reason we're here, I had this vision and saw two ways this conversation could turn out. One was really bad unless I was really honest. The other of course you may have figured out, it was better. Again if I were real with you about our problem, it even had two more outcomes. I'm hoping for the real good one though. So I have no idea what you're thinking of us right now. But I surely hope this is coming out in a good way."

I had my cooler secure, and slammed the trunk before turning around and saying. "Well I can see that you're able to learn, that's a plus. So you said you saw this in a vision. Are you like saying in a dream or you had an actual vision?"

He shook his head as he replied. "I don't really know. I think you could call it a vision. Even though in a sense it was sort of like a dream too."

I had to ask, "Did this vision, slash dream tell you anything else?"

He simply replied, "Yeah, kind of."

"Well then if it told you to be completely honest. Don't you think you should tell me that as well?"

"Ok, ok. But this is the part I'm not really sure about. You see if this doesn't go well, I see us all dying a really horrible death, or deaths I should say. You see some of us seemed to be eaten, and then two of us seem to be flayed. I can't really say what happens to Billy though. I have no clue what that was that I saw, and I'm not sure he died either."

Ok my mind was screaming more four letter words than I care to write right now. I had a feeling I knew exactly what kind of creature he may have been talking about. Nevertheless, in my job description it was to face down evil things like this. So I acted with my coolest intent as I asked, "So as you've inferred and I have perceived from your story, that there are more of you?"

He looked at me with one eyebrow raised. Then he asked me the obvious question, "Is this some kind of test? You know to see if I'll tell you before you say yes or whatever?"

I had to smile at him, as I saw him catching on so quickly. But I had to tell him the truth, "No. You already gave that tidbit away. At least though you're beginning to think correctly. I have to know though to see what I'm up against if I do decide to help you out."

Billy then said. "I don't know about this Arty?"

Arty then said. "Billy we have to trust him. I mean I don't know about you? But I think I want to live."

I then interjected, "Billy it's good that you're being suspicious about me. But I do have to know. I mean would you just run without knowing what's in front of you?"

He shook his head no as Arty replied, "There's a total of six of us."

With this I saw that it was going to be a bit difficult to train them, but six wasn't undoable. At least it would of sort of give us a numbers edge, and that was a good thing if my suspicions were correct about this city. Plus if they hadn't made any headway, I could get this done with ease, and just be on my way. I had no real pending contracts though, so I figured I could help them out for a bit. So I finally said, "I guess I could give you all a few pointers. But if a contract comes up, I have to leave immediately."

With this Arty instantly yelled, "ROAD TRIP! I GET SHOTGUN!"

Chapter 2

They say old things can learn new trick, I wonder?

I almost busted out laughing when I heard that, but I was able to stifle it with a cough. I think Billy knew that I was covering up a laugh, but he didn't say anything. I just have to believe that he may have been trying not to laugh himself. Anyways this is a great place to compare the two boys. As blond as Arty's hair was as dark brown as Billy's was. Both the boys looked unkept, even though of the two I would say Arty was the best dressed. He only wore a tank top in this fall weather, not that actually mattered that much to us. Billy had on a jacket and that was the best look. Even though we couldn't feel the chill, it was better to appear we did.

We had all piled into my old 1969 Chrysler 300, and I had just turned it over. When I half turned around, so they could both see me. I then asked, "Ok where are we going from here?"

Billy leaned over the seat and replied. "Just go down here till you get to the freeway on ramp. You should be heading north. Then when you get to the I-40 exchange go east, but it's not really that far. Look for MLK then head north again. Once you go under one bridge then just barely past the over pass…"

I interrupted him with, "What's an MLK?"

Arty replied at once, "That's Martin Luther King avenue, but really one way is Eastern. If you see an Eastern sign, you've gone the wrong way."

Billy then smiled and said, "Oh yeah, my bad. Well anyways just look for an old broken gate. Once we go down to the bottom, of the little drive you see where you have to move. But it's better if we tell you get there, so you can see what I mean."

So I set my car into gear, and drove to the place with the broken gate. As soon as I saw that it was almost completely hidden by scrub, I can tell you I had a bad feeling about this. Then I got to the bottom, hoping that we weren't headed for the railroad tracks that were there. I was mistaken again. I looked around and saw that the surroundings, and I thought to myself, maybe this wasn't that bad. We back tracked to the bridge we went over, but when we got past it, I saw that it was even worse then I thought. Open fields and old oil derrick's, it wasn't open as far as the eye could see, but close enough for government work. They directed me to park in an old loading dock. That was the first only real thing I felt good about.

Once we climbed out of the short drive to the loading dock where we had parked. I could see there was no straightforward way to get to my car. Arty ran up the hill and Billy and I just walked. I couldn't help notice that the two of them were very enthusiastic to show me what they could do. As we walked to the old iron door that was peeling paint and rusted. I could see that there wasn't really anyway to escape this building without having subject yourself to some kind of attack. I already knew things had to be changed. Arty waited by the door for us, and as we got just feet away he started to knock with his fist, and kick with his foot. All I could do was shake my head, as we moved closer to the door. This was telling me all too well just how green these kids really were. I had to hope they had better trained kids inside at least, even though I knew better. As I also knew that these two were most likely their best.

Then I had to let out a big sigh, as a kid that had greasy hair like he was straight out of the 50's. Can you believe he actually just poked his head out to find out who was there. I knew if I had been a bad guy, this would have been my chance to take has head. Not to say that I would have used the front door actually. With all the holes in the building I could have just walked directly in any of them instead. Then Arty directed me to follow him, so I did as he said. Well if I hadn't got them at the doorway, at least this hallway was a good sign. I didn't know how they made it so dark until I got to the end. I think they must've gotten every cardboard box, and crate they could find to make the hallway. It was a good idea, if somewhat of a flimsy defense, to say the least.

I didn't have much time to really focus on that though, As I saw two young girls were moving about, trying to help a very large vampire who had a stomach wound. There must have been water under the floor, as one move back and forth wetting rags. The other one seemed to be trying to get the blood to stop, as she was wiping where the blood was coming from. That is when I noticed a strange thing about her hair, her hands looked almost as red as her hair did. In truth though, this was a simple thing to fix for vampires. So I looked to the two young guys I had walked in with. With a quick decision that Billy would probably be my best choice. I took my keys and said. "Run to my car Billy, and get the cooler out of my trunk. Be careful, but make you move as fast as you can."

I held out the proper key to show him, with that I threw it to him, and he nimbly plucked it out of the air as I expected him to. That done I turned back to the girls and instructed the red headed one, "Wad up a rag, and place it over the wound. Then place the next rag over top of that. You? " Then I pointed at the big guy and went on, "Use both hands and press down hard no matter how much it hurts." I then turned back to Arty and continued, "As soon as Billy gets back you grab one of the cups, and give it to him. You may have to open it to help him out." Looking back at the big guy I then added, "Then drink all of it. Don't worry about it whether or not you'll like it. Once you taste it, you'll want to have more, I can assure you of that."

The only boy that I hadn't really talked to me. Just seemed to snort at this, as all seemed to just do what I told them. Billy seconds later just came running in, Arty then went straight into the cooler. Billy looked straight at me, so I simply nodded my head. The red headed girl had done all I had told her. The largest, and possibly the only adult in the group, did what I had told him to, as he drank the cup of blood. I could tell you that if I hadn't been told they were newly formed vampires though, I wouldn't have been able to tell any of them were one of our kind. I don't know how to describe it, but once you reach about five year mark, you acquire a certain smell. None of these guys had it at all.

Finally the guy that looked like he would be more at home in the 50's spoke, "I don't know why you're all listening to this guy. As far as we all know. He could be in league with those guys that have been trying to kill us."

I was about to speak to what he had said, when Billy beat me to it. "Dude both Arty and I saw him move. He is so damn fast. If he wanted to kill us, we would probably be just dead."

"So you thought it was safer to bring him here?! Real good decision dude!"

Arty then spoke up, "Dude I had one of my vision. Well two technically. One we talked to him and he just killed me and Billy. But the other one showed that he could really help to us."

"You and your damned visions. Did you think about what may have happened if you just didn't talk to him at all?"

"Yeah ass whip, I did. What I saw wasn't a pretty sight. Dude you really don't want to know what I saw, it was terrible. I can say it was far worse than the other two visions."

Then the very pretty, and very young blond girl spoke in a low voice. But as a vampire we can hear a lot better then most humans, "Like it did Jimmy any good."

I knew I should just jump in right here, but Billy spoke as if he just wanted to really hurt her. "You know the only reason he died, was because he didn't listen to what Arty said. No way did he tell him to go that way, he did that all on his own."

The girl with the red hair then blasted him, "He wouldn't have been there at all! If he hadn't been trying to avoid what Arty said! He may not have been the direct cause of it! But he had just as much to do with what happened!"

The big guy then said, "Caty we've all made mistakes. Now you have to let it go, or we'll be at each others throats."

The red head girl seemed to flash at him, as she snorted before she spoke directly at him. "Yeah I guess you got that right. If anyone knows how to make mistakes, you sure do."

Finally the very young blond girl almost screamed and cried at the same time. Even though I suspected that it was sort of her intent, "SHUT IT! JUST SHUT THE HELL UP! WE HAVE TO FIGURE OUT HOW TO PULL OURSELVES TOGETHER!"

By this time, I had moved to a box that looked like it maybe a table, So I was just sitting down as the kid with the greasy hair said, "I still don't think we should trust this guy."

I had to shake my head as I looked at him with my replied, "I can tell you though. That in a sense, you're right. Just like Billy was right, in his assumption that if I wanted you dead, you'd be that way. But from what I'm seeing, all I would of had to do, is wait until all of you just self-destruct. It may be a good thing I told your two friends I would help. I will say you may need more help then I was prepared to give you though."

"Then why are you even here?"

"Well to tell you the truth. I beginning to wonder that myself. I guess you could say, I'm a sucker for lost causes."

I think both Billy and Arty were a little surprised by what I said. It seemed as if they both asked, "So are you going to help us?"

I nodded my head as I replied, "I guess that's what that means. Well first order of business is to get out of this death trap. I don't know if you fathom what kind of mess you guys are in, but this is one of the worst places you could of used as a hide out."

The greasy kid was the first one to ask. "Why's that?"

"Well you don't see much in these areas in general, because its a prefect entrance point. First it's too out of the way for common traffic, which also means it's easy to hide things, bad things. You never know when you're going to need a fast meal, or an easy hiding place. I think the worst problem of being here is that its such an exposed area, and attracts the worst kind of company. We maybe the proverbial things that go bump in the night, but we aren't the only things. There are worse things you really don't want to run into, things that may even make the Devil look like a good guy." I then took in all their faces, as I sighed I asked. "Let me know your names, and anything you may have noticed strange about you? If I got Arty right, you are all young vampires. So you can tell me the age as a vampire if you really like to, but I'm not sure it will be relevant." I then looked at both Arty and Billy, "I may have figured out already your families you two belong too. So just tell anything you haven't told me since we met, anything that you might feel is relevant also."

I figure Billy would go first again, but instead Arty took the bull by the horns. "You already know my name, and I guess I'll go first. Oh and you know about my visions, even though I'm not sure that's what they should be called…"

I interrupted him with, "If I'm right about your kind, they call it insight not visions."

"Ok that sounds better. There was this one time I was caught dead to rights, by these guys. I don't know exactly what happened. I mean he walked right up to me, but I don't think he could even see me. Well anyways, other then that I don't think I have anything else really to say. Oh except I had just turned sixteen when I was made, I mean turned. That was just barely over three months ago now."

I then said, "Good, good Arty. Billy your turn, then when he's done, someone just pick it up right behind him."

Billy then answered, "Ok I'm not like Arty at all. I seem to be able to do things when I get angry. Different then you Caty though, but kind of along the same lines. Plus I seem to be able to see things too.

Not like you Arty, but it seems like I can see the heat coming off things. You know kind of like their heat signature or something. Oh and even though we don't use them my name its actually William." He looked at Arty as if he were looking for permission, and Arty nodded his head. So he then went on, "Arty's real name is Archibald. He really hates it so we just call him Arty. Oh he also hates Archie too mister. Oh I'm older then Arty, but younger as a vamp, even though I'm sixteen too."

"Wow Billy we kind of have something in common. You see my last name is Williamson, and I don't like my first names either Arty. You see my mother named me Jonathan. I don't like the shortened down name of Jonah, but John will be cool with me. I'll tell you more about myself as we move on. So who's next?"

The girl with the red hair stood up and started with, "Well I guess that should be me since you already know my name. My real name is Cathrinia, before you ask, yeah I hate it too. My dad called me his wild child, and he called my little sister his babygirl, yeah I have problems with that also. But as angry as it makes me, I guess that's why this life is good for me. I do have to say that I really love how strong I am too. Today though, when we couldn't find Billy and Arty Joe anywhere, and I went out to look for them. That's when I may have found another thing to, what I found out is I can really run fast."

I smiled at her and as I looked the big guy, I asked, "Are you Joe?"

He replied, "Joseph, but everyone calls me Joe."

"You'll be next then, and Caty you seem like we may actually come from the same house. Now remember this is just my preliminary judgment, I will make a farther one as I get to know you. I do think this will be a good start for us though. Now you Joe."

He cleared his throat as he began to speak, "Ok you all know me, and how I am. I seemed to have this kind of level headedness about things. I can kind of see things too, but no where like Billy. I guess you could say I can see things that most can't see, kind of like Pepper there." He moved his head toward the blonde as he continued, "But she seems to be way better at it then me. Like Caty, I would have never known I had any other powers until today. That guy that did this to me, he had me dead to rights, and I knew I was dead. Then something seemed to happen inside me, I can't explain what though. But the guys eye's got really big, like he was really scared of something. With that I saw smoke, and he just turned black. He was frozen in place, and I was wondering why he didn't just finish me off. So I used all my strength, and punched him as hard as I could. Weirdly he just seem to turn to ash, and blow away with the wind. Caty didn't this you see, because she came back as it had blown away."

I had to looked at Caty as I asked, "Caty if I'm I hearing right, you weren't there when Joe was fighting his opponent?"

She looked very almost embarrassed as she replied, "Yeah there were three of them. We figured it would be a good idea if we split up. It partially worked, I got two of them to follow me. I did come back after him though, I figured that the two of us could take them out better if we were together. I do have to admit though when I left him, it felt really wrong as I did it."

I decided to be gentle with her since she did seem to know what she had done wrong. So I said to them, "I know the both of you are young and really don't know this. I will show you ways to move so you never have to leave, and get in multiple hits, even if its just with your fists. It's never a good idea to leave a man alone to fight multiple enemies. You don't know what they may have done, the situation was far to unpredictable. What if those other two had decided to double back on you? Or worse, what if you had only attracted one instead?"

"Well that's what I thought. So that's why I pick him up and ran him back here."

Joe then interjected, "Plus it was my idea to split up John. But unlike Caty I knew that I may have drawn the lot of those guys."

I had to applaud his will to throw himself on his sword for her. I had to tell them the truth, "I can tell you if I'm right about Joe and Arty, they maybe the most valuable among us. I think from here on out, we should try to protect them. I also know that you didn't know any of this though Caty, from now on, until they come into their own, we do this for them as well as for us. Joe if I'm right, you can remove your band-aid now. Pepper it's your turn to tell me your story."

Joe then lifted the blood soaked rags, and saw that his wound was now just a pink splotch, both Caty and Pepper had to look as well. Pepper starter to speak, "I don't know that there's anything special about me really, except for me eye sight thingy. I seem to be able to see beyond the person though, sort of like I can see things. I seem to be able to tell if someone is alive or dead, even though I'm not sure that's really right. To be truthful I don't think that really describe it, but that's the closest I can come to what it maybe like."

"Oh, do you mean kind of like the amount of life they have within them?"

She gave me a sweet smile as she said, "Yeah, kind of like that."

I looked straight at her, "Remember this just a start, but I think your family calls that augur. It's an ancient Roman word, which means to be able to see the future. But in truth that's a misnomer, you see back then your kind could almost predict what a person was going to do. Its truly because you can almost see how a persons life force as it moves through their bodies. This why you can tell if someone is alive or not, or possibly lying or not. I do have to say, that we must be alive, because of this ability, even though to a lesser degree then normal humans. We'll see in the end, even though one good sign is if you can almost keep up with Caty when you run. Your family was never as fast as our family though. But then again we maybe similar in other certain ways. Both our families stress the physical aspects of our bodies. Whereas mine and what I believe is Caty's family is, stresses strength, agility, and other things like that. Your family doesn't stress that side as much, but they do stress their physical looks. With this though, because of your normal litheness, that's why you're as fast us also. I don't think speed is a good word for this though. Lets just say its agility more then speed of movement. Well the only one I don't know the name of is you."

I was looking straight at the guy that looked like he was straight out of the 50's. He then said, "Well I don't know that this is the smartest thing to do. Yeah you said you could have already killed us. I have to wonder if any of this is smart at all really. I mean for one thing, how do we even know your name is really John?"

"To be truthful you don't. Ask yourself though, how do I know truly know that all of you are telling me the truth? I can tell you that in my job, I destroy unwarranted or those that are created against the law. I have every reason in the world to have already destroyed each and everyone of you."

"How do we even know you could of killed us all too. I mean maybe one of us could of taken you down."

"I have seen stranger things happen, even though the likelihood of that happening is unlikely. You don't have to believe me, but I have been known to take out entire coven's. This small group isn't even a brood, now would you please tell me what I asked. I really am trying to help."

"Oh ok, since you said please. Well my name is Paavali, that's Finnish. I think my Granddad said it means Paul in Englander, that's what he called the English language. Plus you guys didn't tell him your ages, I'm sixteen almost seventeen. Caty says shes twenty, even though to me she looks way younger then that. Pepper was just short of eighteen by two weeks. Joe was turned right after his twenty second birth day, I think. But of all of us technically four of us are truly under age, which kind of makes me wonder why us. Now about the things I've noticed about myself, well nothing exceptional really. Caty said I have a weird way of looking at things, she says I can be really anal about stuff. If that helps you at all, there you have it."

Immediately after he ended Arty spoke up, "Oh yeah, and what you did to that guard wasn't anything exceptional?"

I asked, "What do you mean?"

Joe replied, "It was like that Obi-Wan in Star Wars. I mean that security guard caught us dead to rights, and could of called the police. The next thing though old Paul here started to talk to him, then it was like, 'these aren't the droids you're looking for'. Man, he was repeating everything Paul was saying to him. John that was really cool."

I looked at him and said, "Paul even if you think it isn't important, tell me, it might just save your life. Plus this gave me a good idea of what family you maybe from. Even though I may not be able to help you with what you really need to know. I can however help you learn to fight with the best vampires, are you willing to allow me to teach you?" He nodded his head, so I turned to the rest of them and asked, "What about the rest of you?"

Everyone said their yes, in their own ways. I then went on with, "Ok now more about me. I really don't think you need to know my age, because if you know as your strongest link, it can be used against us. Just to be fair though, I will give you the fact that I'm just over three centuries in age. I even think that maybe you shouldn't know what my job is, but in a sense I'm kind of well known, so some where you'll hear me called an Enforcer. My house that I belong to is best not said, in fact only your own house members are supposed to know any of this. Again though you already know that Caty and I maybe related, so much for hiding that fact. Even though for us to start this we have to have some honesty here." Joe's hand went straight up then, so I asked, "Yes Joe?"

He asked in turn, "Is the term Enforcer supposed to be important to us?"

Chapter 3

So know we know each other.

I had to give it to him, it was an important question. So I answered with, "Well yeah kind of. But if your sire did tell you about it, it would most likely be to keep you in line. You know kind of like a warning, if you don't do what I tell you, then enforcer will come and hunt you down. You know like the boggy man is used for humans as a way to get kids to listen. There are so few of us, you'll rarely actually meet one. Well I guess you got the meeting part over, and done with now."

I didn't mean it as a joke, but it seemed that everyone giggled or chuckled in someway as Caty asked. "What do you do to make yourself so scary to other vamps?"

"Well vamps have laws. You'll have to learn these laws over time, we really don't have the time now. Within vamp society they technically police themselves, you can see that at times they may get out of control, or a higher then thou attitude. They have systems to even try to control this, but not everything can be policed, and what happens if it is in fact the leadership. That's where I come in, I make sure everything is right. Does that kind of make it clear enough for you Caty?"

She nodded her head as Arty stated, "That would make you a vamp bad ass then."

I nodded my head as I also added, "But never think of yourself as invincible, or that you can't be destroyed. Like I said earlier, I've seen stranger things happen. I have a lot to show you, and you have a lot of rules to learned. I guess what is the weirdest thing about us, is even though there are only six basic laws, There are traditions that go along with these same laws, they seem to be endless. We maybe at the top of the food chain, even though not alone. There's a lot we have to do to stay there though. It may help you to remember that even though we are here, we really aren't alone."

Paul then asked, "Is that why you said we have to leave here?"

I again nodded as I said, "We have three days to get out of here, even though I think getting blood maybe more important. The time is to short for this though, and I think we have to push finding a place first. I'm going to take two with me every day until we find a place, also be prepared to move everyday till I'm sure we are safe. I'll leave it to all of you to decide though, but I think we can't to include Arty or Joe in this. Plus I think Billy and Caty should be included into each group, on my first outing I'm going to be taking those two so I can gauge who's better. Now on these outings, I want you to rely on me first, and Billy or Caty second. While we're gone I want the four of you to make up your minds on what you want. Joe set out a close patrol, but keep it close so you can quickly call them in just in case we find some place. Oh, and change your shirt if you can."

Joe then said, "Sure John, I'll take care of it. Guys lets go with the door signal number three."

I then interjected, "Joe door signals aren't really necessary. If someone or something really wants in here with all these holes in the walls, they would just come in. They're not going to be using the front door to come in. Billy get my cooler, and put it in the trunk as Caty and I get into the car. Then I can have it started by the time you get in."

So we moved out, and Joe asked, "What are we supposed to do if someone wants to come in here."

Caty replied as I smiled and shrugged my shoulder's, "Run like hell."

Billy then added, "And hope they don't have guns."

Arty said as we got to the door, "Thanks, but that wasn't very reassuring."

As we walked to my car, I said to Billy, "Right under the mate where the cooler was at, there's a sheathed knife there. Get it, and bring it with you when you come to the front seat. Caty I want us all to be alert, so you'll be in between Billy and me. If we do run into trouble come out my side, but then attack Billy's assailant from the side. Don't even give him any time to really think, hit him hard, and hit him fast."

She nodded to me as we all separated to make this faster, and headed to our different parts of the car. We then all got into the car, as we did I realized that I had forgot an important part of this plan. I turned to the two of them a little embarrassed, as I said, "Well this is terrible. We have a plan, but I don't really know this city. Where are we going to look first?"

Caty smiled as she replied, "I had an Idea about a week ago, but Joe thought that old warehouse was a far better idea. If you go out the way you came in, and just continued down Martin Luther King avenue. Let me think...I think it's four lights, but it maybe better to look for 30th street. Then turn left and go till you find the street light on Shartel street. Now I think its a left hand turn, but I maybe wrong there. I do know it isn't very far off 30th street though. What you're looking for are these old set of abandoned apartments. I think there's like four of them. So will they do?"

I had to smile as I replied, "Perfect. Now no radio, we're trying to be as quiet as church mice."

I then started to drive, as I did they seemed to talk a lot. Caty's directions were spot on, I knew I was getting close as soon as the two of them shut up. I drove around the block trying to get the lay of the land, I saw that one of the gates were unlocked. I also knew that was way to obvious an entrance, but it would be good to know later on. Finally I pulled down the street that was just past them, as to use them to be hidden away from these duplex's.

As I turned off the car, I turned to them and spoke, "Billy I saw a fence over there, I want you to leave us when we're about twenty feet from it. Go over the fence, and head right into the shadows, and wait. Keep an eye out for Caty and I find a way in, if you see something I want you to bark like a dog. This will distract whatever as Caty and I try to come to your rescue. We will have to look at every house one at a time, Caty you take the rear of each duplex buildings. Billy the left side, I'll take the right. When you go to the next house, watch out for any trouble, but what we're really looking for are loose boards. We could make our own entrance, but we don't to leave much trace that we were even here. Ok you guys got that?" Then they both nodded to me, and just like that we were moving. I did whispered to Billy before we got to far, "Give the knife to Caty. If you vamp out, you probably won't have any use for it."

Of course that was if I was right about him, then again all this careful planning would prove to be useless in the end. It is surprising how much things can change in a flash in our world. Billy then ran to the fence and was over it in a flash. I moved to the fence and checked if it had those metal fasteners. It did, so I just reached in, and pulled from the corner. I figured it would look like kids broke in here, then I held the fence up so Caty could get in, then of course I followed her. We met up with Billy, and were about to move when he grabbed my arm. I looked at him as he pointed. I knew how good his eyes were, even though I had to squint mine just to see. It wasn't like my eyes weren't better form when I was a human, just not as good as Billy's.

I then saw the movement in the shadows that had caught his eyes, and could just make out a shadowy figure. With this Billy pointed at another figure near the first figure, but on the fence. He then moved his finger to a small building that may have been a shed, where yet another figure crouched. Caty then pulled my arm and pointed to a dark figure on top of one of the duplex's. With this I could see we were out numbered, so I pointed to the dark figure and with my other hand tapped Caty. Then I got Billy's attention, and pointed at the one on the small building. I figured I could easily take on two of them, of course now that we had a plan. This would be the prefect time for things to go array.

The one that was on the small building made a sound, and the first dark figure looked up. With that, the one on the fence jumped down, and the first shadow then screamed. We were already moving as it turned, and ran toward the house. I then said, "Caty don't kill her, just follow her."

She never replied to me, as my blade came out. I could see Billy's fingers extending, and knew he was vamping out. I saw the guy on the roof then jump, but for some reason the dark figure moved. He came crashing down to the ground then, so Caty could easily get by him. I didn't have much time to think on this, as I past my knife through my targets neck. I knew he was dead, as I move to the one I knew would probably follow Caty. I looked back at Billy, and saw him getting the best of the fight with the other being. I turned on the speed, but realized I didn't have to. The other being had decide a good attack, was better then running after those other two.

I easily dodged his first blow, but because he moved my knife caught his shoulder. I turned, and I think he was about to say something, as my knife pasted through his neck. He barely had time to register what had happened to him, before his head was traveling to the ground. With the end of the fight, we quickly moved the bodies to one corner of the fencing. With vampires it isn't like we dissolve into dust, but we do rot abnormally fast. It is while we're doing this, that I notice their harsh stench also. Of all the being of our kind in this city, why did it have to be these guys. I really didn't have time to think about it though.

I turned to Billy and said, "Go out front, and see if you can pick up Caty's scent. We need to follow her, and see what's up."

Billy then asked, "Why didn't you just have Caty kill the lady John?"

I replied with, "I'm going to go get my car, and meet you out front. To answer your question though. When you get old enough, you too will be able to tell a human scream from a vampire one. It is a little hard to explain, and we have to catch up to Caty just in case."

Billy nodded his head as he then moved out. I'm sure since he was a young vampire, it didn't dawn on him why I didn't just killed a human. Or maybe he did see how the three vamps hardly bled though, and that maybe a human would bleed way worse then them. I move to my car at speed, and had just pulled around the corner as Billy was turning around his own corner. I pulled up next to him as I asked, "I take it you got the scent?"

He replied, "Don't have to. One of them is wearing a whole lot of pretty strong perfume. I never smelled it on Caty, so I figured it the lady shes following."

"Can you follow it even with car fumes?"

"I think you could follow it with car fumes."

"Good get in, we'll use the car to make it faster."

We didn't have to travel that far though, because she just went to a local dive. I mean this was a real dive, I wouldn't have even known it was there, if Caty hadn't flagged us down. So I pulled into the small make shift parking lot, she looked at Billy who was having trouble phasing back into his more human like form. She then said, "She went into there. I guess you'll have to go it by yourself from here on out."

I said back to her, "I need back up just in case there's some of our friends in there, and as you can see Billy's not exactly ready for company. Even though I don't thing he could possible pass for whatever the drinking age is here, that really only leaves you Caty. But don't worry I think you can handle it, all I want you to do is watch my back. If anyone should give you guff, you just give it back in return." I looked at Billy when I was getting out and said, "Just try to relax. You'll find it really easy once you relax."

I didn't tell him that blood could help him relax a little to, it's surprising what blood can do for us. We really didn't have the time to explain right now, plus what was he going to do, troll houses to see if he could find a donor. As we walked up to the front door of this dive, I could see that it was a house made into a bar. I couldn't tell, but I bet the side door, if it had one, was boarded up to. I could see Caty was very nervous, so I whispered, "Just stick close, and keep looking around. You'll do fine, plus I bet we are the badest vamps, if not the only vamp in this place."

I said that to try and calm her nerves though, I think it worked a little. As we came in the door, she grabbed my arm and asked, "What if they ask for my I. D.?"

I reassured her with, "Relax Caty, we're here only to see what she knows, then we're gone. After all we aren't savages, we just don't go around killing innocents."

We then looked around the joint, it was easy to see where our targets were at. Everyone looked ancient in here, she was the only young lady in the place. Plus I could see the deer in the head lights look on her face, as soon as my eyes hit her. Her reaction was to put her head down acting like she was asleep, like the other lady at her table. We moved to her table, and I sat down as Caty still nervously stood. Without lifting her head she asked, "If you're going to kill me, do it now. I don't want to see it coming."

I said in a whisper, "Is that what you want, because I only came in here to talk."

She tilted her head as she answered, "I particularly don't want to die, if I have a choice in the matter."

"You always have a choice. Isn't life technically of our own choosing, and in the end its what we make of it."

"Not always. Sometimes its what a friend does that makes it for you."

I had to smile at this as I said, "That's the sound of a person that has had hard times as of late, I guess that's why you were out there like we were. If we hadn't been looking for someplace to flop like you, we would of never been there to help you out."

She lifted her head so she was sitting, "You could say that. Our land lord raised the rent, and one of our room mates bail right when we need her the most. Then I lose my job a week ago, and Cheryl loses her a month ago. All in the name of reducing the work force, so we don't even have the money to look for a new place. Yeah you could say we've had a rough time of it, as of late."

"So what are you doing here if you don't have any money?"

"Cheryl was really depressed, so I figured a few drinks would help her a bit. I never took in account that this was the first time for her to drink, so like you, I was looking for a place close, so I wouldn't have to drag her all over town."

"We had just gotten there, when you were attacked. So we hadn't had a chance to look ourselves. You wouldn't mind sharing one of those duplex's for the night, would you?"

"I don't know."

"Oh well, I took a shot, but its to late to go someplace else. So excuse us if we search a little, I will apologize if any of my boys walk in on you."

I expected her not to say no, but more like hell no!

In a way this would be better in the long run though. Heck a lot of things would of probably been better in the long run, like her and her friend never meeting us. She did think about it for a few minutes though, all my question would soon be settled though, after what she said. She looked directly into my eyes and said, "You look like you can be trusted, but what about those other guys? I don't think I'd be very good in a fight, and I'm sure Cheryl wouldn't."

Well I had to tell her the truth, if not the whole truth. Well we kind of came to an understanding, plus I explained that technically we weren't alone, and that we are just a small group. Of course I lied. "I'm only telling you this so you know, I'm basically an honest person."

"What about her though? I mean you've been in here a few minutes, and she hasn't really sat down."

"Oh I asked her to keep an eye out while we talk., she's kind of nervous because shes a little short on age to be in here. She's only twenty."

"Oh ok, so just you and her talked to those guys then."

"Well no. I sent her after you and Billy and I took care of those three guys. Billy's watching my car right now."

"Speaking of cars, do you have a few extra buck's, so I can move my car to the house."

This is where I knew I had her, even though she could also want her car for a quick get away. Which if I were her, I would want to do the same thing. I then told her, "I have a few bucks, but not much. I maybe able to give you a ten spot if that will help."

I had barely over $48, I figure that would be easy enough. Even though I also had to wonder if I would sorely miss the amount later on. She then said, "Well you would be hard pressed to find a place to stay. I went to every house except for the one closes to the road, I thought that one was way to open for our own security. I only found one loose board, and that only barely had a wiggle to it. I figured I would have to struggle even with that one though, but its by the door handle, and I figured I would be able to pull the door loose."

"Well I have Billy with us. I'm sure the two of us could work it loose, plus if you like you can take one floor, and I can keep the other kids on another."

"That sounds good. I mean I wasn't sure what to do about

young boys, with Cheryl being passed out like she is."

I had to smile as I made another offer, "Oh I could put Caty here in between you and the boys, I don't know if the other girl will be any help. But if you like it I can put her there to, I'm sure though that Caty can handle the boys all by herself."

She looked at Caty and asked, "Would you be willing to do such a thing? It means you may have take on you own brothers so to speak."

Caty was still looking around so she barely spoke, "Ah what? Oh I mean sure." Then her eyes locked on someone and said, "John I think that lady is coming over here."

I then looked to see a bar maid coming our way. So I whispered to the lady right then, "I'm here to help you with Cheryl, you called me to do that."

She whispered back, "Good, then for show you can help me carry her out. Shes really heavy for how slight she is."

I nodded my head as the lady came to the table and asked, "There's a two drink minimum, so what will you have to drink?"

I gave her a closed mouth smile as I replied, "Nothing really, my friend here just called me to help get Cheryl home."

She gave me a very good plastic smile as she said, "Ok then, but you might want to make it fast. The bar tender almost called the cops when I found her asleep."

I nodded my head as I got up, the other lady got up to and we both helped Cheryl to her feet. I was taller then her, so this allowed me to take most of her weight off her. She woke up, but you could instantly tell she was still in a drunken stupor. She looked at the lady and said, "Mary you're so good to me. And why are you so cold."

I had instantly knew she had given me away, but Mary actually saved me with, "Cheryl its cold out, and I was looking for a place for us to stay. I just got back, and I'm bound to be a bit cold."

Good she thought she was talking to her, Caty held the door open for us. As soon as we got past it, I said to her, "Go tell Billy to get in the back seat, I think we'll put Cheryl in between you and him. Caty tell him hands off or you'll get him, plus I want you to watch her while I drive the short distance. You get in after we put Cheryl in."

She nodded her head and ran off, I kept my speed with that of Mary's. I figured I would make a comment about her weight, even though she was light as a feather to me. "I dare say even though you told me, I still wouldn't have figured that she would be quite this heavy myself. Not that she weights much to me, but it is a surprise."

She turned her head and smiled as she said, "See what I said. Even though I can feel that you're taking some of her weight off for me."

I smile a close mouth smile as I replied, "Well I could carry her by myself, but I figured you would feel safer like this."

She nodded her head as we continued on, we got to the car and Caty was right there with the door. She then said, "John I threatened Billy within an inch of his life. I'll help with her feet to make it easier on the two of you."

And with that she grabbed her feet, and I saw Billy take them from her. Then with his help we got her into the back seat, I looked at him, and could see he wasn't quite done vamping out. I looked him in the eyes, and said just loud enough so Mary could hear. "Be Careful there Billy. I think Mary might want to check on her friend, and we don't want to leave any unsightly bruises."

Well she didn't make a liar of me, as I watched Billy closely. He turned his head as she checked Cheryl out, then she withdrew so Caty could get in. I held the door for her, as Caty pulled the seat into place. Finally Mary got in, and I moved around the car as she closed her door. I started it as she told me it was the closest house to the gate. I then moved my car to the gate.

Chapter 4

New friends are always nice.

      We then took the very short drive to the houses. I had Billy get out and open and close the gate, and we found a good place to hide the car. I then turned to Caty and said, "Billy and I will carry Cheryl. I need you to take my car, and go get the others. Now be careful with my bomb, this is the only car we have."

      She nodded her head, and we all piled out of the car. I made Billy get back in and said, "You pass her to Mary and me. Then you get out and take Cheryl from Mary."

      Mary instantly said, "I can handle her."

      I came back with, "I know you can, but you have to show us the house." She realized I was telling her the truth, so she nodded her head. I also added, "Plus we may have to pass her to you. We'll make up our minds once we get to that point."

      So we did as I had said, as she said, "Caty I'll leave this gate open for you, just drive the car to this spot again."

      Caty looked at me so I just added, "That's a good idea Mary. That way we won't be interrupted while we sleep." I then winked at her and hoped she knew what I really meant by that. I thought of her comfort also, so I add one more layer to this. As I said, "Billy they won't know where to go, so as soon as we get Cheryl settled you go out and wait on them. Make sure she hides the car well too, then direct them to where you leave us at."

      As we moved I made small talk, "Isn't it funny that we were both looking for a place to sleep for the night? Plus if we hadn't arrived when we did, you might have been killed. I'm not sure about this Mary, but I think your luck maybe turning around for you."

She let out a slight giggle combined with a cough as she said, "The door is where I found the loose board, it's right over here. I was just thinking to check it to be sure though, when all the hairs went up on my arms. That was just barely before I got jumped." She seemed to sniff the air as she asked, "What's that smell?"

I replied, "It kind of smells like a dead dog. Darn that stinks, do you smell it Billy?"

I looked at him as he was about ready to replied, he caught my eye, and immediately knew what to say. "Well it's definitely some kind of dead animal."

Mary asked, "Do think it could be a pack of dogs or worse wolves around here?"

I replied to her question simply with a, "Maybe."

I can tell you know that may have been the wrong thing to say, but Billy seemed to know better as he spoke. "No. You rarely see a wolf let alone a pack of wolves in the city. Now if you're talking about a pack of coyote's, then there's a chance with them. I'm pretty sure we'll be safe in the house though. I've never heard of them going into any houses."

I could hear in his voice that he was still having a slight problem, but it was good enough where she didn't notice. She then said in a low voice, "Well at least that's refreshing."

I decided to add, "I guess we'll have to put up a watch, just in case."

We then walked up a three step porch, made of wood. It was easy to tell, as every step made a creek as we walked up. She then started to struggle with a board, I reached up with one hand not wanting to put Cheryl down. I knew I could easily do this with my one hand, but I allowed her to help so I would look human. I may have used to much force, as the board came free to easily. So I quickly added, "Oh, you must have loosened it."

That was a good enough argument for her, then she started to pull on the door even though there were still two boards there. I helped with pushing in and out, I was really not wanting to show my strength. I then said, "Billy lend a hand and lets see if we can at least weaken it up a little."

He then reached up, and we all pulled together. I knew I could of done this again easily by myself, but using little force, I allowed her to think she had worked it loose. She then moved something, and threw it aside. It was an old mattress, then we were able to get past the door. The house was full of debris, so I spoke, "Mary take the lead and find a relatively clear room where we can set Cheryl down."

I think she had thought the same thing though, because she was already on it, as Billy and I followed her. I could see she was having trouble moving in the dark, whereas Billy and I were having no problems. Even though I am not as adept at this as Billy, I knew I had to speak to this fact. "Take it slow Billy. This place has some tricky footing."

He said under his breath, "Yeah, if you're a human."

I had to look at her, to see if she heard him. She was still looking around at everything, so it was apparent she hadn't. So I said in a low tone so only he could hear, "Careful. We have to seem human to her."

He nodded his head as she asked, "What was that?"

I had to looked, and replied after I scanned the area well. "I was just telling Billy to watch his step, I keep seeing things flash on the floor. I think there might be glass here and there, not that he has to worry with those thick combat boots he wears."

She then said, "Here." I saw her scanning a room as she went on, "I think this will be good, especially if we use that stinky mattress."

I then said to Billy, "Help me put her down against the wall, then go and grab the mattress. Once we get her on that, then go outside and wait on the kids."

He nodded as we did exactly that, he then left as I allowed Mary to check up on her friend. I took a look around to see a pile of something, so I moved to the pile and moved whatever it was to another room. I came back to seeing Billy setting the mattress down. I dusted my hands off as I said, "Good, I hope that stuff didn't have any bugs in it." Even though I knew we kind of naturally repelled insects, "Help me with Cheryl, then go watch for the kids."

He then bent over, and we moved Cheryl to the mattress. While we were doing that he said, "I saw some broken down old chairs in what looked like a kitchen, I figured you could use the chair if you like."

"Good idea Billy. There we go Billy." As we lowered he to the mattress, and it really did stink. Kind of like someone had peed on it all its life, with just a hint of mold. So I just had to ask, "Are you sure she won't wake up with that stink? Jimmeny Crickets!"

She had to openly laugh as she replied, "I think she's to drunk to care. Did you actually just say Jimmeny Crickets?"

"Oops, showing my age."

I said that as Billy was leaving the room, so we started to retrace our steps along the same way he was going. Once we got to the room that appeared to be the kitchen, I immediately picked up what looked like the best of three chairs. I dusted it off and said, "Here you go my lady."

She smiled and replied, "Thank you kind sir." I then took a

chair, and figured I could sit on any as long as I turned it backwards. She then asked, "He's kind of young isn't he. I mean shouldn't he be in foster care?"

I put my head down, as I acted like I was freely admitting something. As I said, "Well they have all had a hard time of it, and barely escaped the system. I have became their defacto leader of sorts, but there are only four of them that are truly young. I think only three of them are school aged though, but they trust me enough though, and with what they've been trough that's huge. They are a bit stand offish though. Well not all of them, but most of them." I had to chuckle as I had to add, "Well unless they get to arguing, then they're very open."

She then giggled as she said, "I bet that's fun with two girls."

"Well Caty can hold her own, and Pepper she just says things under her breath a lot. Even though as much of a spitfire that she is, I think she could hold her own also."

"Her mom must of hated her."

"Why do you say that?"

She gave me a knowing smile as she replied, "Wouldn't you think that a name like Pepper is…I don't know, like she should have her legs wrapped around a stripper pole."

That made me smile really big, then as I remembered what I was, I covered my mouth fast. I then had to confess to her, "No I had never thought about that, I guess it could be considered a stripper name."

She then looked toward the room and said, "I really should look in on her, to make sure that she's ok."

I knew she was concerned, so I set out to try and comfort her. "When they get back we'll send Pepper in, she may have a stripper name, but she seems a natural when it comes to taking care of people.

In fact we have a guy named Joe that got hurt bad, her and Caty nursed him back to health."

Of course I didn't tell her my part in all of that, as she said, "Wow Joe, he sounds like a bouncer or something tough like that."

"He even looks tough enough, but really I would call him more of a diplomat then a fighter. He seems to have a way of solving problems. I'm glad he the oldest, he helps me keep the other kids in line."

Of course I was using what I suspect was his family ties, I had no idea if I was right. She then said, "Kind of sounds like Cheryl. I mean our roommate that left us high and dry, I don't think I would have been friends with. What is weird is she can keep really good records, but she had to have me or Stevie do her check book. Never could figure that one out myself. Caty is a weird name."

I nodded as I said. "It's short for what I think is a Slavic name. Arty has a strange Scandinavian name too, Finnish I think. Even though its easy to figure out what Joe and Billy is short for. Is Mary your real name or is it short for something?"

"Marylynn-Abigail, it's hyphenated which actually makes that my entire first name. Mouth full isn't it? My momma was from eastern Oklahoma, and liked the down home feel of my name. I technically don't have a middle name, which is kind of normal here."

I had to smile, as I hadn't heard a name like that in a very long time. I figure I would let out a little more truth, "Well Arty is the youngest, I think it goes Paul then Billy. Pepper is just short of her 18th birthday, I don't know how close to 20 Caty is. All she'll say is shes 20, then Joe is the oldest. Even though I don't think he was in foster care, he's just had a rough life. That might be why he's so diplomatic like."

She nodded her head as I went on, and then she said when I had finished. "Well I'm the oldest. Cheryl and I have been the same age for about a month now. I'll be a year older in just under three months now, but you did forget one persons age."

"I did? Let me think."

I thought for a few minutes, and as I came up with whom I forgot we spoke at the same time. I said, "Oh me."

As she said, "You, silly."

"Oh well I would be the oldest of course at thirty four."

"Oh wow, you don't look it. I'm just thirty three myself."

"Yeah, but the oldest kid is twenty two."

"Wow. That is young."

I wanted to blurt out that, and yeah he would be that age forever. But then again that was, and wasn't a lie. You see when our system starts to work with the blood, we basically turn back the clock. We basically will look in our twenties after about five years, kids under that age usually seem to age at a normal rate, until they look like that at least. Strange thing is that kids that aren't in or going through puberty won't age, that's why its forbidden to turn a mere child. I saw her look to the back of the house, and start to get up. I them reached out very quickly and said, "Don't leave." She with drew her hand back, and I immediately knew what was wrong. So I just used her excuse from bar, as I blew onto my hands as I said, "It is getting cold isn't it? I wish we had a blanket for Cheryl."

"Why did you grab my hand?"

"Well its been such a long time since I've had real adult conversation. I just didn't want it to end." I gave he a contrite look as I added, "I'm sorry if I scared you."

"No, with so many young kids, I guess I can understand that.

Let me just check on her really fast, and I'll be right back." I nodded my head, and she did as she said she would. Then she said, "She's looking really pale, but she seems to be breathing ok."

I smiled again, and had to cover my mouth also. This time I quickly blew into my hand as I said, "I'm glad shes ok, like I said I can have Pepper have a look at her."

"Good, I think I would like that, now tell me about yourself."

"Me? Well there really isn't much to tell. I got my start in Los Angeles, I'm a bit of a nomad though. The last city I was in before coming here was New Orleans. I'm kind of a trouble shooter, I stayed there until a new job called. I don't get paid much for what I do though, so I'm forced to keep traveling." I figure if I mixed in some truth with just as much vagueness, would be a good thing. I also new I had to redirect the conversation really away from me, this is where I think I made my first mistake. "Hey this may be a little forward, but I really am over my head here, I could use some help. They need a mother figure or type here to help them, especially the girls. Would you be willing to help out?"

I could see that she was completely uncomfortable with the question, as she replied. "Me a mommy, I'm no mommy. I can barely take care of myself, I had Cheryl for that."

I knew the question was wrong as soon as it left my mouth, I could hear a welcome sound as I went on though. "Yeah I guess I could see that, you seem to be really close to her. You know like a mother protecting a child, so I took a stab in the dark."

She smiled, "We're very close. In fact Stevie used to say we were like sisters, even though I have German in me and shes from some Native American tribe. I think the Choctaw Nation or something like that, when my mom died she was right there for me. Just like I was there when her husband was killed on the freeway, he was just changing a flat tire." I could see her eyes gloss up as she added, "She and I don't like to talk about it much though. I mean we start crying and stuff."

I saw the hidden darkness in her past, as she looked off while telling the story, and at the end I could hear a bit of a crackle in her voice. I said in a low tone. "That's when you really know who your friends really are, I know that it hurts. Why don't you just stay here when Pepper get her, I know it would be easier to just sit still for awhile. Plus you could help, since I am so starved for adult conversation. If anything goes wrong, I'll make sure she comes after us so we can help."

She looked at me as she spoke, "I would like that, besides I don't think we have much time. Is that your car I hear?"

I already knew it was, but I tilted my head like I had just heard it too. And replied, "Well I'll be, I think it is. You have good ears."

She nodded her head with a smile, it was such a sweet smile. I would get to see that smile one more time. We made a little more small talk until the kids came into the room. I Immediately said to Pepper, "Pepper go to the room where Cheryl is in, Billy please show her the right room. Paul if you please could help Pepper, and help with whatever you can." I then pointed at the blond girl and said, "Mary that's Pepper," then I changed whom I was pointing at and added, "And that's Paul."

Each of them said their hi's in turn. then I turned to the main groups and pointed each out. Starting with Arty I continued, "That's Arty and that's of course Joe." I move my hand and put it down once each of them said hi. I continue just a little with, "And you already met Caty and Billy." Joe then grabbed an old box and Arty sat on the last chair, I gave each of them a stern look. As I spoke with a little bit of a harsh tone, "Guys aren't you going to be gentlemen and get Caty someplace to sit?"

Joe immediately jumped up and said, "Oh, I'm sorry Caty. Here you can take mine, and I'll see if that box is alright just outside."

With this He left the room, and Caty sat as she said, "John I could of done that."

I then spoke to her, "Yeah, but I thought Mary would be more comfortable with you sitting here."

She turned to Mary and said, "Hi again. We just met John a little while ago. He's been a great help, I think we would be dead if it wasn't for him."

"Stop that Caty, you're making me blush." I let it get quiet for just long enough for the silence to register, then I continued on with, "Ok you can say more about me."

I let out a little chuckle, as Billy came in and said, "John, Pepper and Paul are settled in with Cheryl. I told them to keep a close eye on her, and even though you didn't say anything. I told her to run in here if there's any problems."

"Good Billy. I meant to say that, but I forgot."

Mary then asked with a questioning look on her face, "Keeping a close eye on her? What's that supposed to mean?"

I looked at her as I replied, "Pepper's not a nurse or anything. So I figured it is a good thing if she asks us if its ok first, I think-"

Pepper came into the room in a flash, I realized two things right then. One she had found her speed, and second something must have been wrong. She spoke in a bit of a tizzy, "John I think her heart is about to stop! What do I do?"

I jumped to my feet, as I said with almost as much emotion. "We have to take her to the hospital! Billy give me a hand! I'm sorry Mary this may have been a bad idea! I think she may have alcohol poisoning! We have to move fast! I just hope we're in time!"

We all started to move while I was talking. I allowed Mary to get in front of us, as I knew she would question us moving faster then her. What would be worse is if she saw Caty, Pepper, or me move. Mary said with tears running down her face, "Noooo. She's all I have left in this world."

We entered the room, and instantly saw immediately what no human would perceive. One I think you would have to be a vampire to even smell and see the sight we all saw. Paul had a small streak of blood running down the side of his mouth. My eye's went right to her mouth then and not her neck, Which I was willing to bet that's where everyone else's eye's went to, when you're a vampire its hard to shut out the smell of blood. I looked directly at Paul and asked, "What have you done?"

Paul innocently replied, "You said to help Pepper, and she told me to keep her alive. I was listening to her heart, and it was all fluttery, it even stopped a few times. This was all I could think to do John, at least to keep her alive. So I gave her our gift."

Mary pulled her out of Paul's arms, and I saw that he was about ready to snarl at her. So I said to him, "Let her have Cheryl so she can see for herself."

Mary automatically started to move her hair, and almost pet it. She started to rock her and say, "Why are so cold honey. Don't worry, I'm here now honey. You can't leave me now."

I put my hand on her shoulder and said, "You know what's happened to her Hun. You have to let her go now."

"No! No! She can't be dead!"

I looked at Paul and said, "No matter what Paul they have to be given the choice. Did you give her the choice?"

He shook his head as Mary asked, "Choice? Choice for what?"

I had to give her a smile as I was about to explain.

Chapter 5

How to or can you explain this life?

<u>Mary</u>

I saw the painted look on his face as he replied to my question. "She's started a new journey that you will be given a choice over." He looked around the room at everyone, and spoke to everyone there. "Children you see the change. I didn't have time to explain this part, but all have to be given the choice. She now walks the journey of this unlife, as her life was, so it will seem the same. But like all living things, they must all die."

I was beside myself with grief, as I cried out, "Nooo, she can't be dead! She's all I have in the world! She can't be dead!"

He went on, like he hadn't even heard me, "From this life she now passes, and even though she will be dead, she can never give her family closure. For the undead leave no corpse, we never share this with humans. So this day he has caused two deaths, without any knowledge of his crime, but it is a crime, and he must be judged for this crime."

Then she moved with a jolt in my arms, it was like she was having an extreme seizure. I yelled, "LOOK SHE'S STILL ALIVE! WE CAN STILL GET HER TO THE HOSPITAL!"

He then took my face in his cold dead hands, he looked as if he was going to cry also. He then spoke in a gentle voice, "No Mary. This is only her first steps into our unlife. Paul went far beyond the measure of our law, and this is our first sign that what he did his work well. Here body is hers, and the journey has now started.

Nothing can reverse this from happening, it always starts this way. Shes one of the damned now, and nothing can save her from this unlife."

I then said in a very strong voice, "What do you mean Journey? What do you mean? What the hell is going on here? And why in the hell are your damn hands so cold?"

He looked at me with knowing eyes, as he replied, "I could explain, but it's usually better for you to see."

"Oh the hell with that! I want to see you explain this to me now! Or I'm going to go get a cop! I bet he'll make you explain dammit!"

"Caty I know you like her, so you have charge over her until we can show and allow her own eye's to explain. Until then she doesn't leave your sight."

I couldn't believe it. She was across the room from me one second, and the next right next to me. She then openly smiled at me and said, "Now Mary be a good girl, and don't make me chase you. John just how long does she have to wait?"

He then replied, "It usually takes in between two to three hours after her second convulsion."

With that Cheryl suddenly convulsed and this was a bad one. She screamed so loud I thought for sure that would bring the police. Even though I had to admit, I had never heard her scream like that before. It seemed to have an emptiness to it, sort of like what you would think the howling banshee would sound like. I knew though I had been beaten in this, so I was going to have to sit here and just watch my best friend in the world die. I thought I would wait for the police at first, but when it became obvious that they weren't coming, and Caty had left the room I made a break for it. I barely made it to the fence we came in at, when Caty just appeared out of now where right in front of me. She then said, "Mary I like you. So I really don't want to hurt you."

She was a small woman, so I thought I would just bowl her over. Running into her though, was like running into a brick wall, and I fell on my butt. She helped me up, and as she did she whispered to me. "Mary, John's really good at this. You really don't want him to have to hunt you down. He's nice and all, but I don't know what he would do to you, and I don't even want to think of what he may do to me."

I whispered bad to her, "If he's so bad, why don't you just leave?"

She smiled and replied, "He's a lot nicer then some, I think he'll be good as our head honcho. Like I said though, I don't know him that well. Our kinds have some pretty drastic punishments, I'm thinking I don't want to know just how strict he is until after we see what happens to Paul."

"Well I would hate to be led around by the nose, he'll never be my boss that's for sure."

"John's not our boss. We just needed his help is all, and he gave it to us. Technically he's only the head honcho by default though, once we get to a certain point we'll be able to declare our own leader." She smiled at me again and said, "Now you be a good girl, and go sit down. I know it has to be close by now."

She walked back with me to my chair, I had to think my eye's were playing tricks on me though. I swear I saw teeth, not normal human teeth, but like vampire teeth. That couldn't be right, right? There's no such thing as vampires, right? Well I also knew I had to be tired, I did have to admit though John had a cold touch. Hers was cold as she grabbed my elbow, and wow she was really strong. Truly all I really wanted to do was cry, but I just couldn't give into my captors. Plus I think Caty would probably ripe apart a crying girl, if I didn't tell you I wasn't a bit scared I know I would be lying to you. I mean this whole show seemed straight out of a horror show, as Caty leaned up against the counter. I just had to ask, "Hey exactly what are you guys?"

She seemed to chuckle as she replied, "I'll tell you what my sire said to me. We are the things that which nightmares are made of. We are those things that go bump in the night. We are those things that lurk in the shadows, you don't want to think about. We are the damned of this world personified."

I had to admit that was a mouth full, her answered to my question was good, even though at the time, I hadn't a clue. I decided to just ask stick to the basic questions then, "Hey what time is it?"

She put up her arm in show me she had no watch. So I asked, "What does that mean?"

"I was showing you I don't have a watch."

"Oh ok. I just wanted to know how late it was?"

She turned to me to say something, but right then that guy I think they called Arty came in. He then said, "It'll be soon. Shes twitching so John sent me out after his cooler." He stopped and looked at me as he said, "This is so exciting, you should feel lucky to be one of the witnesses."

Then he ran out the door and I asked, "Witness to what?"

She smiled and said, "John wants you to see by example. So I can't tell you, but its really cool."

I had to think, what do I need to see by example, and of course you can probably guess that my mine would go to the worst possible examples. Boy was I completely wrong, Arty came back in as Billy came into the room. Billy wave his hand for him to come on as he spoke, "Hurry up Arty, shes sitting up, and John told me to hurry you up."

They both then ran down the hall. I had to ask, "Caty why does John have you guarding me?"

She smiled as she replied, "He probably knew I was the least likely to hurt you, even though with my strength I could hurt anyone here. Well except for John of course."

Pepper then came into the room and said, "It won't be long now sis. John is explaining things to her now, Mary I will have to take your chair for the next part. I'm sorry about this. Wow, John just explained we could have two in one day. I envy you Mary." She then waved as she took my chair and said, "See you two in a few."

Then I said, "I know being a prisoner you have to keep me in the dark, but darn I wish I knew what was going on. Can't you tell me anything Caty? I mean we are kind of friends."

She shook her head as she replied, "No. John didn't tell me not to tell you. When he said it, I knew he was right, its best if you see by example."

Right then Joe came in and said, " John says its time. You are to escort Mary in since shes human, I'll bring up the rear to make sure everyone is within the room. Once we get seated, then John will start. He says he's going to do it the normal way, so we know what to expect in the future."

Caty moved me in front of her, she stayed just close enough to help me know the way. I figured Joe was just behind her, she moved me to a crate, as she sat next to me. I then looked around to see Joe hadn't followed us. Paul was sitting in my chair, and John stood next to him. He waited for just a minute, then he nodded his head as he started. He started with, "All have come to witness, and see a broken law. This law calls for immediate destruction."

Oh my god he was going to kill this poor boy.

"But there are circumstances that cause this to go to a council judgment, as we have no elders, and I am the chief elder amongst you, it falls on me to stand in a judges place."

So he was going to be judge and executioner.

"I need my council though to set judgment though. We need six of our own, so I have to not start in exact order this must be done. So because this is usually is the last thing we do, it has became the first in that order. Paul will you happily announce your progeny?"

Ok this was getting strange, this boy wasn't old enough to have children.

He stood up and said, "Cheryl as I am your maker, will you come forth and introduce yourself?"

My head snapped around as the most gorgeous figure I had ever seen came walking into the room. There was my best friend alive and well, She strutted down the aisle like she owned the place, she seemed to bow to everyone. To me she bow with a wonderful smile, and lastly a whimsical wink. I was so over joyed that I didn't know I was crying until Caty gave me a Kleenex. Then she turned and spoke. I've heard her speak before, but never had I ever heard how wonderful her voice really sounded. "I am Cheryl TombiOhoyo, I have entered through my sire Paul. I am now his child, and from this day forward I am his ward."

What the hell?

Everyone then said, "Welcome to our brood."

Whatever a brood is, but I was so happy I really didn't care.

John then asked, "Cheryl since you weren't asked to be part of this unlife, I will ask you. Do you except this unlife that you have been given?"

She looked around the room as she spoke, "As I have been advised what I can say, and what I can't. We aren't in the right order to say my comment now. I understand why we have to be asked when we enter this unlife, and in what you did I find you guilty of this crime.

What I have found out, I don't want to loose though. I'm told that it is also bad form to reject your teacher, so even though I would like to cast my vote no, I'm forced to say yes. Now that you know my vote, and why I say that it would be my pleasure to join your brood. I now surrender the floor back to you John."

I had to think exactly what all this really meant.

John then spoke again, "We now have our six, if there is a tie I will render my judgment. Know that if it does go to my judgment, it isn't good for you. Now we start from the youngest sired and Cheryl already rendered her vote. So it now it falls on you Caty."

Caty then spoke, "As you know I never got a chance to know Cheryl, I would like to think shes as good as I feel Mary is though. Knowing this I'm sorry Mary, but I have to say yes for Paul's sake."

I can tell you I was completely lost here.

"As you know this is designed so that the oldest doesn't have to vote if it is decided before the last vote is drawn. Joe I was told that you and Caty are the same age, I gave her the first vote so yours would decide hers. Now how say you."

Joe stood up and said, "As you all know I'm all about the rules. I like Paul a lot, but rules are rules. So even though I feel for him, I cast a no vote."

"Billy I heard you were just a little younger then Pepper, so you are the next to cast. Now how say you?"

"I know we're like newbies at this bro, but really with the way you are, you knew to ask someone, any one. The law of the land says I have to cast no also."

I really had no idea what was going on truly, but I knew this young kids life seemed to hang in the balance of what the next two said.

"This means that you're next Pepper. How say you?"

Pepper stood up and I realized she had the same tone to her voice Cheryl had. "I can't say that I ever really liked you much Paul, but then again I never really hated you either. So I can't in my right mind cast a no vote, so I say yes."

Oh wow, this could end up being John as the deciding vote, and he already said how he would vote.

He then looked at Arty and said, "Arty this is it. If you vote no Paul will die. If you vote yes he lives this unlife. So how say you?"

He sat there and said, "I'm kind of in the same boat Pepper is in, but like you said because of my special kind I have a third way to vote. So as myself trying to honor my kind, I choose the only vote we usually do. I cast a no vote at all as it may affect the future."

John then said, "As there has to be a minimum of six votes cast, I'm forced to cast my vote which as you know is no. Like both Arty and Pepper I haven't a care about Paul's fate, so as head of this tribunal I say that the vote cast is a none decision. This means that Paul retains his life for now, if at anytime someone comes up with evidence that may change someones vote. Bring it up before your future leader of this brood, then his fate will be finally decided. Paul you may sit on the other side of Mary. Mary will you come and take Paul's place, Cheryl you can take Mary's seat as we give her, her choices."

I know now how it would go, but you can see how I thought I was going to be tried as I sat nervously down. I looked at John as he smiled at me. Then he spoke to me in such a gentle voice, it made me want to love what I suspected would be my killer. "You've seen to much Mary, and like Caty I have grown to like you too. Because of this I discussed it with her, and shes sponsored you, I have also seconded it. Like I just said though, you do get to decided. So let me tell you plainly about this. The choice that isn't yours though is whether you have to be put to death. There is the good news Mary, Caty you can now put it to her."

Caty stood up and asked, "Mary would you please become part of our brood?"

"This would do two things for this brood. One it would make them a coven, and second it would give them a great member I think. It is your decision though. So you can pick this unlife or just plain death. What say you?"

Oh wow, I didn't really expect this at all. I knew I did want to be with Cheryl, plus I didn't exactly want to die. So my decision was a very easy one. I heard myself say what I wanted, "I want to join the brood."

John's smile became so intoxicating it was unbelievable. He then asked, "Like I said it's always your choice, so you may choose your infector. Now know that you can choose anyone you like to do the deed, that even means Cheryl could be your choice, even though that would be an unwise one. But like I always say, its your choice."

Well I wanted everyone to think I was really thinking about, then shout out Cheryl's name. I tapped my chin with my finger, as I scrunched my face in my mock thinking. I then got up, and paced back and forth making a good show of it. So when I opened my mouth, I was as surprised as everyone else was. As I said, "I choose John."

My mine screamed what the hell, but as he spoke I never opened my mouth. "You do me an honor. Mary from now on you may call me what you will, but to me you will always be my daughter. As your sire, just like a father, I will always try to protect you from all things within my power. Plus you have given the children their first teaching tool, this is a personal act and can only be seen by other if you say yes. I see it as a teaching tool so my answer is yes also, since this is something just between you and me, you can just say no."

I then said to him, "I'm new at this, but I will bend my will to your judgment."

He smiled that 100% smile that I think melted my heart and said, "I think it would be best, so we don't have anymore occurrences like Paul and Cheryl. Even though this a very private thing, and I truly wish not to share it. Like you, I will bend my will toward the house, and commit this in public."

My mind was going wild again, as I had to think commit what. The only thing I could think of that you committed to was a sex act, was he going to rape me in front of all these kids. He helped me to my feet, as we walked to the room where I saw Cheryl die in. This was really sick, he was going to rape me right where they killed Cheryl. He then stopped and spoke, "Oh my. I'm such a dolt. That's where you saw your friend get violated. Would you rather do this in another room?"

Yeah, like in my old bedroom, without all the company. I knew that couldn't happen though, so I figured if it had to happen that place was as good as any. So I said, "No, if we have to do it, that's as good as any spot."

Then we moved into the room. He sat down putting me on his lap, I had to think this was an unusual way to be raped. He then took out a very big knife that was curved the wrong way. He handed it to the guy Joe and said, "Be careful with that, It's very sharp. Because of what I suspect you are I want you to do the honors." He turned to all of them, and spoke more to them then to me. "Joe do this one at a time. Because we don't want Mary to bleed out, I will drink just a little, then stench the wound. He starts with me and moves to her, but we have to wait for her reaction first. Now watch closely, because this is the correct way to do this."

He looked at me and asked, "Are you ready Mary?" I nodded my head so he went on, "Now just do exactly what I tell you to do." He looked at Joe and said, "We're ready, just use the words I told you."

It was then that I knew he knew I would choose him, but I didn't have time to ponder my thoughts though. As Joe said, "As all things that live, one day they must reach a time of decision. Mary your time of decision is right now. Will you choose to except this gift?"

He then sliced John's arm with that wicked knife as John whispered, "Drink my blood." I figured this was some kind of crazy initiation, even though I know better now. So I drank from his arm, then he whispered to me again, "Steel yourself for when Joe cuts your arm, it won't hurt though because of how sharp I keep my knife is. We do have to wait for your reaction."

I thought this was really crazy, and I wasn't thrilled about having my arm sliced. Then the first prongs of the first pain came, I thought it was so bad, I just wanted to die. I could barely hear Joe say, "As the gift is given so it must be given in return so the act may continue."

Then he sliced my arm, John was instantly drinking my blood. Then he licked the wound, and I was surprised that it healed right in front of my eyes. I saw his eyes, as it seemed like he was getting a high from my blood, they had an almost red hue to them. I guess the good thing was the pain was gone. Joe then said, "As life passes to death, so must we all be drawn close to the darkness."

He then quickly sliced John's other arm, I knew what to do now, so even though John whispered to me I was already drinking his blood. When the pain came on me this time, I thought I would shrivel up and die. To bad the worse pain was yet to come. He repeated what he said before when he cut my arm. This time I think I was floating in between consciousness and unconsciousness. But I heard his next line, "Now as you walk the line between life and your knew unlife make the final leap into the unknown."

I could feel John putting something in my mouth. I drank as best as I could, as I wasn't sure if I was drinking or not. But the pain that hit me when it took hold told me, I had done it right. Even though at the time I had no way of really think, the pain was so bad it seemed to travel through every part of my body. I think even my hair hurt, but I may have even felt a pain through my very soul. If that were possible. Then I barely heard Joe say, "Now take her right before the door of death and allow her to finish her journey."

I seemed to float as everything turned dark, then I felt this lightness. And once I was consumed by a grayness that took hold. I don't know, but I think that's when I died.

Chapter 6

Who am I? Or better what am I?

Now this all happened the very first day. In a normal vampires life this may of taken a week. But for some reason we were put on an accelerate. You'll see as this story continues.

<u>Mary</u>

I can't tell you how much time past by when I finally woke up, as I laid there I knew that at least part of it hadn't been just an ugly dream. I could smell the mattress I was on, but I didn't remember it smelling exactly this badly. It smelled like some one had peed on it every day of its life, with just a hint of mold. Then I felt my throat, it felt like I had been in the Sahara desert, I was also so dang hungry too. It was then that I spoke my mind, "Jeesh I could really eat a burger right now and drink a huge bottle of coke right now."

Then a mans voiced scared me half to death, "You can never eat or drink that anymore." I couldn't believe it, my fingers had dug into the ceiling like about an inch. He then added, "Well unless you want to get sick really that is."

I had to ask the obvious, since I was a bit confused about this. "How did I get on the ceiling, and especially how did my fingers go an inch into the same said ceiling?"

As I looked down he was smiling at me as he replied, "You and I are the same now. It was your strength that cause you to jump, and subsequently your strength that helped you dig your nails into the ceiling."

"Wow, exactly how strong are you?"

"Pretty strong, but you'll realize your strength as well."

"Realize my strength?"

"Well we are all the same technically, but certain families have centered on certain things. Our family has focused on our physical side, we are faster and stronger then most. When going from human to vampire we still have our human mind set. I wouldn't say that you're stronger then me, because men tend to be stronger then women. But you could technically maybe quicker then me, I think Caty maybe faster then me. Now you and her will tend to be stronger then every other woman in our little coven, but always remember that with age usually comes realization. Some may not ever realize their true potential, but we all have the ability. Oh we tend to call these disciplines, because it takes discipline to realize your true potential. Any other questions?"

"Yeah, how do I get down?"

"Just let go."

I did, and he surprised me with catching me as I fell. I did scream as I did, and a little squeak as he caught me. He said then, "I could of let you just hit the floor, but we don't know how strong the floor is. I can assure you that there isn't much that can hurt you anymore, after awhile I can teach you techniques to even resist a bullet hitting you. It won't stop the pain, but you can turn it into a plus. You see that's why I'm here, I need to train all of you how to be vampires."

Oh great the only reason he caught me, was because he didn't want me to hurt the house. Well I guess it good to know, I'm a bad ass now. As if he heard what I said he said, "But it takes times to realize your strength like I have."

There was his smile again, but why doesn't it affect me like it did before. I do have to admit, it is a sweet smile. But it doesn't make me melt like before. Then I realized that I saw his face, I saw it before, but not this clearly. I looked out the window to see if the sun was up. He saw me and asked, "Are you worried about the sun, because of the human lies?"

I had no idea what he was talking about as I asked, "What lies?"

"Ever since cinemary started, they have perpetuated lies about our kind. I don't know if its on purpose, or just ignorance. But one of them is, that if sun light hits, us we burst into flames."

"And we don't?"

"Nope. We don't."

"Good to know. Well does the sun do anything to us at all? I mean lies usually come from somewhere."

"Yes, this one kind of does too. Sun light causes us discomfort, but nothing we can't stand. As long as we avoid direct sun light, we're ok. It seems that anything that can cause us to rot, does so much faster."

"So no sauna's then?"

"Definitely." I had to giggle at that, he handed me a cup and said, "You must be tired and hungry. Here drink this, it will help."

I started to drink, and it kind of exploded in my mouth. It was the best tasting stuff I had ever drank, in a salty kind of way, and I swear I could taste a metal flavor too. I never ate, or let alone licked metal, so I had to wonder how I knew that flavor was metallic. One thing was for sure, it really tasted good. I had to draw it away from my face so I could speak, "This is fantastic. What is it?"

He simply replied, "Oh negative. It keeps better." My head snapped down to see the dark liquid barely falling down the sides if the syrofoam cup. I lifted my head as he added, "It's never as good as the first time."

I knew the answer, but I had to ask anyways, "Are you telling me this is blood?"

"Not the best though, positives taste far better, even though the negatives are far better for us."

"I'm not sure how I feel about feeding from a human vein."

He chuckled as he said, "We only have to do that in an emergency, most of our blood today is harvested. Like we have a running agreement that about a week before it goes bad, blood institutes will sell us their left over blood. Plus even though its rare to get it from the source, there are a few blood farms. We no longer have to skulk to get our blood. Even though I dare say, we might have to resort to that until I can get us set up."

I looked at how bright the light was getting under the door as I said, "I'm not sure I like the idea of that."

He put his head down as he added, "I know, but I feel if I have to tell anyone its you and Cheryl. The others chose this life, but you two had it thrust upon you."

"Maybe not Cheryl. I mean she gets squeamish even if she gets a paper cut."

"Oh I'm sorry. I spoke to her about what was going to happen. You know just before I gave you your choice? And as she was drinking I think she seemed to relish the idea. Well at least the drinking of the blood, and what it does to us."

"What's that?"

"We call it the vampire affect, you could say for a person in their nineties, its like the fountain of youth. But as soon as we start to drink blood, it has an affect on us that takes about five years to be fully realized. The older you are the more pronounced it is, the younger you are the less. Adolescents seem to age at a normal rate, it is extremely forbidden though to change someone that hasn't reached adolescents though. For some reason it causes them to be suspended in time, we don't even know if they could learn how to use their disciplines either. The High Council figures its safer this way."

"Oh then what you're saying is that in about fives years I'll look twenty something. What if what you memory of your twenties isn't exactly a good thought?"

"Well technically you won't be twenty, after all I'm just past of three hundred and I definitely wouldn't call myself twenty." He then put his hand to his chin and added, "Well once you get there, it is safer to pick an age between twenty two and twenty eight and stick with it. Only admit your true age as a vampire to another vampire."

I had to look at him as I moved and sat barely on the window sill. Like I had already said I didn't have a great young adult life, but what could it hurt now that I know better. I had to look at him as I asked, "So what you did is what turned me into a vampire, and because you killed me there's no going back now?"

"Well no. Do you want to go back?"

"Not exactly, but I can say I would of chosen death over turning. There are only two reasons I chose to turn, Cheryl is good, but she isn't really good at life. Ah I mean un-life. Plus what you said about the kids intrigued me, I told you I'm no mother, and I really don't want them thinking of me that way. I do like taking care of people, I think though, because I barely caught some of that, I may have to ask you to explain it to me, the reasons why."

"Well I'll try to give the basics about why, let me think." He sat for a few minutes then he started in, "When we started many years ago, they really didn't know how to turn humans into vampires. Every generation had their own way to sire humans, but through this experimentation they got no where really fast. There were only a few hundred for years though. We aren't exact sure, but we think it all started in the 12th century. There were these people called the Dacian's that the Roman cast declared war against, we vampires declare war its a form of genocide. Now these weren't Romans as in Roman, these were just the vampires. They found they had to protect themselves, and we know it was just one vampire, but he was the one that discovered the way to turn vampires. The problem was he still had a high failure rate, and we would find out that you had to kill the body, for the change to be complete. Where there should of only been one or two vampires all of a sudden the numbers were even. This would also present a problem also, but for the time period it helped them." He then interrupted with, "You should really finish your drink."

I then answered, "I will, I'm just finding this story interesting."

Then to prove it, I tipped my cup up, and drank some of the wonderful elixir. So he went on, "So anyways, over time others were able to discover the way to make vampires. But the Dacian vampires started to think their people owed them something, so they started to miss treat their humans. Vampires back then were ok with this because most vampires looked at humans as cattle, this belief spread through that part of Europe. Some of those that would be, even saw it as away to take over the human world. So they started to raise armies of vampires with no thought of feeding them, they lesser vampire went out of control. So the vampires of the world saw they had to do something to stop this, all the vampires banded together to get rid of all the rogue vampires. You may have already figured this took some time. This is how the inquisition got its start, but like us they had to make as many mistakes as we had. The problem was, they learned far faster then we did."

He moved to the window, where I was sitting and said, "We'll have to rest soon." He looked at me, and as he moved back to the filthy mattress he continued, "So the vampires of the world, after slaughtering all the Romanian vampires, decided they had to do something. They decided that every year there would be a Moot, during these moots two new High Council members would be picked, and every two years there would be a Proconsul Member chosen. This would make sure the members of the High Council were always nine. They set all the rules which came through trial and error, then they have three levels of laws, first level are called the basic laws. Sort of like the ten commandments, that's why there's only six of them I think. Then you have the lay laws, these are generally called the traditions. Kind of like add on's, but don't necessarily have to be followed. And lastly the prime laws which are set by the local leaders and magistrates."

"Who are our leaders and magistrate's?"

"All their sires are missing, so I truly don't know."

"Does anyone have an idea where they are?"

"I do, and it isn't a good thing."

"Can you tell me?"

"You kind of know. You know those guys we had to destroy to save you Mary?" I simply nodded my head, so he went on, "I think those are the minions of those that escaped the Romanian purge."

I blinked my eyes as I said, "But you said that vampires commit genocide when they go to war?"

He sighed as he went on, "So did they, but there wasn't enough vampires to do the job. Like mud threw an iron fist, one or two escaped. When it came to finishing the job after they discovered their mistake always seemed to take to long. So after that they seemed to finish the job, just to find out they only went into hiding. The old world was able to keep them from exploding. Then a terrible thing happened, the new world was discovered. We had no over riding authority here so one or two turned into small groups. The free world was still ruled by the authority of the High Council, but slowly as our population grew from this free world so did the ranks of those few. In recent years they have asserted their own authority over the free world, and are now gaining control. When you face a group you usually face three to four true vampires, they have a way of making cannon fodder. In a sense they barely even know they're vampires, they say they hit them over the head with a shovel, and turn them into vampires. So as a general term we just call all these guys Shovelhead's."

"So what you're saying is that those were Shovelhead's?"

"I could tell the type of vampire they were threw their stench, but I faced a few of their real vampires, and I can tell you it was far to easy to destroy those guys. I can't tell you beyond that what kind of control they have over the city though. Heck since these guys still had their freshness smell, I can't even tell you what type they were. All I can tell you is like cockroaches if theirs one, then there are more. I just hope not far more."

I sat there for a bit, and I could actually feel a sort of twitching to my skin. I don't know how to explain it better then that though, I looked at John and asked, "What is this uncomfortable feeling I'm feeling?"

He replied, "Its you animalistic nature, we usually call it the beast. You see it only gains strength as we loose strength, our strength comes from our blood. We keep drinking blood on a normal basis, and you have no problem. But when you loose control of the beast, you do unspeakable things. Though Mary vampires have lived their entire unlives without ever giving into the beast."

"Unlives? But I thought we could live forever."

"Nope. You see no one is perfect, and over time you loose tissue. There are two ways to kill a vampire. One is to remove its thinking ability, then the tissue dies, and we rot away, like corpse. Two is about the same, over time you finally stop being able to drink, and you just die. You can last about 600 years, keeping up with everything, and possibly 800 years. There are rumors of those that might live to a thousand years old, they only say the originals have lived longer then that."

"The originals?"

"Yeah, but I've never met anyone that's really met one, so I think they're myths. When we get that far I'll tell you the tales, and what I believe, and let you make your own mind up. I think they're just tales like children's tales are to scare you. So I don't put much stock into the tales."

I figured I would go find Cheryl, so I moved to the door. John then said, "Where are you going?"

I told him, "I'm going to find Cheryl."

He smiled and said, "You can't leave for a few days. Just like she has to sleep within a hundred feet of Paul, so do you, with me."

"For how long?"

"They think it takes three days for the inner bond to be broken. If you leave my side for to long you'll feel sick, then start puking up blood. I figure you can be away from me for like two or three hours, then you have to come back."

"Or what?"

"Or die the final death."

"As in dead, dead?"

"Pretty much so."

I looked down as I said, "Oh." Then I asked, "Does this mean I have to do whatever you say?"

He nodded as he was saying, "During the three days, but don't worry Mary, I'm a firm believer in a persons choice. So I will never make you do what you don't want to, well except when we start your training. Then all new vampires will have to do exactly what I tell them to do. I know a few of you will be destroyed in our endeavor, but I hope you all survive to become good vampires. What is weird is that the best vampire tries to live as much like a human as possible. Why this is so strange is we are far from human anymore."

"That makes sense, so what do we do know? I mean do we just lay down on the mattress?"

He smiled and replied, "Until we can seal these windows we have to protect ourselves from direct sun light. Right now we don't have any blankets, so we'll tilt it up and lay under it. Now we could sleep in the sun light one day, but we don't know when we'll get our next blood donation. So its better to conserve our blood, and try not to get to damaged. So until we can truly find a permanent place to stay, and set up some kind of blood delivery, we really need to conserve."

"Can this cause us to die?"

"Yeah. That's why I've already decided to teach you guys how to get blood with the little sip, I know you guys may fail the first few times you try. But if I can get all of you to do it right, then we can feed without killing anyone. This is so we don't attract the watchful eyes of the church or government, plus I know its far easier if you don't have the deaths of innocents on your mind. One thing I will definitely have to teach you guys is, that these Shovelhead's are basically already dead. So you you're not killing someone, but destroying what is already dead."

"Does that really make it easier?"

"Remember me telling you that you have to forget your human world?"

I vaguely remembered that so I replied, "Yeah."

He nodded as he went on, and I got under the mattress with him. "It isn't easy at first, but as you go on and start to realize your disciplines, you also begin to understand the truth of this also. So yeah at first you have problems, but you kind of grow out of it. I think the real realization, is when you realize we are no way even close to being human anymore. Once that day occurs, then you're really on your way to being a vampire. The only problem is, that a lot of vampires forget a simple parable. With great power comes great responsibility."

I had a lot to think about, and a strange bed to lie on. I wrapped my arm's around me, and really didn't feel secure. I then asked John, "Can I ask you a favor?"

"Your my child, if I can do it, I'll try."

"Can you put your arm's around me without anything sexual happening?"

"Sure," He put his arm's around me and asked, "Is this ok?"

"Fine." I replied. I asked one more question until, later that night. "You said we need to rest. Why rest instead of the word sleep? I realized there's a meaning behind everything you do, or say."

"Well we can stay up for days without sleep, as long as you have blood. Some of us never actually sleep, so the term rest fits far better. So now you know."

He was right, I would actually sleep for two to three hours a night. Well except this first day which would be my last full night of sleep. Oh I mean full days worth of sleep.

Chapter 7

Day 2

Much needed information.

John

      He had known he had only laid down just a few hours ago. He rested for a little while and could feel his hunger welling up deep inside. He was older then the rest, so he knew he would feel the hunger more, but his training would allow him to control it far better. He felt the sunlight waning so he crawled out from under the mattress. The sun was still bright, but it was at the apex of setting.

      He had to shake his head, as he realized he had eight new vampires to train all by himself. He then stared at her as she laid there sprawled out. Her first night as a vampire had been a restless one, as her skirt had hiked up far enough to show her rib cage. To try spar her any embarrassment for her, he tugged it down for her own modesty.

      He did then start to wonder exactly how good of a vampire she might be, or if she would just be cannon fodder like so many others. He had to hope this was only be a small invasion, and not a major war, but just this few said other wise. It appeared that the Shovelhead's wanted this city for some God forsaken reason. But who could really figure out their motive really?

      They relish their vampirism like in some B rated movie, heck a lot of them were nothing but cannon fodder themselves. Plus what reason could anyone want this backwoods town anyways. No he had to be wrong, they ha to be a renegade band, like most with no rhyme or reason. Plus he had no real way to know if it was these guys that were attacking them either, so in truth he had only seen three Shovelhead's.

He could see her starting to stir, so he moved to the window to watch the sunset. He always loved this time of the day, the turquoises and purples just before their eyes really started to work. It was a wondrous as well as beautiful sight. Not that his life had ever been anything to write a story about. He watched the lingering sunshine as the terrible darkness took over his and their lives as it would always did, even though technically they weren't condemned to this. She then spoke through a sleepy voice, "It's quite beautiful isn't it?"

He turned his head as he replied, "Yeah. And I've seen quite a few. So are you feeling better today?"

Mary then replied, "I guess so, but you were kind of right. Does this hunger ever go away?"

John smiled as he answered, "You can quench it. It's easier for the young, but you still have to drink a lot of blood. Even going without blood is easier for you. You lack the control you need though, so you can go maybe two, possibly three days. I have had a lot of time to learn this kind of control, so I could go may go two or three weeks. I have never had to test that theory though. The longest I have actually gone without food has been a week. Took almost three weeks to quench my thirst though."

"Why? I mean I think I know why. What I mean is why haven't you eaten recently or didn't eaten for a week?"

I looked at her with my usual smile on my face. Some of those I fought said that was what unnerved them the most. I replied, "This time I was in transit to this city. I bring blood just in case I need it, but usually I wait for them to give me blood. I did have to use some of my blood to help Joe, and to help you and Cheryl threw the change." I didn't tell her the gravity of the situation, as to really how little blood we really had. So I just added, "But don't worry about that, I've already decided to take care of this small problem."

As she smiled back she said, "Don't worry about Cheryl and me right now. We just ate last night and I'll explain to her our problem. No matter what they should go first."

I had to chuckle as I said, "Have you thought about the fact that Cheryl and you are now the kids, among all these kids. You two do have more life experience then them, but as vampires you're just youngest. But you are right though, out of the six, five haven't eaten. Plus the way they didn't know the basics about the blood, I don't think they know that its best to feed every day. I guess what the worse part is that Arty has been using his discipline unknowingly. Billy is so good at what he does too, I'm sure he's been using it a lot too. This means those two have to be the hungriest of the lot."

"The worst part is they are the most hungry? Are you saying they are close to being a monster?"

"I think so, even though I can't be sure how close. Arty, Joe, and Billy have unusual disciplines, as in no one else has or can have them. Arty's is always on because its like part of his natural mind, and I think Joe and Billy's powers use a lot of blood. Of course there are two problems with this assumption. One I can't really be sure that I'm right about their family house's, and second is that even though I do know their families. I have no idea how to train them in these special disciplines."

"Well then, if you had to decide, who would eat first?"

"What do you mean?"

"Well if you know this then you can concentrate on that one first, then go up the line till everyone is fed. Hmm. Well you did say Joe ate last night, so you would only have to choose between Arty and Billy technically."

I had to shake my head as I replied, "I used my reserves literally. I think even though we're out of danger right now, we still have to concentrate on finding a better house to stay in, until I can get all of you trained."

She looked at me with a strange look as she asked, "If this is such a problem? Then why help? I know it's the Okie way, but you aren't an Okie. Most normal people I met outside our area I think would just let us die on our own."

"I kind of told you why, even though its sort of different. Everyone has to have a chance to survive. I can tell you I have taken a lot of unlives away from vampires." I don't know why, but it just felt so right as I spoke. "I have had to take away blood in order to survive at times, but I only really take the lives that deserve it. I have came close to destruction a few times, and somethings got me through it every time to reach this point. If I can pass this onto one new vampire, and he or she lives a good unlife I know this is a good thing. You told me about Cheryl, and because of that I think I can help her. Does this mean I know how this all plays out? Of course not. I would like to help it have the best ending though, if it can possibly happen."

"Well shes not really the same since she fell apart. Even though I do have to admit she seemed different last night."

"Exactly how different?"

"She just seemed so much stronger, like the confident lady I use to know. Like something that had been destroyed inside had been turned back on."

I had to smile at her again as I said, "Oh that might be the vampire blood Paul gave her. It's like it takes your best attributes and enhances them. Like I said though, she has to still realize her strengths, I mean disciplines. In a sense the change makes us better and worse people then what we were before."

"Strengths are a very good place to start though. I'm not trying to second guess you, but in my life that's always been the good place to start."

"I guess that maybe right, but then again I'm not a trainer."

"What's that mean? Can you teach us or what?"

"A trainer knows thing that I technically don't, and they usually have years on them. Each family as I have said have certain abilities, and when we mentor, we're expected to relay these abilities. But a mentor knows far less then a trainer, like how to get to the heart of a situation. This is in a sense of how the final relationship of truly being a vampire comes out. Like Joe could have the ability to be the best of his kind, but its the trainer that finds a way to make their acts easy. Even though in my job, we don't rely on trainers as much. From day one when we are turned it starts to manifest, and our mentor will realize this. So he will bring in another mentor to take over for them, but that person is never really a trainer. They're just another one of us, and through their experiences we realize our own ability. So in the end we really never see a trainer ourselves. I think in a sense though, we are better trained then what a true trainer could do. As an Enforcer you have to realize your abilities fast, but this also forces us not to totally rely on our abilities too. In a sense its a sort of sink or swim attitude."

"Oh." Then she had to giggle as she spoke, "So what you're saying is that a true vampire is gently guided into what they are, but you kind are thrown into the deep end of the pool and you just sink or swim?"

I nodded my head as I said, "Exactly."

"Wait? Technically except for the mentor part, isn't that kind of like how the Shovelhead's are trained?"

"Yeah, I guess you could say that."

"So looking at it from this prospective, isn't that kind of like sending the goose after the gander?"

I had to raise one eye brow as I said, "We are nothing like Shovelhead's. Plus shouldn't be the gander after the goose?"

She started to laugh...at me...I may have been getting a bit angry. Then she regained control of herself and said with a little chuckle, "Don't worry I think I got it...mother."

She started to laugh again, and I didn't find it funny at all. As I sat there though it did begin to seem funny to me for some reason. I let out a little chuckle as I said, "Ok you might be right on that, even I handle the heavy lifting of the training. If you begin to realize our special abilities and you wonder why it doesn't work on us. Most of the disciplines have a problem getting to us, unless its directly related to our physical side. So the only way I can think of covering this is by taking them out, and seeing if it works on humans for them."

She sobered up real quick and said, "Oh ok. That means you want us to take them out, and make a judgment call on this and that?"

I smiled at her and replied, "Yes, but not me or the person that sees it. The test has to be free of opinion. You know like a court of law is supposed to be."

"Makes sense. We can do that."

"Mary I do have to warn you about something about yourself now."

"What's that?

"Watch your temper. You haven't realized it yet, but with special control you could rip the door off a bank vault. We are so strong just by our nature, that many of our kind have hurt a friend just by not think of what they're doing. You could say that like Billy, Arty, Joe, and Pepper this is our special power, and we don't always realize we're using it until its much to late. I tell you this, because I see a control in you I don't see in Caty. You may have to help me keep a close eye on her. I guess you could say this is a generalization thing, but she seems like a very angry young girl."

"I bet we all seem like very young girls to you?"

"Well that would be a yes and no. I'm really sure about you, because I made you, and I can concentrate to see your differences. So even though you will be your what you will be, I have an idea of what to do to help you. Even within this though, I won't be able to teach you everything, because I also hold a special office. The powers of this office are more on what we would call the basic side of things. Still different though, but like all sires I'll teach you what you need to know. If at any time I feel a special pull from you, then I'll teach you the skills of my office. My realization happened in Los Angeles, yet I got my start barely south of Detroit. The last town I had been in was New Orleans, but then again I'm called to a lot of cities. I will have to admit, I didn't expect to see such a problem in such a small city like this. Then again I'm usually directed or drawn to a city, it's all part of my job."

I think the smile that she showed was filled with appreciation, and wonder as she asked. "And just what kind of job would that be?"

I was a bit wary when I replied to her, but I knew I had to tell her all the truth. In fact I think I would always tell her the truth as I replied to her, "I'm called the Enforcer. It's kind of the vampire version of a sheriff, even though its far deeper then that, but even more for me then most others. Most are called in by whatever force controls the city, as you heard me say I'm usually drawn. Most leaders of a city are glad to see an enforcer show up. Yet I walk into town, and they pale at the sight of me. It's our job to get rid of the root of problems when they show up, even if it leads directly to the local leader. I felt the problem when I came to this city, but in a sense, I had no idea why I wasn't called, like I am most of the time. Being here was a mistake, I almost never make any mistakes when I'm reading a map. Because I've live in a world where there aren't any coincidences, I have to think there's a meaning or will why I'm here. I just don't really know why, at first I thought it was the kids. They're so young, and it is a very unusual thing. Then I had to save you from those Shovelhead's, so now I'm thinking this maybe the reason. But to tell you the truth, I can't really be one hundred percent sure of any of this."

It was strange that it was so easy to tell her this, and she nodded her head the entire time, with the occasional, "Yeah I think I understand," and. "Uh-hun I see."

Then we could hear the girls giggling as they walked down the hall. I had to give her a knowing smile as I then added, "I think you are about to be welcomed into this new existence. I know I've told you a lot, but be reserved in the information you actually tell them. I guess the next thing to say is, I hope you'll be good friends with them. I think you know that friends can be a good resource to ones self. Especially in this world, where so many of our kind would rather see young vampires dead, or worse just used as cannon fodder."

Right then, the door burst open as Cheryl came in, and wrapped herself around Mary's neck. She then drew back and asked, "Mary isn't this life great?"

She corrected her with, "You mean Un-life?"

"Yeah, yeah. But we can do anything, and see things, oh. My. God. We can live way past where we should die, and the best thing is once we reach like five years, we'll look twenty again."

They both hugged again, and she kind of looked at me. I nodded and made my way to the door as she said, "Cheryl we have to talk."

I was barely out the door where Caty, and Pepper had stationed themselves. I then said, "Hey knock first, but go in, and welcome your new sister. I want to see all four of you downstairs in a very short bit though. After all we have to start to work on things."

I could see that Caty stayed just outside the door as Pepper went in. I knew she was trying to be careful and reserved. So I added, "Don't worry Caty, I don't think you'll be interrupting. I'm sure Mary would be happy to see you. You were just doing your job I asked you to do."

~ o ~

I didn't wait to see if it went ok, I just moved down to what we were calling the kitchen. I was glad to see where I had asked them to leave my cooler. I knew what was in it, but I picked it up to make an assessment of what we had left. So I popped it open to see the last of our blood, just enough to quench the thirst of one vampire. I thought of up ending it, and just stopping my thirst, but I knew it wasn't enough or fair to the others. So all I did was shake my head as I said in a low voice, "We just don't have what we need, but then again I didn't think I would be feeding three this soon. We just have to find away to get more."

Then a barely recognizable voice that came from right beside me, "We had a couple of refrigerators full of that stuff at our old house."

I had to rear up, even though I wasn't as reactive if I hadn't barely recognized his voice. "Dammit Joe! Don't ever sneak up on me! I could accidentally kill you!"

I could see he was aware of how I moved and said, "Sorry. I thought you heard me come in."

"I guess its alright. No harm done. So what are you talking about?"

"Oh our house we came from. It has like two refrigerators just dedicated to carrying blood, plus each freezer is full, with a separate freezer. I think there's a wine cooler too, even though that maybe just for wine. Samuel always had me help him fill the fridge, Paul did it to. I think it was kind of our sires jobs, even though my master got balled out for not doing the paperwork. I think my sire and Paul's drank it with wine, that's why I said that about the wine cooler. They were all metal like, whereas the freezer was off the landing and was just a white one. Oh and in each freezer above the refrigerators they had an area sectioned off, for what he called special mix, and to never touch that."

At first it was barely a thought, but in seconds as I stood there it started to grow. I had to wonder if this is one of those feelings like

Arty's kin usually got. Was it be possible, then I had to think about the ramifications if I was wrong. I then thought about Arty then, and with him was the ever presence of Billy. I knew they were both about to tip over the edge, and that can be really bad for someone so young. I knew I had to ask the obvious question though. "How long have you been gone out of the house?"

He had to think before he replied, but the news was actually about fifty, fifty. "Oh maybe three weeks, possibly a month. Why?"

"Well the refrigerated blood may have gone bad. Hmm. Though we maybe able to raid your old house and get the frozen blood."

"That maybe a good idea. I see Caty getting more out of control every day, plus maybe we can grab a few clothes, we kind of left in a hurry. The way we were dying there, I have to wonder why our sires told us to stay there. I mean they even said it was safer, but we lost three there."

"Well it might not be for anything, but it sounds like you already got raided. We'll probably get in there, and there won't be any blood left."

"We didn't get raided, they were killed away from the house, but we sent out Billy every time to find them. They were never far from the house. It didn't seem like we really didn't start to get hit until we left the house. In fact for the first few days Arty, and Pepper were all for going back home. Back then we may have actually listened to Arty if he had ever said it was one of his visions, but then we got here, and all the attacks seemed to just stop. I mean the warehouse not here."

I pulled up a chair and asked, "And how hard would you say you were hit until then?"

"Well we were hit almost every day there abouts. Why?"

He then pulled up a chair ,and sat down too as I replied, "Joe I can't be sure, but you may have put me onto something. It is common to try and protect others as well as yourself. There maybe a protective point or possibly a spell over the house. Most magical vampires like your sire can feel it, so as to avoid it, or get invited into the area. People have long believed vampires couldn't come into homes, but most often it was just a place of power. Now a normal vampire can get past it, even though it makes a home almost impossible to enter. That's only if it were an actual human home, I'm thinking that your sire enhanced it so it would be like a human house. Like I said though, this is just a guess, because I can't be sure about your family. Once you became a vampire, did one of the elders have to invite them into the house? And bare in mind, that you were under your sires auspice, so you probably didn't have to be invited."

"Yeah, those they called the Lords had free access. But we would have knights come over, and they would sit out until our Lords asked them in."

"Good. I think this might be the break we were looking for, I have to think of a plan now. I think though all of you maybe going home, of course never count your eggs before they're hatched. First I'll have to check the area out before I say anything definitively, so for now all we're doing is a simple raid."

"What are we going to do?"

"Right now just get food and possibly clothes, but don't tell anyone truly about what we talked about. I wouldn't want them to get over excited, that's when mistakes are made."

Billy then asked as he entered the room, "Make mistakes where?"

I simply replied, "I have an idea how we maybe able to get the blood we need. So Billy will you go, and get Arty, while Joe goes and gets the girls?"

"I'm right here," Said Arty as he went on with, "I think the girls are coming also. Even though with all their clucking I can't be sure."

I could now hear them also as I said, "Arty never say that where a girl could hear you, I shutter what the possibilities could be." Then I said in a louder voice, "Could you all join us? I think I have an Idea of how to get us our much needed blood."

Chapter 8

A plan to an old life.

Caty led the way so I offered her my seat first, Joe did the same. But the other two just sat there, so I cleared my throat. When that didn't work I asked in a low voice, "Billy and Arty are you two going to be gentlemen?"

I was about ready to say something in a stronger voice, when Paul came in and said bluntly. "Oh for God's sake. Will you two stop being morons, and give your seats up. Cheryl and Pepper should be sitting, am I the only sane kid here."

With that Billy jumped up, and gave his seat to Cheryl. Arty just jumped up on the counter and sat down, so Pepper sat in his chair as she gave him a look. I watch Billy and Paul join him then, whereas Joe just pulled up a crate. So then I felt free to actually talk. So I started with, "Ok, I have to reason this out first. I guess the first thing that should be said, is you all are going home."

The only ones that didn't cheer were of course Cheryl and Mary, with Joe because I think he knew it already. Once everyone calmed down I went on, "Ok I'll take Caty and Mary with me to check the outside. This could take awhile Caty, so you might want to set Cheryl on looking for something for you to wear after you finish our main job. Now Billy I would love for you to come with us, but we need your nose. Pepper you look at the blood in the refrigerators, then Billy you smell them. This is all to make sure these are ok, if not just trash them. Paul your job will be to keep count."

I then handed him my cooler and said, "Fill this, but we need to know exactly how much is in there, plus we'll have to have 9 extras to drink when we're completely done. Arty its your job to search the house for unusual spot, but you'll have to set Cheryl to looking for spot you already know about. Unlike Arty, Cheryl your job will be to judge accessibility to the spots he tells you about. Now for you Joe, I don't expect you to hit a home run off the bat. But you go to the library, and if anything even remotely looks like it maybe about magic, grab it."

I then looked at Mary and Caty and said, "Ok here is how we'll work. I'll check the area, while I do that you check the outside of the houses out. Then which ever direction I come from you then check out the house right there, this way I won't have to speak to you. Once we get done with that then we'll move across the street. I'll go to the right of the first house I want you to check. Then just do the same as we did before as I meet you. I have no idea where they are watching the house from, but I'm sure they are. If I get into a fight that means you two come running. But once, and if we find, and deal with any problems, we may find. After that we'll decide what to do beyond that."

I then moved around as I finished up, "I said we're going home, but unless we do this right we may just have to leave again. Plus we'll have to be on guard there, after-all to just make sure they aren't watching us all again. Any questions?"

Mary then asked, "Yeah just one. How are we going to get there?"

I thought that was kind of a strange question so I simply replied, "My car."

"You think you can fit nine of us in there?"

"Oh shoot! Well I hadn't figured on that problem. Oh wait. Didn't you say you had a car?"

"Yep, out of gas though."

I pulled out my bank roll of barely over $49 and pealed off a ten spot and handed it to her. I then said to her, "Go put this in your tank, and come right back. Then we'll get started."

	Now she could of said that she wanted Cheryl to go with her, I'm surprised she didn't. If you think about it I gave her the perfect avenue to just escape from us. I knew that if she did it would be with Cheryl though, so all I can say is that somewhere in all I said to her help her make up her mind. Which might have been the second best thing to happen to this group. The first best thing was yet to happen, and came in from a surprising place. Not that I care though, well maybe I should say I really care. Now you can see how this group just seemed to be the right mix.

	I wasn't as surprised about what Mary had done until someone mentioned it to me though. Then I worried about it a little, but only in secret so the kids wouldn't know I had made a mistake. I guess the most reassuring thing was as close as she was with Cheryl, she didn't think to take her. Well to be truthful, since I don't know if her intent was run or not, I can't really say that either. I can say that I was glad to see her show up, after about twenty minutes. To be safe I sent Paul, Billy, and Caty to go with her. I told her that if Paul didn't know the way, then I was sure Caty could get her there. I also had to wonder if she had made a mistake too, and that sooner or later she would figure out a way to escape. I can say, that I really wasn't so concerned for her though, when I really thought about it. With what she told me about Cheryl, she was really the one I was concerned about. My family cast, even those that aren't trained, tend to do well on their own.

	I took the lead, and was followed by her. I was glad I had Pepper in my car, whenever Joe was unsure, she knew exactly where to turn. At first I thought we were going back to the warehouse, but then the turns went a different direction. We were driving in an area with very dilapidated houses and businesses. I knew this wasn't the area though, we loved to hide our houses in plain sight though. For a vampire to actually own their own houses, it usually had to show just how wealthy they were. So when we turned into a neighborhood just off this street I had to wonder. Even as I saw the sign Heritage House editions I was wondering, then that changed as all the houses became the old Victorian style. There were a few more modern house, but I was sure it was going to be one of these Victorian's. As we turned into a very old, very big, as well as very dark Victorian houses, it wasn't that much of a surprise. We all then piled out of our respective cars.

  I didn't say a word, but just pointed so they would move. I had decided to take the long way around, so I directed the girls to get started. As they moved out I turned and was over the fences in a blink, as I moved along I look under every bush, barely up in the trees, and other area's that were far to obvious. One thing I can say about Shovelhead's, they maybe tough to kill, but I haven't ever really met a smart one. This would be really fast to though, I knew I couldn't allow Mary and Caty to hang to long. I was approaching them from of the house, then I noticed two things. First the kids in the house were turning on all the lights, I would have to scold them on that later on. Secondly the girls were in the shadows, but they weren't really trying to hide. Well I could correct this right now, and I would of done that right then if every hair on my skin hadn't gone up. Immediately I stopped, and started to scour the area for Shovelhead's. I finally found a well hidden being, that I knew couldn't be a Shovelhead. At first I couldn't really tell anything about what, or whom this might be.

  Then I seemed to just catch that glint of yellow eyes. I couldn't tell though if they glowed or not. So I said in my normal voice, "Ok. I have found you. You can come out and face me."

  Then a voice that was between human and beast said, "Then who are your friends, a trap for me to walk into."

  I could tell that this was one of the border line families, you could tell by how close they were to sounding like an animal. I thought to reassure whatever sex this thing was. "Listen here you don't want to do anything, our not attacking you outright should show you our intentions."

  A wolf then came out of the bushes, I could now see the golden glow of its eyes. I tried to use a special ability to see if I could see any red tint in her eyes, I think she may have been doing the same to me. I knew the trouble she was having keeping this form, as I heard a hint of a woman's voice. "I show you my form, will you now run from me or treat me with honor?"

"If that's your true form then I'm Chicken Little, I know what family you're from. All I really want to know though, is are you with the Shovelhead's, or will you truly be truthful to me?"

The wolf then went into the bushes as she laughed. I knew it would take her a few minutes to come back to her true form, so I folded my arms, as I waited. If nothing else she maybe able to help to us, then a very bronze looking black woman stepped out from behind the bushes. She was wearing a very tight natural leather almost Indian style garment. For her kind it was natural for them to want to look like the woods. Her dark hair I could see was placed in a long pig tail, that was so she could move through the woods better. Like the kids I had no idea what kind of vampire she was, but her style and clothes gave me a good idea. She then put her hands on her hips and spoke in what I could only figure to be a Jamaican accent. "Now you see me for what I am, and as for Shovelhead's, I eat them for my breakfast. Only fools would side with other fools. Now you see my bare arms what will you do?"

I knew the way she spoke, she had figured out my family as well. So I opened my jacket to expose my Glokk and Kukri knife. I then put my hand in my empty holster to show it was empty. I knew she wouldn't even come close unless I said to the girls what was right, but first I figured to see how good she really was, which for my two girls wouldn't be that hard. So I turned and offered her my back, I also knew if she had figured out what house I was, she was probably smart enough to have already seen the girls as well as know about my families famed speed. I then said so she could hear, "I offer you my back in good conscience. I'm no threat to you."

Then she showed just how good she was, "What of your two friends? Do they choose to honor me too? Do they still not pose a threat to me?"

Well I had no choice now, but I decided that I may use the excuse of youth. "They're still young, one is just one day old. The other even being as I am, has just been found, and she is truly young too. Maybe a month or more."

"How can I truly decide whether they have been truthful to you? Or if this is even a lie to you as well?"

"Well one was made just recently, I know because I made her. The other I can say isn't truly a threat to you, you have the word of the Enforcer."

She was right next to me when she spoke next, "The Enforcer, those would be very big shoes to fill if you truly are he. You must of made a mistake and meant an enforcer, besides I heard he was seven feet tall."

"I have heard that, and he never offers his back to anyone. His lightning speed is beyond any real claim, even beyond his own family, with a strength to match. In truth I didn't make any mistakes, and I have had to fight many unwanted fights. Will you except my truce though through my act?"

"How can I know you are you, or just one that pretends?"

"You can't, but you have probably figured out my family by now." I sighed and continued on. "If I wanted you dead you would be so, and in this environment, you probably couldn't escape me."

"His blade is renowned, even though many have copied it. When I see it for myself strike true, then I will know it is you. Until then, I'll just think of you as one of your lot."

"I could show you now, but the only target are my children. I know you wouldn't want me to strike one of your children, so you have to know, I wouldn't do it to my own then. Then again if you stay with us long enough, you may see me use it. We have a strange problem in a city so small."

She now sighed and confessed, "Yes I know. I knew this house was here, and sought comfort for the night. As you know we are very careful, so I wanted to see if there was any trouble. I saw three of that same said trouble, they did not expect how fast I would attack. So two died as one fled, but I followed him and made sure he told no one about me. But this city is far larger then I think you suspect, it took me a while to get here, and had to board up one night. I had decided to come here to get direction to my next target, but at last I have realized that they might not know of their own problem, so this time I came to make them aware of it."

"I see, then you just did this out of the goodness of your heart?"

"I know you know that isn't true. As you know we don't have need for money, but a dollar here or two there, I thought I could make a few bob if they didn't know."

"Then again you could be one of them, I offered a treaty and yet you have to reply to me."

"Well I guess the better part of valor is to say yes, I except, and to show my trust in your offer, I also offer my title as well, I'm known as a huntress. Like you though, you will have to see me in action to know I'm telling you the truth."

"Then I suspect that we can now walk to the house, so I can present some more hidden truths."

"I don't like the sound of that, but I guess I have to trust you since you offered the truce first. Now as a resident of this house will you invite me in?"

Oh my I forgot about that, I then turned to Caty and said, "Caty can you invite Mary, me and...I didn't get your name Huntress?"

She then said in a loud voice, "Child it is Naomi. Keep it to yourself though. I don't commonly spread my name around to the air."

Then Caty came out of the darkness and asked, "Will you

Naomi, along with our new defunct leader John, and my new friend come into our house."

As we walked up to where Mary and Caty now stood Naomi then asked, "Do these children always follow orders this well?"

I knew if I didn't speak I'm sure Caty would rip into Naomi. So I replied over Caty's voice, "No. I've told them I want them all to be totally independent."

She had to giggle as she said, "Ah so you knew my game and you headed me off."

I smiled at her as I replied, "They haven't eaten in days and she is one of mine."

"Oh so you did it to protect me. I dare say that I could carry the day in one so young. You are right I can smell the ripeness on them."

Mary then asked me, "Whats that supposed to mean?! If you were slamming her again, she may have to beat me."

I could hear the slight tone of irritation in her voice, so I quickly spoke, "No Mary. What Naomi meant was that you still smell like a human. I guess I should of told you. You don't gain the true vampire smell until after about that five years, you remember I told you about that. Naomi and I probably don't smell like anyone else, but unlike us Billy and Naomi have this heighten nose that can pick it up."

"Oh, I guess that's a good thing then."

Naomi shook here head as she said, "Oh they're really that new then. I thought they would at least have some formal training."

I then had to admit as we reached the back door that we were using, "Well except for me, there really isn't anyone here of age or of any experience. But we have two that have shown ability, I can't really make a judgment as I have only been with them for two days. I've seen that mine, and she seems to have natural ability, but then again like I said shes only a day old."

She let out a low laugh, even though I think she tried to cover up. Everyone in the house were clearly still busy, so they barely lifted their heads. I then said, "I want to introduce Pepper, Billy, and Paul to you Naomi. Guys this is Naomi. Naomi as soon as they get done I would like you to look at Billy. I took a guess on my own, and think he maybe your type. Even though it was a loose guess, and thus far he's proven me completely right. Now you guys say hi to Naomi, then I need to talk to her."

They all said their hi's and went right back to work. Naomi then asked, "What do you have them doing?"

"Pepper seems to be one of the beautiful vampires, so I have her looking for impurities. Billy is then sniffing whatever she approves, and if it doesn't smell strange, he hands it to Paul. From there he accounts for it, and I was thinking of allowing him the control over our blood."

Pepper then spoke up and said, "John as of yet we haven't really had but like two or three pass. This maybe a bust."

I smiled at her and answered her even though it wasn't a question, "There wasn't really that much hope Pepper, but if we can increase that number to now ten, then we can all have a drink before we have to go out again. That is one of the reasons I brought you in here Naomi. I know how cautious your kind are, so I would ask you how much you were actually able to actually search around us?"

It didn't take her but about a second to start, "Well you know my kind well. I search the outer perimeter, and all of the inner, but I only found this three when I approach the house from the west. I took my time getting back, so I could cover the destruction I caused. So no trace of those three will ever be found, but on my second approach I found no one, even though I wasn't really looking. I figured to tell those of this house, and then they could complete my job. Then I could get a good days sleep."

Joe walked in with an arm full of books, so I said, "Joe you can put those back, plus I think you can do me two favors. Go around the house, and turn off any lights not in use. I don't think we have anything to worry about since you six have returned, but its better to be safe then sorry. And I know you knew about the house, but just in case you forgot could you please invite Cheryl into the house."

He looked wide eyed at me. So I nodded my head, and he ran off saying, "Sure thing John. Hey guys we're here to stay, start to put things back."

I then turned back to Billy and said, "Billy you go around, and sniff for any strange smells just to be sure. Caty hes real vulnerable when he does this, so can you follow him, and get his back just in case of trouble. Mary most everyone is here, but can you go around checking on the others. Plus tell them there's a meeting after they're done. Paul after the meeting, you'll have to show me to that freezer you told me about. I know most house put a lock on it, to keep it safe from prying public eyes. We may have to find away into it though without breaking it to terribly badly."

Mary looked at me and asked, "When will I have time to move in my clothes?"

I looked at Caty and said, "You can take over for Mary after the meeting." I then looked at Pepper and asked, "Do you know all the rooms with shutters and those that only have heavy drapes?" She nodded her head so I continued, "Good make sure Cheryl and Paul put their stuff into one room. Then make sure Mary puts all her stuff into another shuttered room. Once you're sure that you have done this then come back here. But we do have one more thing to do before the night leaves us."

Naomi then asked, "Ah I see. Then you are making sure they don't forget to train?"

"Absolutely not. I was hoping that you might give us a bit of your expertise, and help out about half of us."

"Why not, I saw a park just a bit away, plus it will give me time to get my vehicle."

We kind of talked a bit as we waited, from what I gleamed from her, she certainly had a hard life. I also could see that she was old, but she must have been changed in the last hundred years. It was kind of strange that she had taken on such a modern look on, and yet had this certain elegance to her. Some times this does happen that someone that isn't meant for their new life is picked. I had to figure she was one of those, even though when she talked about being a huntress, she had a lot of knowledge. As an enforcer they tend to talk to much, but as The Enforcer I didn't like to talk about my job much at all. She even asked me about this, and I told her the truth, 'When so many can tell my exploits so much more better then me. Really, why waist the time, and allow the fear not be theirs.'

I guess what was kind weird, is how excepting she was of that answer. Anyways, once everyone got into the room I spoke, "Ok is everyone here?"

I got a few yup's and I think so's, so I went on. "This is Naomi, and she has followed the order of the truce, so that means she is protected under my auspice. Now for the good news, the Shovelhead's only had three guys watching the place." I looked around to take a dramatic pause then went on, "Naomi here was able to surprise them, and they couldn't tell anyone we that we have come back here to live. Better yet is, that she took care of this even before we got here. This means that no one has any idea where we are, so we're safe to stay, for now."

I knew there would be some concern, but I wanted everyone to get their cheering done first. After they were done I went on, "Now this doesn't mean we are totally safe though, this only means we have a window of freedom for right now. I can tell you that this has told me that they don't respect your ability, and that's where my next part will come in. If we start now, the next time someone tries to separate you, and destroy you, we can give them an unwelcome surprise. Not only that, but as long as they keep under estimating you, this gives you a window to even get better. This will give us the time to get you better through training, and possibly give you a fighting chance at survival."

 Naomi then said, "If it is giving those Shovelhead's an upset stomachs, you can count me in. They have bullied my kind into joining them for far to long, I have long hunted them one at a time when they cross my path. It's now time for their reckoning."

Chapter 9

They really are like cockroaches.

I tried not to show how happy I was, to actually have another elder to help me. I'm not sure I did well though. I then added, "You could also call me an expert at handling Shovelhead's too. I've destroyed a few in my un-life."

She openly laughed as she said, "A few? Kiddo's if what he has told me is true, hes known for destroying hundreds and possibly thousands. You may not know this children, but in the vampire world, we have a God's honest rock star here. The way he doesn't toot his own horn, is making believe him more and more."

I looked at every face and said carefully to every kid, "Its best if you try to forget that though. Naomi and I are old enough so vampires like Paul can't easily get into our thoughts, but all of you are still very young. If I know Naomi she has ways to even suppress your inner turmoil very well. So even though it will be mandatory for Billy, everyone else can go to her and ask for help in this. Now this doesn't mean just to intrude on Billy and her though, be courteous, and ask first, after all we aren't savages here."

"Good point John. I will handle hand to hand and concealment too. I know John's two best subjects are hand to hand with weapons and all the physical side. So if I have what I heard John saying earlier right, we'll be leaving in a few minutes, and covering some of the basics."

"Yeah, a simple game of hide and seek at first. This will give both Naomi and I an idea of where you stand on this. Then we'll go into sparing, but just simply wrestling for today. We can get into Karate and Wistenese later. I'll teach all of you also how to use a blade, I use a pistol, but most of our kind usually don't like these. We prefer to fight with our hands instead, I will use my experience in pistols to try, and help some of you out. Again not now, but later. Now all we have to do is make four two man groups. You may ask why four groups, well that's simple. We usually fight in two man groups so one can cover the back of the other, two divides into eight is four."

"Well with you ,and me John that would make five."

"Oh yeah, Ok four groups for training and later five."

"Good idea for now."

I took Billy, Caty, and Mary, I then said, "These are the basis for the battle groups. We only know whom will lead two groups now, that will be Naomi and me. I also want to make it mixed groups, so we have Pepper and Cheryl left. I have no idea who can take care of themselves yet, so just not to break you guys up. Pepper you join Billy and Cheryl you'll be on me, but Cheryl whomever gets picked to be with Naomi, will be your training partner. Naomi, Arty seems to have some experience, but I really don't know Paul or Joe's experience level. I do believe we really need to defend Joe though. I'm not sure, but thus far he's shown all the abilities of being a blood mage."

"Well then that's simple, Joe you're my partner and Cheryl's my partner for training. Since Mary is so new, I think Arty should go with her, that leaves Paul to go with Caty. So I think we're as set here as we can be, John you take the team of Cheryl and Joe. I have to look at Billy so I'll take that team."

I quickly added, "I think it would be best if I take Paul's team just because of what he is, that leave my daughter in your care Naomi."

"I don't know if I like that John. That would put an untold burden on me to protect her."

I smiled at her as I replied, "Well I though of not telling you this Naomi, but lets just say, that our family has been in more disputes with what I believe Paul's family is to be. That is if I'm right about his lineage."

She had to smile at that, and then said, "Why don't we compromise then. We'll do a rotation of our training classes until we figure what they're best at."

"Actually that sounds like a good idea, then we get them into more training, and can make our decisions quicker."

"Then its decided. So everyone get ready to move. When we get back, everyone that doesn't have a job come to the aid of Paul, Cheryl, and Mary. Once this is done the rest of the night is all to yourselves. Now let's get under way."

With this we all moved to the door, since I knew that Naomi had a plan I would of course start mine, just around the house. I couldn't decide which might be the worse, so I mentally flipped a coin and Joe won. So I then said, "Paul I want you to go hide, do the best you can to keep Joe from finding you."

With that Paul took off, and I was glad he was taking it so seriously. I then looked at Joe and said, "Give him all the time you think you need, then go after him like your life depended on it."

I'm not sure he knew what I meant, but then my instruction were meant to be ambiguous. I waited for him to go, and then turned to Cheryl and said, "You basically have the same instruction that I just gave to Joe, but if you find Joe before he finds Paul, then you continue, and search for Paul."

After Cheryl left Caty asked, "Why did you do that?"

I looked at her and without an answer I said, "You have the same instructions as Cheryl, but I'll give you a clue."

Then I took off my jacket and laid all my equipment on the front seat. Then I turned back to her and said, "Dang I love a good game of vampire hide and seek. See you in a few minutes."

She started to walk away, and as she ran off, I knew she finally understood. If only she knew that was my clue to start to seeking them also. She didn't have much time to hide, so I found her almost immediately. After I did so I whispered to her in a voice I knew only vampires could hear, and told her to get back to the car. As you probably already know my next target was Cheryl. I tried to give them a chance to do good, then I would tell them to get back to the car. Next was Joe, he was a bit harder even though when I did find him he looked like he was confused. So after I whispered to him, he whispered back to me. "John Paul was doing so well," He pointed to a shrub, "Then he eased his way out of there, and started to look at that other shrub."

He moved his finger to the shrub he was standing in front of. So I whispered to him, "Go get the rest we may need back up."

Joe took off the way I pointed, so then I moved up to Paul. I got close enough so he could hear me. Then I said in a low voice, "Paul what's going om?"

He turned his head and replied, "I think they're dead John. Why they haven't been discovered, or rotting hasn't taken over yet, I don't know."

I slowly creep to his side, and I saw the two dark figures. I knew though I couldn't quite see them as well as Paul, but I whispered to him. "Do you see any aura around them at all?"

He nodded his head as he replied, "Yeah, but one is extremely weak. Whereas the little one has a very strong one."

I got up and said, "You grab the small one arms and I'll grab the big ones. We need to drag them out here so we can look at them better."

He nodded his head, and then made a sound of disgust. I knew he had no idea what he was looking at, but these two didn't seem dead.

All he saw were their died up shriveled bodies. Now I knew they were close to death though, and were also very close to the beast. So I moved him away, and knew one of them must have been very powerful to keep them this long from the beast. I saw both Caty and Cheryl draw up as they got close, and Joe simply said, "Ugh disgusting."

I knew I couldn't do anything until we all got back, but I had to make sure they would help me. So I told them the truth, "This is what happens to you when you haven't had blood in a long time. Now technically because of the hospitality laws of our kind, we must take them in, and help them. I can't tell if they will survive this, but again we must try. Now you four take the big guy, and if he tries to bite you just drop him. You have to continue to bring him into the house, I'm hoping if you drop him enough he'll learn his lesson. Of course my top hope is that he won't try to bite you at all, but before we move tell me what floor has the most secure room."

Joe replied, "The top floor, I mean the third floor. The top floor would be the attic."

I nodded my head and said, "Lets move."

So they moved like clock work. I used my speed, and they were almost to the house as I rested the small one on the floor. I then ran downstairs, and grabbed two bags of blood, but didn't take the time to check the blood count. Then I was just able to move back upstairs, and to find the room. I placed the blood in a near by room, and moved back to her. Finally I moved her to the room just as the four of them got to this floor. I place the small one on the rug next to the bed, I instructed them to do the same thing as I went after the blood. Finally I said to them, "Ok Caty, and I will back up Cheryl and Paul, Joe you've got the door. Cheryl and Paul you two put these bags in their hands." I then handed them the bags of blood. Then I continued on, "Now they'll want more blood and probably come after it, that's why you move right behind Caty and me. Joe we'll back out, as soon as we clear the door, you slam that baby shut. Caty you, and I will hold the door until he has shut it and locked it."

I knew they were scared as they did exactly what I told them. With a precision I had for the first time had glance within these four when they did as I asked. I then said to them, "Ok onto our next hide and go seek game. Everyone to my car."

I think they were surprised at how whatever, I was about this whole situation. I really wasn't but they didn't have to know that. I took them to a little place near our first hide out. I didn't actually want to tempt going there, but it did seem like a good place.

I then had them all get out, and I looked at each of them as I spoke, "Oh I'm going to change it up. We're going to still do it Paul, Joe, Cheryl and then Caty. The real difference will be in that you don't want to get caught. So this means that you fight like hell, so not to get caught. The only exception is, that if you are tapped by me, you come back to the car. I'm doing that, well because you really don't want to be fighting me. Also there is going to be a time limit to when you start hunting, once I tell Paul go you'll have four minutes until Joe comes hunting for you. Remember you don't want to hurt each other yet, so if you feel you can't win just say uncle. Do any of you have any questions?"

They all stood in literal silence, so I went on with, "Paul I would run when I say now, and remember I mean literally." I looked at my watch and as it came up to the twelve I said, "Now!"

Paul was then off like a shot, I kept my eyes on my watch, and one at a time I said the word now. I figured it would have the same result, especially because now they knew better an would hide much better. I gave Caty the promised four minutes, but as I did I took my fighting gear back off. No point of accidentally destroying one of them before their time, if you have never seen a real vampire go to the shadows, I did just that right then. It wasn't as if we could use them to transport from one to another, but for some reason we could move from one to another without being seen. The best way of explaining this, is that normal humans won't look up on us. So as long as it was over distance, this was a simple trick. As a vampire ages he learns to look for this to protect ourselves, but these guys were way to young to know how to do this. I also knew what do look for, you would be surprised how easy it is to hunt at night. Of course it does help us that we have the eyes of a vampire, and as most races this was better in some then others.

I crept up on Caty, and I got really close as I knew she might be my hardest target. Not in the hiding part, we aren't known to be that good at concealment. I knew it would be awhile before she could get her anger under control also, which might present a problem right now. That's the one problem with our kind, even though we had great abilities, we tended to have anger issues. I got close enough, and said just loud enough so she could hear me. "Caty I found you, now I could touch you, but I'm sure you would just rather walk to the car."

Now for Cheryl, I could tell she might be good at this. Right now though she was having problems with getting dirty, her kind are known to have to get this mind set, so I found her easily. I moved up and tapped her on the ankle and said, "Got you Cheryl back to the car."

She jumped and said a four letter word, I won't repeat it though. Next would be Joe, even though I knew he didn't need this training as badly as everyone else did. If I was right about him, he would be the power behind our attacks, kind of like the hammer. When you think about it, how I fight, you could probably call me the anvil. When I found him he was doing ok, but I knew he might not ever really get any better. I tugged the back of his shirt, and said the same as I did to Cheryl.

Paul would be last, and even though his kind weren't known for fighting with their hands. They did like to use cover when firing their weapons, so I knew this would help him. I had to wonder though as I moved, if his sire hadn't trained him to hide. I was having a heck of a time finding him, but then I saw him stand straight up, and move to another bush. This was a terrible move, and I really had to wonder what he was doing. I wanted to make sure he didn't get away with this, so I started to move toward him. I figured if I tackled him, that would probably teach him not to just stand up like that. As I was about to move, and tackle him, I saw movement out of the corner of my eye. I looked that direction to see a small figure getting ready to jump this one, and he was well hidden. That is when I realized that the small figure was Paul, and the other one was someone else. I used something I learned from a friend to help focus my eyes. This help me realize that this guy was not only a vampire, he might not be a good guy.

    I really didn't have much time after that though, Paul jumped up, and rushed him. All I could think was he thought this guy was Joe. This was my fault, because I didn't think any vampires would be out here yet this close to the old warehouse, how stupid could I have been. I then moved as fast as I could, as the other vampire threw Paul off him. I think he was really thinking of what to do next, when I came on the scene. I used my strength, and ripped his head off his shoulders. Paul was wide eyed as he slowly crumpled to the ground, then I dropped his head. I didn't think, I then moved everything of our foe under a shrub. Then I came back to Paul and said, "This may have been a mistake, move to the car.?"

    As he did, I back tracked and made sure no one was following us. When I got back to the car, Paul I think was explaining what had just happened. I immediately barked orders, "Get into my car, NOW!"

    I dove home with my eyes shooting everywhere, I really didn't want to be followed. I pulled into the garage right next to a new car, I saw Mary's car on the other side of this one. It was one of those yellow jeeps, with the big black covers over the top of it. I really didn't question it, because I figured Naomi would bring her car to the house. Normally we would have been more careful to make sure it was truly her car. I didn't have time to look though, and see that the trunk of Mary's car was open. I then said to my kids, "If you see Naomi before me tell her we have to talk real fast."

    I was trying not to sound like I was worried, not that I really was. It is that after hurrying them, and not running, but moving rather rapidly into the house may have excite them. I was glad to hear Naomi's voice say, "I'm her John, what's wrong?"

    "We had Shovelhead troubles. I didn't stay around to see if any of his friends were there, I figured it was best to get the kids home first."

Paul then said, "You should of seen it. John just ripped his head off his body."

Naomi said, "We did too. Billy was forced to attack one, but he didn't see the second one. Good thing I was there to take him out, before he was able to do worse to him."

"Hows Billy, is he ok?"

"He's a little shell shocked, but none worse for the wear."

"Paul also, but I caught him before he could do anything. He was molting when I left him, and got the heck out of there. I did do a general sweep of the area, I think he was a lone wolf. I couldn't be sure, so I kept an eye out for possible trailers, but more importantly I got the kids home safe."

"I did the same also, even though I gave their heads a good kick. I don't think there was no helping them at all."

I couldn't believe she was thinking more outside the box, then I was. I said, "I should of done that, all I did was hide its head with its body."

She smile and said, "Arty found a key to the weapons safe, I don't know how well it was hidden though. He seemed to find it rather quickly. He said he saw it while we did our training, and as we played he thought about it."

"Good what did you find?"

"I maybe a fighter, but I had no clue what I was looking at. You can go look at it later."

Arty came in and said, "I know the rifles, because I saw them in an SOF magazine. There were two rifles, an AR-15 and a HK-33. I can tell you there are a few blade, nothing bigger then your knife. Plus 4 handguns, but I really didn't see much ammo at all. I think there are a few mags for the rifles, but the only gun ammo was loose. You may have to look at it, and really see what we got there."

I then said to Arty, "The Rifles are called assault rifles, and yes I will have to do that. Well we can just lock it all back up."

He smiled at me as he said, "It took some tweaking to get it to open. The gears maybe rusted, but I broke off the key in the lock."

"Oh well what is done is done. We'll try to use it like that. Maybe we should have Paul or Cheryl regulate it."

Arty shrugged his shoulder's and said, "Yeah sure that's probably a good idea."

Then came from the hall, "What are we to guard, and can someone tell me why that room on the third floor is locked?"

We all turn our heads to see Mary and Cheryl coming out of the hall way. It was very easy to figure it was Cheryl that had talked. Naomi then replied, "Oh Cheryl, dear we thought you or Paul could take control of the gun cabinet upstairs. As for the room I have no idea why a room would be locked at all. John do you know anything about this?"

I was going to talk directly to that fact, so I was glad Naomi beat me to the punch. It may have been answering the first question, with a question of our own so to speak. I was nodding my head as I replied, "Yes Paul found two strangers. I couldn't be sure, but I think they were trying to get to someplace. Since the only thing in the general neighborhood was this house, I figured they were coming here like you did Naomi. There is a bit of a problem though, I think they found out about our problem, and hid till they could find away in. They were past starvation, we took the first step to solve that. They maybe a little animalistic, so I was going to wait till you got home to do more with them."

Had to take a second look at them as they were both wearing dresses. To describe the dresses, Cheryl's was all business woman like, whereas Mary was more like a mom's dress. Cheryl shrugged her shoulder's and said, "Naomi said we had to wear what was wearing when we trained, but our time was our time, and we could wear what we liked. I do think she meant whatever was comfortable to us, but I hadn't worn this in a long time."

Well I had to admit that she was right about that. So I had to say the obvious, "Oh she was right, I have just seen you and Mary in slacks before, it was kind of pleasant to see you in dresses for once. Naomi was right except for one additive, your work out clothes have to be rugged. Your battle clothes have to be rugged to, useful, and seemingly normal for day to day use. You see what I wear, it's mainly so it can help me soak punishment. Naomi has to be more ready to their approach when moving through rough terrian, and yet she also looks at punishment also. Of course we wouldn't walk into a night club with these on, but they are close enough to look like day to day clothes."

She smiled at me as Mary said, "I think we can do that."

I saw the rest of the kids coming so I started with a simple plan. "Caty and Billy you'll back both of us up, the rest of you stay out of the way just in case they have been taken over by the beast. Now don't worry their only thoughts will be to get away from us, Caty and Billy it'll be your job to rush them to the nearest window if they are. We can always fix a broken window later, but it might take a bit to fix one of you. Now Mary and Joe I want you at the flight of stairs just down from us. I'll tell you its highly unlikely they'll get past us, but if they do I can assure you they'll be really hurt, and Caty and Billy should be able to handle them with ease. There has been weirder things that have happened in this un-life. So as the Boy Scouts always say, 'Be prepared.'"

Everyone then said their sure's and yup's. So I added, "We move when Paul gets us two more bloods, then we'll be ready. Oh and Paul I never marked off those two earlier bloods, and make sure that there's ten bloods for just before we go to sleep."

Naomi the added, "Make that twelve Paul, just in case they decided to actually stay."

Paul asked right then, "John why are they called Shovelhead's?"

"Well it's because," I started to reply, and then changed up with, "Paul we can cover that later on, right now we have more pressing issues." Then I went on with the solemn issue, "Ok everyone I'm sure you all know by now both of our groups ran into Shovelhead's. I was more concerned about getting you kids out of there, then find out just how many they were. I would like to think they were small groups, but both Naomi and I know not to delude ourselves with that thought, but if you think about it they tracked you to an area where they thought you would be taken care of. So in this, both Naomi and I have intervened, so for the time being this gives us an advantage. Even though with recent events, I'm sure they'll see several members of their gang are missing. So this will cause them to look at their first possible target, which are all of you. Once they see this, you can be rest assured that they'll start searching for you. Another good thing though is to hide someplace they are sure you aren't, hence this house gives a few more days probably."

Chapter 10

In the frying pan out of the fire. Wait is that right?

I then looked at each one with every word that came out, to emphasize what I was saying, "This. Does. Not. Mean. We. Are. Safe. Got it!" With all their nods and such I continued, "This means they could discover us at any time now, so we train like they have already found us. Another words like there isn't a tomorrow, now Naomi it seems you know whats going on with this shield. Can you explain it to the kids?"

Pepper instantly asked, "Shield? What kind of Shield?"

Naomi said as she rose, "If you give me a moment, I'll explain it to you young one. This isn't a shield in the truest form, to give it a physical reality, lets just call it a force. The force around this house was centered on a single person, he started the ring, and as long as you remain in the house you're ok. Once you leave your connection starts to fade, I think it takes about three months for it to fully fade though. Like most vampire novels would say, you have to be invited to enter, but also in another sense it has no truth to it. I can tell you that if a human should tell you to get out of their house, we do have a physical reaction. But again if there isn't a place of power, it has little affect on us, it's like a cross-"

I cut her off with this little one, "Naomi we can discuss that with them later."

She nodded her head, and went on with, "But truly it's just like a natural reaction. You'll not ever see a vampire go flying through the air out of a house, I guess you could say it's like a thought. You have this overwhelming urge to leave the house, like John said though we'll get into our unusual powers that come naturally to all vampires later. One thing you may ask yourself though. Why are there no true photos of a vampire, and why when describing vampires, do the terms seem so general? Right now isn't the time to cover this."

Pepper put her hand up, so I asked, "Yes Pepper?"

She asked, "I know this sounds stupid, but is it because of the silver in the film?"

I had to smile at her as I replied, "Not really, but I bet you knew that? I mean you've looked at mirrors, and they're usually backed with some kind of silver. Humans don't use any silver to see, but like we said we'll get into that later. We really have more pressing business to take care of right now. I just wanted to cover a few things before we moved on."

Naomi then said, "Pepper you seem to be good with clothes. Why don't you start a slow clearing all of the rooms, take Paul and Cheryl with you, you put the clothes in categories you understand. Paul and Cheryl can tag for a later date, so if someone needs something you'll know where and what to get them."

"That's a good idea, but Pepper you don't have to do this in one night. Take your time and do as good of a job as you can." I turned to Cheryl and Paul and continued, "Once you know the system only one of you needs to help a night, but until then, I expect the both of you to help her." I watched them all nod to me, Naomi and finally Pepper. I then added, "I don't know what we have in paper products though. So blood will always come first."

They both said, "Ok."

So I said, "Ok we all know our jobs, so lets get started."

Then the six of us moved to the second floor. Naomi and I placed Joe to the back of Mary, then the rest of us moved to the third floor. I looked both ways, and across our backs was best. Then Naomi and I moved to the door, she place herself on the side of the door handle. I was on the back of the door as I unlocked the door, Naomi looked at me after a few minutes. Then asked in a whisper, "What are we waiting for?"

I whispered back, "Paul has to bring me the blood."

Right then he was coming down the hall saying in a loud voice, "I knew you guys forgot this stuff."

He then walked up and handed them to me, and Naomi shushed him. I simply gave him a look and said, "Thanks." I then waved him off, and I was glad he understood me, as he backed off. I opened the door, and as it was fully open I swear I heard a little girl giggle. I then said so they could hear me well enough, "We're coming in, and we have blood, so try to keep calm."

Naomi and I then entered the room ready to fight, what we saw though wasn't the worse we expected. I saw the head of a single person, and she was gaunt, but look like a little girl. She wasn't looking at us, in fact she was looking down. Then she asked the strangest question, "Does it do that all the time?"

I cleared my voice and asked, "Does it do what all the time?"

A deeper voice then suddenly said, "Oh shit, shit. Why didn't you tell me someone had come in." Then the head of a man with wavy brown hair popped his head up, and waved as he said, "Oh hello."

The little girl then said, "Oh save your breathe Blue Stranger." I thought that was weird, but she went on, "He already hates you."

I do have to tell you this was strange, and before I could ask he did, "Why does he hate me?"

"Oh he loves the blue ones, but he hates Gumba's. To his majesty you're the lowest life form." I can tell you I was getting confused. I turned to Naomi to ask her and he said, "Don't worry about her dude, she has that stuff they call insight. I was told to defend her with my life, and I think we came very close to that."

She then said, "No worries Blue Teacher, you know much naughty naughty. Your essence though is for another path, plus Demon Lord no kill you. He just watchy watchy. Oh is there another, hello Mistress of the Forest."

Naomi then leaned to me and asked, "Is that supposed to be me?"

I was about ready to answer her, when the little girl stood up, and started to walk over. The guy with the wavy hair tried to stop her, the reason why was blazingly apparent as soon as she stood up. She didn't have a stitch of clothing on, not that I had expected her to have any on really. She put her hand out for me to shake as she gave me such a genuine smile, in the vampire world she would be called an anomaly. You see, it was apparent that she was a lot older then sixteen, but she still retained the young body of a sixteen year old. I knew this some times happens if the vampire became a vampire when they had barely hit puberty. The guy then said, "You might want to get her clothes, and its very hard to control her when she wants to do something."

I took her hand and shook it quickly, I then made my way to the hall where I saw Paul gawking. I pushed him away and said, "Caty come, and get Paul. Then as you take him away from here, send Mary back with a robe or something." I looked back in and re-said, "Ah make that two, one for a guy too."

By this time she was shaking Naomi's hand, and Caty said, "I see why."

She then yanked him away, and I said to Billy, "Billy I think we're safe, but take up Mary's place just in case." I then returned to the room and said, "We have three very young boys, and well you just saw one gawking at...who are the two of you?"

The guy then said, "I'm Anthony, but I go by Tony. I heard one guy call her Cynthia, but most just call her Kitty. You'll see once you start to really talk to her, I still have a heck of a time understanding her though. Like this last time she wanted to go for a dream walk. I swear if I had to deal with the sun one more day I was going to go nuts."

Kitty was looking around like she was in a different world as she said, "Sunny make pretty color, pretty colors here too. Ooo! Dolly! Dolly! Dolly's" She then opened one of the dresser drawers and almost exploded with happiness. "DOLLY'S!"

I don't know why I felt the need, but I had to look. The drawer was full of dolls, but not whole ones, I think I saw doll parts of every kind. I looked at Naomi, and she must of read my mind, because she went right to the draws too. She pulled out underwear that fit her perfectly, with a little skirt. She looked everywhere but no bras, so she just put a kids T-shirt on her. After she was done Kitty started to dance around, that's when I saw that she had a straight razor in her other hand. I moved closer to Naomi and asked, "Do you think we should trust her with Arty?"

I do have to say though, Mary had come in and thrown a robe to Tony. He and her then left, to try and find him something to really wear. Well back to this, it seemed she sensed what I was thinking, and she said, "No worries I not hurt Boy Toy. He be of the ribbon and I see and teach in my lively unness." I wasn't sure what to think, but I knew her kind well enough to know once they said something they'd carry it out or die in the attempt. So if nothing else, I had to trust in that. At that she stared at me and said, "You almost goodie, but need turn from rough hues. Oh beautiful white princess come, and she help you. Demon Lord become great Dark Shadow, no one safe after this, he be badder thener. Anyone darn cross his path will see results, but even look wrongly at white princess. Ooo he even give all for her, he be Dark Knight then. Kitty love you great sir."

I knew all of what she said was for me, but I was sure I wouldn't know until over time. To be truthful their insight could be for yesterday, today, or tomorrow. It was over time that you could really tell, and especially when they're over a long period of time. In fact it's usually when some other person says to you, wow that prophecy really came true. Well except they would be the first one to tell you, it really isn't a prophecy. I knew the time was getting late, and I looked at my watch. Then said, "Its less then thirty minutes till sunrise. I want the kids to get used to sleeping then, so why don't you come down, and have your bags of blood."

She skipped out the door saying, "Goodie goodie juicy juice time."

As we walked through the house I said on every floor. "Dinner time kiddies." And by the time we got to the kitchen we had a following. Paul and Cheryl handed out all the blood, and as we drank I spoke. "Guys these guys are Kitty and Tony. Kitty and Tony this is," and I pointed as I said their names, "Caty, Joe, Arty, Billy, Paul, Cheryl, Mary, and over there is Pepper. You've already met Naomi and I'm John. Kids they're as of now going to stay over at least one night, but hospitality says our door is always open as long as they're civil."

I then did the bow thing, I really hated that. Kitty then said, "Me stay. Me no come just to visit. We have certain purpose. No leave till purpose happen."

They all looked at her like she was from a very foreign country. I then told them, "She means shes here to stay until shes fulfill her purpose. Which is a good thing, we believe she is the same kind as Arty. She can teach him stuff Naomi and I can't dream of, they say having one person with insight is a good thing, can you imagine having two of them."

Everyone started to say hi to her, and move over to welcome her. But then Naomi said, "I wouldn't do that. They aren't known to be good in crowds, and they have a nasty bite."

I could see, but what she said made the right impression, as everyone backed off. That wasn't what really got to me, it was how fast they listened to her. I then turned to the Tony guy and asked, "So what family are you from?"

He replied, "Well I think her kind calls us the beautiful people."

He pointed at Naomi, I really didn't like the way he said that. I mean common courtesy would have been to say Naomi's people, I knew she probably felt the way I did. So I asked, "Where were you raised?"

He replied, "Why does that matter?"

"Normal people would have said Naomi's people, but hell you're pissing me off now. So Kitty he may die even before we get started."

"That's what I thought, you're kind can't appreciate the full insight of our kind. We were made this way to exist among humans, not vampires. We are the true predators, all your kind know how to do, is stir up trouble. That's why one day, my kind will rule the vampire world, because no other vampire understands this."

I was about ready to jump, and rip his head off, when Naomi grabbed my shoulder and whispered, "He's not worth it John."

Of course she was right, even though I did think to punch him squarely in the face. I also knew we would need him to train possibly Pepper, and maybe help with Paul and Cheryl. You can imagine as I decided to start hating him now, from that point we all drank our blood in silence. I moved out to my car just as the sun was cracking the plain of the earth, I always loved this time of the day, even though I knew without a full blood dose it was better for me to go in, then to watch it. So I returned to the room, I knew Mary was in, with my bed roll.

I did make a mistake, even though I'm still not sure what I did. When I made it to our room Mary was in her bra and panties, I told her that, that was good, and it would save on more blood if she took them off. Then she took them off, and acted like she was putting on a show or something for me. I can tell you that I wanted to take her right there, whether she wanted me to or not. I'm not that kind of a vampire, and I always ask, but she was also my child, and I saw this as a bad thing, not the sex part though. The truth is that its rare for a sire to stay together with their child, the normal thing that happens, is that they go through their training, and by the end of that, they're ready to go out on their own. I almost never take children just for this fact though, I mean most of the time a vampire makes a new child, its because they're in love with same said child. I never enjoyed the pain of our separation though, so I just didn't do it. I should of taken into account though that we never really had the time to fall in love though. So in a sense when I made my bed on the floor, and told her this was safer, that probably was the wrong thing to say to her.

But like all clueless men, I thought she was ok with it. I wouldn't find out until the next morning, so I went to sleep thinking Mary was just having a restless night.

Chapter 11

Day 3

When John got up Mary was awake to, and she gave him an almost evil smile. Even if he had thought he had done something wrong, he knew how this day had to start. After all this was a lot to take in, well at least in just two days. The first thing he had to do was go to the refrigerator, and retrieved twelve blood packs. He would have to teach Paul how to set up for each day though, as this would normally fall to him. He took them to the table, and set them out so everyone could have a thawed bag, without affecting the bag next to it. Then he picked one up and started to roll it around in his hands so as to thaw it out that much quicker. Joe then came into the room, he saw what John was doing so he started to do the same thing. He then gave me a knowing look as he said, "I heard what happened between you and Caty last night."

Of course this totally took me by surprise, so I asked, "What happened between Caty and me?"

"She said she offered herself up to you on a platter, and you were so clueless that you just spoke and did nothing."

"Joe Caty wasn't even in my room last n..." Then I had to ask him another question, "Exactly how did she say that Joe?"

"Well she sound like she was talking in the third person, and even though she never really mentioned her name. I kind of figured she was talking about herself. Well especially as mad as she was."

"Joe I do believe she wasn't talking about herself." I couldn't believe with all we had to do today, I managed to anger the one person

I was depending on with these kids. I had to shake my head, as I also added, "I can't believe I already messed up this badly. Well I maybe better at everything then you guys. A better fighter, better at just being a plain old vampire, but when I mess up, no one is in a league with me."

Cheryl came in and asked, "Who's out of your league?"

"Oh were talking about how easily I'm at messing things up. I told Joe that when I mess up, I'm in a league of my own. I do hope she finds forgiveness in her heart for me."

I couldn't believe, that right then Naomi came in asking, "Forgiveness for what?"

Joe replied for me, "Something that happened between him and Mary. But John dude, I think she'll forgive you man, it wasn't like you were looking for anything. Now if it had been what had happened in between Caty and me, then I would say you were in trouble man. We had to find a way to work around it though, as we were the two oldest people at the time."

"That's good for you Joe. Its bad to have unresolved issues. John you should go to Mary. Even if this can't be resolved, you should show you're trying."

I had to give her a look, because I knew she was right, but I had to tell the whole truth. "I don't know what I did wrong really Naomi. I was the perfect gentleman last night. I even explained to why its better for us to sleep nude then with clothes on."

Cheryl Gave me a strange look, and then she was out of the room in a shot. Naomi then said, "It might be best if I run damage control on this, so it doesn't get out of control."

I was a bit worried though, I never had to have damage control done for me before. I was really worried, when Arty came into the room. I had been so worried about my own issues, to even notice he was a bit worn for wear. He started to do what Joe and I were doing, even though our bloods were about ready to drink. Billy came in speaking as he looked in the refrigerator, "What is there for breakfast around here?"

Joe then replied, "John already took them out, but they have to be worked out to drink."

He straddled a chair as he said, "I don't mind a bloodcycle that much."

With that Joe and Billy started to drink and eat their breakfast, respectfully. They both used their teeth, I had to smile as I got up and went to the drawer, then I pulled out a pair of scissors out and just cut the bag open. I saw that Arty was torn in between both ways, so I handed him the scissors and said, "Keep your teeth sharp, its hard enough to pierce the skin as it is." I knew that was sort of a lie, so I continued with, "It isn't that you teeth won't ever really be sharp enough to do the job, but truly you guys are still to young to have them toughened up yet. It is possible for you to loose a tooth still, it is a bit rare though, it's really bad if its one of your canines though. Plus this is plastic, even in the middle of a fight tearing open a bag can be distracting."

Tony came in with, "Yep, it's just like John's kind to be sprouting how to win a fight. We though prefer to get what we want through persuasion more then physical force like his kind."

"Tony have I told you the gravity of this situation?"

"Not exactly, but I bet I can guess."

"Well then why don't you just enlighten us then?"

"You've seen some kind of corrupting force that is threatening to take over the city. So everyone is barking at their very own shadows, and seeing thing where nothing truly exists. With these phantoms you have been able to conjure up the fear you need, then you begin to turn this place into an armed death camp. All the while never ever really thinking of a diplomatic solution. The worse thing is my kind seems to be more gullible to the shadows you have us chase."

I turned to Joe and asked, "What kind of shadow sliced open your belly Joe? Caty and Mary witnessed it themselves, Billy actually helped me fight off three." I turned back to Tony and said, "You maybe right about some of my kind, but this was happening to them long before I even arrived. Why don't one of you tell Tony how many members you had before I came along, I mean even with all the elders within this house?"

I didn't really expect any of them to answer, but was glad when Billy replied, "Twenty seven. I mean we were twenty seven vampire John."

As vampires we can't blush or pale, but I can tell you Tony looked a little more white after he was told this. I truly didn't know this either, and was surprised by the number. But I went on with, "Twenty seven no small number, but then if we follow your train of thought, they all left their own kids on their very own. Something no self respecting vampire would ever do, so if one did it would be very uncommon, but to have I'm guessing twelve to fourteen just get up and leave. Well, then those lovely sire need to be investigated by the High Council, wouldn't you say? So what would you say were these few kids chances without any of our help?"

He then asked, "What makes you think any of us can survive, if twenty seven couldn't bring then down?"

"Well for one, this is a safe house which means this brood was well established. I know of no Shovelhead establishment, which means they probably took the house by surprise. We might not know where they are, but we know they're someplace here. Then you have the fact that they weren't prepared for my and Naomi's help, so in a sense that gives a small advantage too. Even though its a very small advantage, as neither of us are trainers. All of our first meetings have in a way gone very right, both Naomi and I were able to easily take out three

Shovelhead's at two separate times. This to me means they aren't very well train either, if they have received any training at all. With this I have two very powerful tools in Arty and Joe here, with the advent of Kitty I think things are looking way up. You heard her last night too, something has drawn her here, and isn't going to leave until it's all done. You might not want to help, but as her protector that leaves you here anyway you look at it as well. Now I will admit the advantages that the Shovelhead's have right now, seem insurmountable. But every turn things have been getting better, plus the only two that can truly see how this may come out haven't said anything bad yet. So knowing all this how do you think our odds look now?"

By the time I finished my little tyrant Paul had came into the room. Tony then asked, "I still don't know why we just can't talk to these Shovelhead's?"

Naomi came in then and asked, "Have you ever tried to talk to Shovelhead's?"

"I can't say that I have?"

"Well the only ones that I knew that tried that, came home in body bags. John I think shes still upset, but I told her you did it only to protect her. I told all of them, I would explain the lacking of a bond once they got down here. You don't mind if I do that do you?"

I replied, "Ok that's good, oh wait. Tony your kind arc known to go through this worse then our kind. Can you lay it plainly down so they can understand it more easily?"

Tony replied, "Sure I guess so. Why what did you do?"

"Mary's young along with the rest of these kids. I haven't even been able to go into the bonding yet. Last night I was trying to save Mary from that, but I made a mistake and forgot I hadn't told anyone about the three levels of bonding yet. So she completely misunderstood what I was saying to her."

Naomi then came in and added, "You might want to explain the blood thing, and why we do certain thing to conserve our blood also."

He nodded his head, as I could see his wheels turning. I knew it would be a big feather in his cap, if he could get control over one of my kind. I thought he might try to sway Mary from my control, even though I knew it was much to soon. In truth after he talked I had to believe his target was much larger then just Mary. Naomi and I stood as the room started to fill with the kids. There were only eight chairs in here, so I had all the boys get their own chairs from another room. Once everyone was settled in I stood up and said, "We have a lot to accomplish today. But for the first thing we asked Tony to speak to you. Tony go ahead and tell them what we asked."

He actually gave me a warm smile as he stood, and then took my place. Then he turned on his hundred dollar smile, "First you have to understand all of you have a limited blood supplies, so John is trying to stem it with only one bag a day. Normal vampire blood usage is about four a day, and this is without the hurried up training hes giving you. My kind of vampire have long used our humanity to the extreme, so we have had to learn and teach the ways to conserve blood. Day to day activity just like rolling in bed causes blood usage though, but there are still things you can do. Like we don't feel temperature and clothes add to the usage of blood while we sleep. So a lot of my kind have gone to the extreme of never wearing clothing while we sleep at home. I believe this is why the other vampire families have called us the hedonists of the vampire world. So even though no family have made it mandatory, some do it just for the bloods sake. Look at Naomi for an example, she looks all the part of a huntress. I'm sure she won't tell you, but I bet she doesn't wear a stitch of underwear underneath her clothes."

He stopped, I think it was for affect. He then said, "Bonding? What can I say about bonding?"

He took a few steps and then said, "Bonding is one of the best things about being a vampire, even though it will also leave you heart broken too. Ok one of the reasons for making a new vampire is that you've fallen in love with him or her, but the bond created through this will almost always fade, once it does and he or she realizes what you have done to them. This slowly eats away at them and the love they may have had for their sire, then one day she or he will look at you as their sire and only feel hatred. Either way its better for the sire to keep them at a distance, saving themselves from this terrible thing that almost always happens. Completely losing your sires bond before you're five years old can be a terrible thing for both the sire and their child."

"Now there are three other bonds, one is for a human. This means that you will only drink their blood alone, but this can be very bad as it means you go hungry when they aren't around. Well lets just say that never really ends well. Then there is the human bond for a vampire. Basically this means a human get addicted to the healing affects of vampire blood, but getting addicted to vampire blood is an easy thing to occur, so be careful giving human your blood. And there's the third one, but vampires have used this to control other vampires over the centuries. So even though its not the law, it has become a common rule just not to drink the blood of another vampires."

Mary then put up her hand and asked, "Is there anyway drinking vampire blood can be a good thing?"

"Yes Mary. As vampire don't really marry, but we are known to get very close. Once you fully find yourself trusting the man or woman, and you feel you love them you go through this bond. You are very young though Mary, and as a human, you knew sex has it's consequences, this becomes foreign to a vampire. When we make our children we are actually able to select them, but you can never have a baby the human way from this day forward. So the sex act is just that, and it becomes just another act. So when you want to share something special with the lady or gentleman you love, what better way to do this then through our blood bond, but this isn't an advisable act until you're older and sure. The breaking of such a bond can be very difficult and painful."

I waited to see if there were any other question. When I was sure, I got up and said in dismissive, "Thank you Tony, that was very informative. Ok everyone today starts with Naomi, then me, Tony could you show them the basics of shooting?"

"Sure," he replied.

I continued with, "Lastly it will be Kitty. Then we'll do a short field problem and come back here. The four of us will talk, and see where we can stress your training."

Tony then asked, "John wouldn't it be better if we did it in a round robin sort of way."

Naomi then said, "I agree with him John."

I then said, "Yeah that might be the best way to do this. Paul pull blood just in case someone needs it. I think 55 minute intervals would be good and 5 minutes in between classes. Naomi you have physical training, lets call if intro to vampire hand to hand. I'll do hand style with weapons, Tony yours is the basics of fire arms. Kitty you just come up with something, like maybe basic vampire etiquette. These are a good base to see where we go from here, and teachers you'll have to watch them closely. We need to know everything, also think of were you want to take your group for their first outing. Well we have four groups and four teachers. Ok kids we may have to mix up the groups, but we'll see. I definitely know that Arty goes with Kitty, Pepper goes with Tony, Billy goes with Naomi, and Caty and Mary need to go with me. But we really need our power separate, so we need to break up Caty and Mary. But I need to train with each of them, so for this I think we should do a round robin here as well."

"I agree John, and as you know what was, is true for most families, isn't necessarily true for all. So this would be good to see if, like maybe Pepper was good with knives, and like that. Even though technically her family is known to be better with guns."

"Well yeah, even though as Tony has shown, they would prefer not to use them at all."

Tony then came in and said, "We prefer to call it a diplomatic alternative."

"Exactly. Anyways, I think I'll use the dinning room if they have one, otherwise meet me in the living room. So since we are good with weapons of all sorts, Mary you start with Tony. This will show my willingness to trust Tony with my very own child."

Naomi interrupted me before I could go on, "John don't you think he should start with the child we think is closest to him?"

"Sure why do you ask?"

"Well Pepper and Mary aren't in the same group."

"Oh yeah who did we put with her?"

"Billy and that's where the problem comes in. Cheryl and Joe are a group and they have no mentors."

"Oh ok, well then Joe you go with Pepper for training. Billy you go with Cheryl and Naomi. That leaves Mary and Arty shoot, ok Mary and Arty you'll start with Kitty. Lastly that leaves Caty and Paul for me to train. Ok now go get on clothes you won't be mad if you tear them or possibly worse."

With that all the kids left, so I went on as I knew the elders didn't have to leave. "Tony I don't know where it is, but Arty found a gun safe somewhere. You might want to find him, and ask him where it is. I'll look around to see if I can find some practice weapons. Oh and you might want to ask if there's a good sound proof room. Ok I think we all know what to do. Kitty I saw a library on the third floor, that might be good for you. We got less the twenty minutes anything else?"

I knew that Tony probably wanted to say something, but then the adage that, they were a bunch of lovers, and not fighters, was very true. So I had to reset the groups, but this wouldn't be the first time. In a sense though we were set, and even better is we were set into the basic vampire three person fighting groups. So what I really didn't need were more vampires, and like usual I wouldn't get what I wished. Right at that time though I had to get set to train them, so I found two of those bamboo practice swords in an empty room. I also found a room that was better then what I was looking for, it was an actual ballroom. It was perfect for the training we I needed to do, not to mention a large dinning room. I decided this was far better to meet in then the kitchen, but why vampires needed such an elaborate dinning room was beyond me. It was only the rare vampire could actually eat. Which made the living room in comparison was rather small, which to me was weird also. Maybe the size of a room and a half, I would have thought it would be twice that size.

Chapter 12

I could tell you a lot more, but I'm willing to bet you might already be bored. So I leaned a sword against the wall, and had the other one in my hand. A lot of people really don't know these things have to be used two handed. So I went to the center of the room while swinging sword, I was trying to get use to how light it was. Then when I thought I was ready I turned on both Caty and Paul, even though I was swinging the sword one handed. I then said to then, "See what I'm doing?" They both nodded their heads so I went on with, "What if I told you I was handling this sword incorrectly would you believe me?" They again nodded their heads, so I pointed at Paul and asked, "Why?"

He replied, "Because you're the teacher and we aren't."

I then pointed at Caty and asked, "Anything else?"

She replied, "I don't know. Maybe because the handle seems to long."

"Its called a hilt, this above my hand is called the guard, and the bottom is always called the pummel. The hilt is to hold on to, and the guard is to guard your hands. Can either of you tell me why its called a pummel?" They looked at me with blank faces so I just went on, "The pummel is named that so you can pummel your enemy when you can't use the blade. Remember that there are many ways to use any blade. The blade is only one use, even though it is the primary use. Now come here Paul."

I could see he was a bit scared, so I moved him quicker. Then I used my foot to separate his legs and said, " Always keep your feet about shoulder width apart. Also make sure you're comfortable, your feet just a hair out of place, can mess up your stance. Now you can use your lead foot in your attack, but never over extend your reach. I'll show you better as we go along, but next will be how to hold the sword."

I handed Caty the sword I had and said, "Paul go get the other one. Caty which hand do you write with?" She showed me so I put the sword in that hand, and went on, "Now place your hand close to the guard, but leave about two finger space. Once you have this I want you to put your other hand below that, but about an inch apart. Remember comfort is the key to being able to fight well." I then looked at the two of their stances and once I was moderately satisfied I moved on. "Now we'll start with a simple downward strike." I took Caty's sword, took my stance, and then showed them. "Now get into your stances and do this a couple of hundred times." I watch as they did as I had said, I corrected as they went on. I had them doing side swings by the time my time was up, but I knew they would get bored half to death as we went on.

The rest of the classes went close to the same way with a few changes, but that's expected. Then we met in the kitchen after the four hours of training were up. I knew Tony's training would be the loudest, so I did have to wonder how he muffled it so well. I did have to ask though, "Tony to train them better are you going to need some field trips?"

He replied with, "Yeah that would be nice, but I think I can get all the basics in, in three lessons. So some time after that we should do that."

I nodded my head as I spoke to the entire room, "Good we'll have to set that up for you. Everyone this was just the start, we won't even be able to make preliminary choices until you have more training. This is what these outings are for though. they're to put you into situations that you would not normally face. This helps us assess you faster, and make the right choice for you. I can tell you we aren't perfect though, and may make what seems like stupid mistakes. So bare with us, I also know you picked me as your leader. This has to be remedied, but again you need to know one another better. So we'll get to that. Naomi because of Kitty's possible problem with a moving vehicle, I'll take her with me. So that leaves you with Tony. Now the teachers will teach you what we are best at over the next four days." I looked at Tony and added, "Other then the most obvious. Tony knows my kind can kick ass and take names, this wouldn't be fair to all of you, so as mine is on the physical side, I'll teach you the physical side of being a vampire."

Naomi then added, "The reason why we do this as an outing is that it usually takes real physical room. Like my secondary ability is how well I can hide in plain sight, as you can see that wouldn't be easy to do in a ten by ten space. Ok are we clear on this?"

I didn't know, but Kitty had opened up a can of worms. Pepper raised her hand right then. So Naomi then asked, "Yes Pepper?"

"Kitty was talking to us, and what is weird is how easily it is to understand her if you just listen. She said something that has me a bit confused though. She said the we are all made in the image of God. Is that right? I'm mean just like the Bible?"

I think everyone that had a few years on them knew what Kitty meant, but it was easy to see where Pepper was going with this. As Naomi replied, "Well the human bible does say we are all created in the imagine of God, but beyond that you'd have to ask my momma."

"What I mean though as vampire is there a possibility that we can all go to Heaven?"

Tony fielded the question from there, of course what he said was the plain truth. "Well we don't know. There's a saying that my master use to say. We aren't the bad guys in all this, but we can't exactly claim to be the good guys either."

"Bad guy? Do mean like the movies teach us that we are the damned?"

I was no theologian, so I was happy to allow anyone else to answer these questions. "Some say we are the damned, but some say we aren't. I don't think anyone truly knows really, plus it isn't as if our kind has gotten into the religious side of things though."

Here though I had to add something. Which might have been the wrong thing to say, but I felt it had to be added. "Well there are those that are religious, but for some reason its like they forgot about God and have centered around Satan."

I was happy to leave it right there, but I could see that I had gone to far with Naomi's scowl. She said with a little disdained tone, "Now you have to tell them John. You can't drop a bomb shell like that and not expect questions."

Well she was right, and I should of kept my big mouth shut. I cleared my voice as I started, "Ok it's kind of an old story, and no I'm not old enough to have witnessed it. Just about a thousand years ago there was this group of these guys. A very religious group of guys that went to war against the infidels of the day. If any of you do the math, or know history you'll figure it was right around the time of the crusades. But this all got start by a group of Zealot Christians, they weren't vampires yet. A part of the world had gone through a major change, and a lot of our friends had to go under ground literally. There was one group that lived in Jerusalem itself, and their hiding place was uncovered. This group was not trained at all about their beliefs, so in a sense they were very ignorant. They had no idea what they had really found, and only knew one way to take care of it."

I made sure that everyone saw me when I said the next line, "Remember ignorance breeds prejudice, and prejudice usually breeds violence. But this group of vampires felt that they could help them realize what they were doing, whether it was right or wrong. Also they thought that if they took in the most important of them, that it would be easier to help understand the plight they were causing. They were extremely wrong though. It turned out the leaders were even more ignorant then their simple soldiers. so once the leaders knew what they needed to know they figured that they were of the devil or Satan. If they were of the devil that was one thing, but at least they could rid themselves of those that created them. So they destroyed all those that sired them because of their believed evil, and then sire all those that they desired as captains."

I prayed that they were getting what I was telling them. "These guys clung to their beliefs, only now since they obviously weren't of God, they had to be of the devil. So they started to worship the devil in a sorts of ways, but also took it up on themselves to rid the world of other vampires. Also they realized they could gain power from the drinking of another vampires blood. Their favorite thing to do was to slowly drain the blood from a victim or worse. Shortly after their rise they were thought to have all been slaughter, or so we believed. This vampire cult of the devil keeps popping up threw the ages, to this date the cult has risen seven times, and six times we had thought we were rid of them yet again. This last time they came, they had a new trick, they spread themselves so thin no one really saw the rise start."

I got up and moved to the door as I added, "One of their favorite trade marks is to just hit a human over the head and turn them into vampires. They give them barely enough information, so they're lucky to even know that their even a vampire. This are they're storm troops, or as we like to call them Shovelhead's. Now let us get to this training, before we loose the night."

I knew this was the best way, as he left Kitty at an old church. Vampires always trained best in small groups, so it was the right thing to do. I just couldn't shake this uneasy feeling though, I knew all the ins and outs of every kind of vampire, so he didn't fear for himself. When it came to Tony, he feared because his kind were known to take their sensuality way to far. Naomi I was sure could really handle herself, and she was pretty sure Kitty could to if she chose to. It wasn't that Kitty's kind weren't fierce fighters, it was that they so feared changing history they some times would do nothing at all. With his newest kids that just sat there as he drove, even though he was sure they had about a million questions.

I knew with the recent revision it had upset the groups, and he hoped they could settle into their work. Then it wasn't a bad revision, in fact it may have made the groups as a whole better. All his years in his job though, screamed he was completely wrong. Kitty had given him that reassuring nod as she left the car with her kids. It should have been reassuring as he turned into the parking lot to a small park. He could still feel the sting where her nails had dug into his flesh, as he drove. She hadn't drawn blood, but with her nails and grip, it was only a matter of time. Over all this pain though, was this nagging feeling they really didn't need to be there.

He then got out of the car with the kids, and walked to a tree. Then he said, "Our physical ability out weighs what we could do as humans. Yes we can run faster, jump higher, and last long because of things humans need that we just don't. A vampire would only be a sum of his parts, though as he or she were as a human. So if you didn't have much strength, dexterity, or stamina as a human, don't expect to have them as a vampire, There are ways we have an advantage over the beasts in the field though."

I then took a step back from the tree I used it, and I knew it looked like I had just ran up it. "Now I did this because I was able to take advantage of the tree. You can do this to almost anything as we don't have to rest, and can easily fight through the pain. I do have to warn you though, you have to know your own way. Just because you can climb a four story building with ease, doesn't mean we can't make mistakes and fall. Healing as you saw is an easy thing, but it isn't as easy to heal a bone. So if you're being chased by a werewolf you can easily escape by climbing a four story building. With enough training you could easily escape anything, well almost."

They both nodded to me, so I then said as I pointed to a tree, "Ok give it a try on those trees over there."

With this Caty and Paul took off, I knew Paul would be slower then Caty. His abilities just weren't like our kind. I mean he could realize it in time, but for now she was surely the fastest. It was kind of strange how things worked out, you could have one like Paul that ended up being more like me. Then again he would be shunned by his own kind, and yet there is a good chance that if Caty were more like him she would be shunned too. I had always thought my people were of a more freer nature, but at my age I have seen exactly the reverse. Those that seem to have the fewest laws, seem to in the end have the most, and those that have the most, seem to actually have the fewer. I watched them move from tree to tree and then added, "Once you think you have that down packed, move to the fountain and see if you can do the same there." I almost just left it like that, then I decided to add a warning, "Remember fountains have water in then, and a mistake can leave you drenched."

I saw some people walking by, so I moved to the kids and said, "New game, starting with you Caty then next will be you Paul. Every time you see someone walk by, track them until they see you, or are out of the park. You have to use your new special tricks, and you can't just hide. Now try this."

I then jumped up on a fence at speed and ran along the top. Then I jumped down and said, "If you keep your speed up, you can run the length of the rail. Once you get that down, I want you to try, and use the two together."

I could see that they were having fun, then Caty came over and said, "John come here."

I followed her to the other side of the park, and then she asked, "Can we try this on those buildings?"

I saw three four story office buildings and I replied, "Sure, but watch me first, and I want you to do it one at a time, just in case you fall."

So we had to move across six lanes of traffic, but then we made it to the building. I looked at them and said, "This will put a lot of stress on your feet and hands, but just fight through it. Remember speed is your friend here, plus if you don't succeed the first few times, just remember some people it takes years to do this."

I then moved back to give myself a little running start. I came from the side so it looked like I wasn't going for the building. At the last minute I turned into the building, and with my first swing I was going up the building. I was up on top well within a second or two, then almost as fast I descended the building, and was standing with them again. I then said, "Now remember also, I've been doing this for years, and have mastered a twenty story building. That takes a lot to do that, we'll stay with four stories right now."

Caty went first and barely made it to the top. I knew she was wondering why it took her so much longer then me. She did come down faster, she lost her grip about half way down. I moved and was able to catch her. Then Paul tried to do the same thing, but like I said his kind weren't as physical as we are. He nearly made it to the top, but then like most just one misplaced hand and I was catching him as well. We then moved back to the park and I told them as we walked, "Never try that until an elder tells you are ok to do that on your own. As you saw that can be rather difficult going up as well as coming down, and Paul don't let it bother you that Caty did better, remember we are built for the more physical side of things. It kind of comes ease to us. Whereas we do well in climbing buildings, I bet Tony and Pepper are aces at that fence thing I showed you."

I looked at my watch and saw that an hour was almost up. So I said, "Ok on the way to the car move from tree to fence to tree, and keep this up, and try not to touch the ground until you reach the car. I'll be watching the two of you, and use this for a judgment. But don't worry there's no pass or fail. Now hit it."

With that they did as I said, I could see that Caty was the better of the two. Paul did ok as well, I was impressed at how well he moved. That kind of made me wonder, if his kind just chose to hide their ability. I finally decided it must have been just his youth and vigor that made him so good at this. As I got close to the car I said, "Ok the hours almost up so we have to go get Kitty."

They both basically said, "Aww."

I then said as I got in, "Don't worry you'll get another chance." Then I added for good measure, "Well that's if the Shovelhead's give us the time."

We got into my car as I told them this, Caty leaned forward as she said, "That was cool going up that building."

I turned the car over when Paul who was sitting on the other side of the car asked, "John whats that?"

I followed his finger to see a dark shadow, I knew that he more likely saw more then I did. When it moved though, it was an unmistakable figure that looked hunch over. I wasn't scared of one lone figure, what I was afraid of was what he may have seen. So even though I knew this wasn't the reason I was having a bad feeling, I did know I had to take care of this. I put my car in park and turned it off. Then I turned to them and said, "I won't be long. Just watch my back in case there's more."

I guess this kind of sounds stupid, because as I was moving that could have been anyone. Something inside me though told me he was a Shovelhead, but if there was any doubt, as soon as I neared, I smelled him and that reassured me. I could see how he reacted, he wasn't a normal one. So I had to think that someone had actually taken interest in this one, he quickly spun around to try and face me. He then bared his teeth in his best ferro look he could muster. I already knew it was to little to late, so as my blade flashed with the limited light he could barely react. I do have to wonder in all that, if he even had time to comprehend what had just happened to him. My knife pasted with a little effort threw his neck, which told me I was right, he had received some training. With his head traveling toward the ground though told that he didn't have enough though.

I then move his body under a low hanging bush, then I returned to the car. I started up the car and started to drive toward where I left Kitty, as we came closer I saw that they were already out near the road. Instead of just stopping, I pulled into the parking lot behind them and said, "Guys get in the back."

Andy got in the back seat as well, whereas Mary sat next to Kitty as she got next to me. But I turned to her and asked, "Anything unusual happen?"

Kitty nodded her head as she said, "Shadow up on shadow, making waves in what they don't know. Demon Lord is nasty, but they being nasty in wrong way. They not stop bring terrible things down on us, but kiddies aren't ready for show." Then she looked at me and with the first instance of clarity I've heard from her. "John it's bad, they're messing with something they have no idea about."

"Show me."

So she started to point and said, "Follow tippy of de flange."

I did as she said, but as I did I was stopped dead in my tracks by a single sign. The sign read Cathedral of our Lady, I had to shake my head as I only said, "Oh no! No those stupid idiots! What are they thinking about? Well I hope we found out this in time Kitty."

Chapter 13

I then drove to the house, as I drove up I asked Mary and Arty if they had seen anything. I was glad to see that Naomi was already back, as we drove into the old garage. As we got out I told Arty and Paul to make sure the doors were closed. We walked into the house, so I told Caty and Cheryl to tell the others to meet in the dinning room, and to send Naomi and Tony to talk to Kitty and me. So we had to have a kind of show down, even though I knew as well as anyone they weren't ready for this. Tony made it to the room first and he asked, "Is it bad news?"

I replied, "The worst, and it was Kitty that found about it."

"Well hell."

Naomi then came in and asked, "Did any of you run into Shovelhead's?"

I nodded my head as Kitty replied, "A multitude."

"See Tony you thought I was seeing things. I didn't have one in my area, but I swear I saw one in Tony's area."

I then said, "There was one in my area. I would of missed him if Paul hadn't seen a shadow move. I couldn't be sure if he had saw us, so after I made sure he was a Shovelhead, I disposed of him. But what you and I saw I think will pale in comparison of what Kitty saw. Go ahead Hun and tell them?"

She then spoke, "Me saw tree dirty ones dancing and playing butt to butt. I knew bad so I go to ground and follow, seenie they torcher youngily. Was terrible then with a thud thud they go bye bye, so me meanie follow again. Me see them joinie with two more, I keepy distance and watch until totally this many." She held up nine fingers and went on, "Knew Demon Lord would want ya knowie, so me wait as a signal. I knew was real bad, but it be the Demon Lord that find the sign."

She put out her hand so I carried it on, "The sign read the Cathedral of our Lady. You all knows what that means?"

Tony then just said, "Well shit."

Naomi asked, "Do you know their involvement yet?"

I replied, "There's no way of knowing, but them meeting in the neighborhood might be a good sign. So we have to figure the worse and hope for the best."

Tony shook his head and said in a strong voice, "John these kids have had only one day of training! This isn't a sink or swim situation! We can't just throw them into something like this. They'll all get killed!"

I said in a calm voice, which didn't reflex me wanting to pull his head off his shoulder's, like I thought. "I know that Tony, but I see no other way. Plus if you think about whats happened thus far, we have to have a literal infestation in this city. Heck it might be better to move everyone to another city, but truly how can we know unless we have the time to find out. I can assure I'm pretty good at that, not as good as Naomi. I am sure though that they aren't really giving us that time. So you tell me what should I do?"

Before he could speak Naomi spoke, "Tony would you really like to just give this city up to just another Shovelhead advance?"

He finally was able to reply with, "No they've taken control of far to many cities as it is. I might not agree with your methods, but I guess I do have to agree about the Shovelhead problem though. I do think we should keep the groups small so we can help protect them in the long run."

I then said, "Well I think that's a good idea too, and with our numbers it suits the vampire way of fighting."

Naomi then said, "To keep good coherent groups I suggest Billy join you John and Caty join me."

"Yeah I think that's a good idea, and to keep along the lines of talents. I know you would want Pepper Tony, but it might be better if you took Paul and Cheryl."

"I know you would want to use Arty and Kitty as our little surprise. But Kitty who would you like as back up?"

Kitty spoke as Tony nodded, "Bestie to bring it on, but he no be ready so best under Demon Lords wing. So me take hammer that be best to the Demon Lord as she is the kiddie."

Ok I wasn't 100% sure what she meant, but I went with what I thought she meant, "Well I'm sure she means Joe should come with me and that Mary should go with her." I looked at her as she nodded her head, so I went on, "That just leaves Pepper to go with you Naomi. Can anyone else think of better teams for now?"

Everyone nodded their heads except for Tony who said, "I don't see any other way either. I do worry about Joe and Pepper being so close though."

I added to that, "Well once Joe begins to realizing his own strengths, that will pull Mary from us. I don't know if we can free up Pepper though, only time will tell."

"I just wish I had more time so at least she was good with a hand gun. I mean a Beretta is a good weapon to use, but at this phase it maybe just to much."

"I have a Glock 18 you can use, I have a generic holster and can put a Beretta in its place."

"Do you have ammo too? I was only able to dig up like half a magazine worth."

"Yeah I think so, do they both use a parabellum round?" He held up a round, so I pulled out my Glock and compared them. We were right they were almost the same round, then I remembered and said, "Well my back up ammo is Remington, that should fit this better then the true Glock ammo. What about other weapons, I mean Cheryl and Paul will need something."

Tony replied, "We have two assault rifles, but I don't think anyone is ready for them. I have two more semi automatics with little ammo. Ones and old Army issue 45 Caliber pistol, the other is a PPK. Along with a 38 the PPK and snub nose has plenty of ammo."

I looked around and asked, "Has anyone had time to look at the knives?"

He again replied, "Well three look to be knives, but one has an eighteen inch blade. I'm not sure, but doesn't that qualify as a sword?"

"Well Mary and Caty can use the knives. I don't think either of them are ready to use what are called long knives. Arty will need one too, Kitty to you have an inside outside surprise?"

She smiled and said in a sweet almost child's voice, "Me has many surprises, many hear the blap, blap of tommy, tommy."

Well I perfectly understood what she meant by that. So I added, "Send Arty to me so I can give him a toy. It's not a great plan, and we're doing the best we can. But I think we may have an advantage in this though. When I destroyed the one I found he was able to react to me. I think someone took interest in this one so he was of importance. And even though I can't be sure, but he may have been the leader."

Naomi then said, "Finally at least a little good news if you're right. But I don't think we should tell the kids. We should paint it as if half of them may die tomorrow. Well that is if they even show up. You know how unpredictable they can be."

I nodded and added, "I agree and tell them this might take like a week. That is until this one den is cleared out. Everyone talk about it, but no one adds that it took me four days to destroy all those vampires."

I got up as Naomi asked, "Was that the one in Los Angeles?"

Everyone else got up as I replied, "Nope that was the one on the east side of Brooklyn. I couldn't believe that place held almost five hundred vampires."

"Oh that one, I always thought that was a myth."

Tony then asked, "Wait? You're that John?"

I nodded as I replied to Naomi, "Nope, but it was easier then the one in L.A. I mean they were packed like sardines in there. I couldn't fire a bullet without hitting like four or five people. That really help separate the humans from the vamps. I used a can of gasoline with a Molotov cocktail to kill their leader. He must of not been feeding regularly, he went up like cord wood."

Naomi then said, "Well that's one way of getting rid of one of those bastards. I've only fought forth and fifth terr Shovelhead's. What was he?"

As we walked into the room I said, "He was a second terr, but the one in L.A. Was a first terr though. Did you hear he had like seven clones?"

She nodded as we all sat in front of the kids to start talking. I looked at tony and said, "Hey Tony I think you'll be better at this. Do you want to start this?"

He nodded and stood as he started, he went through the recent events without mentioning what Kitty had seen. Then because we hadn't completely covered it as he talked about the history both Naomi and I added what we knew. Now he did cover their past but only briefly as he really wanted to keep to what was going on in the city. Finally he got to what Kitty had seen and with this he had to hit a little more of their history. "Now I can tell you the way they think of their old leaders isn't a good thing." He said. "They think they can bring about the end of the world as long as they provoke the church. Their favorite target is the Catholic church which is a bad thing. So when they do this we have to find a way to stop it or die."

Caty put up her hand and asked, "I can see why we try to rid our city of these crazies. But really why are we worried about humans for?"

I looked at her and said it as plainly as I could, "They have the backing of the church which means ancient resources. They really get into hunting us to the point where they're almost as good as us. Worse is the catholic Church has special units that have been around a long time. Some say they have found a way to age slowly like us. The more experienced ones seem to receive special abilities like our disciplines. And lastly they train their lives on just how to kill one sort of super. That means their knowledge is as complete as any vampire hunter. The short of it is you don't really want any of them hunting you. It would be far easier to have a government agency chasing you. But no matter how good you are all these have one advantage we don't have, and that's numbers."

Everyone got silent after that, and when we were sure no one else had a question Tony went on. "Ok Paul, Cheryl, and Pepper I'll show you the weapons you can use. Joe you're going to be with John, but for your safety I want you to carry what we call a cannon. John its on you."

I stood up and said, "Ok Mary, Caty, and Arty come to me and I'll outfit you with knives. Now for teams, Joe you heard that you'll be on my team, Billy you're also on me. Pepper and Caty are with Naomi. Of course Arty you go with Kitty. Normally Joe would go with them as well, but Joe hasn't came into his own, so we opted for a heavy hitter. That's you Mary. Now Cheryl and Paul you're with Tony as our cover, this means cover. If you see someone sneaking up on like Mary you shoot them. I think the next part should be left up to Naomi."

Naomi then stood up and spoke, "Kitty will start the show if needed. We can't promise you this won't take a while, plus we can't promise some, to all of you maybe destroyed. I can tell you the best way to catch them though. Kitty and Arty will be there in the open with Mary hidden close by. To trap them in this salient though, that means John and I have to be by the side lines. Once everything gets started though, we'll move to push them to the center where Kitty and Arty will be. Tony and his crew will sit just off, you need to leave open one side of a trap. That's his job to close the lid on the trap."

She then put her leg up on the chair and leaned on it as she went around the circle. "We need for this to work. I know we'll make mistakes, none of you are trained well enough. If we can save a vampire life we will, but don't count on it. This isn't the worse situation we could be in, but it's not much better. Foremost though is everyone has to help the other, if he or she sees a problem. If we do that and we somehow get out of this, we will all know the better for the next group we have to face."

She then sat back down and then Tony went on with, "Now break up,and go with your prospective elder. Oh and on more thing, if you can find it tomorrows dress is battle. If you don't understand ask your elder."

With this I walked away, and knew I had all mine following me. I spoke as we made our way up the steps. "We fight primarily with blades and blunt objects. When you think of armor, it isn't like armor of old. Leather should be your first thought, second would be anything with padding. Remember modern clothing won't necessarily stop a blow, but it will lessen the effect. I know the three of you aren't ready for this, but if you can grit your teeth and bare it. The pain does go away in time, and try to never allow the pain to influence what you're doing. This way you might be able to stay on track."

Caty then asked, "John do you really think some of will die?"

We entered the room as I turned and replied, "I won't lie to any of you. None of you are ready for this, so there's a real good possibility. Naomi and I will be there trying to help you out, and I hope you try to help out each other as well. If this works then we all have a chance, and maybe we can keep the deaths to a minimum."

Then I went to the same closet that had the weapons in it. I saw the three knives and I immediately gave Arty the straight razor, and said to him. "Do exactly what Kitty tells you, and use this well." I then pulled out the largest knife, but not that 18" one. I then said to Mary as I handed her the knife, "You're my daughter, and I would rather have you with me. But I know Caty has more experience, and we need our strength on the outside. Don't be scared, and swing this with all your strength. It's not a great way to fight, but with your strength it should be very easy for you."

Then I returned to the closet for the last weapon as Caty cleared her throat and said, "John?"

I replied, "Yes Caty?"

"Can I use this?" I turned around to see what she was talking about, as she pulled out another knife. Then she went on, "I know its small then yours, but I think I can handle it, and I have been practicing that reverse swing you use. I think I'm getting pretty good."

I had to smile at her as I said, "I see no reason why not. We'll just give that to Joe just in case." Then I thought about it and added, "Caty do you know my other blade the bayonet?"

"Yeah John."

"Give that to Pepper, and this one to Joe. This is more balanced, watch them for a moment. Which ever one has problems give this knife, the other one gets my knife."

"Ok, I'll do that right away."

I knew that Tony was coming as they all left. As I passed him I said, "Put the Beretta in my room, I'll put the Glock ammo on the kitchen table for you." I then handed him my Glock, I kind of felt naked as I walked away. I heard him tell Pepper to put the Beretta in my room then get the ammo from the kitchen. I went right out and got the one box that was actually made for my Glock. I decided to find that library I heard of, and see if I could read.

I really did have to wonder if any of these guys would survive their first real encounter with Shovelhead's. At least now they were doing something in the positive state, instead of just running. Running wasn't always a bad thing though, but it never seemed to really help a bad situation. I had fought a lot of fights, and that's how I think I got so good. I am the Enforcer, and a true Enforcer isn't chosen like most of them. None of these kids were even close to actually hold an office.

Then I stopped and thought how Billy had fought. I then realized that unlike Naomi, he might be destined to be a natures warrior. He had no control, but I could easily see him as one. Plus with the ease he goes into his fighting mode. It is kind of funny though, in my long existence I had only ran into one other. It turned out we were searching for the same guy. We fought a nasty fight until we realized that. We hadn't even come close to really hurting one another, but it was tough even getting a blow in. It's a good thing I'm a talker, if I hadn't been talking about him getting in my way. Well yeah, that fight may have ended a lot worse. I do wonder though who was better, and whether he's still alive.

I saw one lady that was ever even close to Caty. She was old when I met her so she had to have past by now. Neither of them are from the same family, but I could see those two butting heads, and having a knock out drag out fight. That kind of made me smile, then I thought of Pepper. Oh yes she was beautiful, and she knew it, but I knew one of her type that truly surpassed her. I kind of remember her having almost as red of hair as Caty's, well except her hair was long, and I think she had a little pink in there too.

Oh poor Salien, she was so determined to keep her humanity. In a lot of ways she was exactly like Arty, even though I think he maybe a bit more human then she was. With this I thought of Paul, I really couldn't think of any of his kind like him truly. In the end this might be a problem for him. They are so bent on keeping their political correctness, that they haven't really seen that they are losing all their power. Most call Paul's type the corporate vampires, but I do have to admit they really know how to make money.

Thinking about this I thought of Cheryl and the way Mary described her, she just might be the perfect of her kind. My kind have never been friends with Paul and Cheryl's kind, which made me think of Mary and Cheryl's friendship. I guess it wasn't a bad friendship, but could it survive if they were pressured by their own kind. Mary was unusual for my kind though, she seemed to always try and look like the mom. But then I realized that in truth she wasn't as I remembered what happened last night. Our kind always prided itself as being the most rebellious, well the way Mary was she sure was the most rebellious without being rebellious.

I had to wonder if this motley group of elders could actually pull this off. He could see that Tony was more of the in line type of vampire of his kind. He couldn't really see where the beauty came in, not that he was the judge of another guy. Naomi he could see that they may have just been pass by night friends. Then again her type was always known for their roaming nature, but truly he felt the closest to Kitty. In the end just before Salien was killed, by that mad woman, she was beginning to sound exactly like Kitty. But he did have to admit they both had a certain beauty, but he couldn't fathom how Kitty stayed so young.

And with this last thought he had another strange thought. It seemed to come from no where, and since he had never thought of this in 347 years. The thought was, wow our family is actually coming together. I had realized that I had been calling them all kids, but in truth could I actually call any of them kids. I mean I had heard the story of

Mary and Cheryl, and in their own way they had already lived their own school of hard knocks. Then you had the original six that were more then that, and these were the last survivors of the lot. Calling them all kids just didn't seem right after all they had suffered. Sure they didn't have the knowledge for this life, but they had a lot of other knowledge. Plus in the end wasn't if life knowledge that made us what we were.

Chapter 14

I then came in this room to read, but wasn't really able to concentrate on the project at hand, so there was no getting any reading done. The I saw Naomi walking by and said, "I wish we had more time."

She stopped dead in her tracks and said, "I know, but there's nothing we can really do about this situation."

"Maybe not." I smiled as I continued, "But I also have to ask if we're doing the right thing? I mean is it really that important to change what they would do normally, are we right in this disruption of their lives?"

She looked at me almost with wonder in her eyes as she replied, "I know all to well. I've only known them for two short days, but they seem to be growing on me too. I showed them how to use the shadows and tree line even though that a later act, and then how to camouflage through being seen. They were very surprised at how easy it can be, and I found myself feeling pride in their discoveries. Billy was like an old master at it, but Cheryl was so excited, that she could actually do this, it didn't matter her mistakes."

"I know what you mean, Caty wanted to see if she could climb a building. I figured it would be ok as long as I was there to catch them. She was so excited that she could do it, I don't think she even thought of how short her skirt was. I think Paul was almost as excited, plus they both did end up falling, but I was there to catch them. When I did that both times it was as if I were saving my own kids. in the end, I feel I showed they could trust me too. I don't know about all this training stuff we have to show them, but I do think that helps us out a lot with them. I also knew Paul wouldn't be as graceful as Pepper, but he did so well on top of the fences. I have to wonder if he's more then the sum of his kind, yep these kids could be quite good."

"I think you may have something there, but we are on a downward trend in this anyways John. We're already having to steal from Peter to pay Paul to make ends meet, plus the little bit of blood we have, we are already rationing. Well we need to set a lot of things up, and get some help, from somewhere. With the way we have to move I don't see it happening anytime soon though, so exactly how can we do this if its an elongated fight?"

I had to look at her in a state of wonder myself as I asked, "Do you really think that they would be any better off in the outside world that we know about then? You know our story, and that I feel more comfortable away from the others, then the common leadership in their scheming and plotting plans. To tell you the truth though, it isn't that I don't like them, which in truth I really don't. The fact that it does seem to do the right thing, at the wrong time, or the wrong thing, exactly at the right time. How can that really happen if there isn't another agenda, or possibly worse a set plan to literally destroy everything."

"Well that is true, but all those anarchist you usually team up with aren't usually any better. I've seen both sides of the coin, and for a group that's so against the authority, or as they like to say The Man. They have rules that set them up for death, and in the end they're of more of a throttle to themselves then any authority. Is this what you think is best for our kids?"

"Well not really. What I meant is maybe they should do this all by themselves. Keep the Prince's and Princess's out of it, or at least any governing body, and just do this for themselves. Hey I have no idea how to do this, but since we know the laws so well. Why don't we actually let them decide for themselves, and all we do is tell them what the real laws are?"

"Hmm." She said as she put her hand to her chin. "That might be an idea. Lets put it to Kitty and Tony."

I then said, "Ok lets go look for them, and meet back here in lets say twenty."

"Sounds great to me too. Ok be back in twenty."

So we both left, and had gotten back within that time frame. Then we laid out what we were thinking to the two of them. Tony was the only one that had any serious questions. Which I had already expected, but in truth it seemed he was into this as we were. So we gathered up all the people, and sat around the second stairs fight as we explained all of it. Everyone was excited about our thoughts, and we were sure to say all this needed to be ironed out. I had Tony explain the few things about the hierarchy of the High Council. Then I told them about the anarchist, and all the problems with them. I think in a way I sounded pro High Council, and Tony sounded Pro anarchist, even though we were the exact opposites in truth. When they finished even though it was bed time everyone were still talking about our ideas.

But we went on because we could see they wanted more. Mary then asked, "If its up to us does this mean everything, I mean even in our own leadership?"

Naomi then replied, "Yes of course it is."

I then asked, "Mary you meant more by what you asked, didn't you?"

"Well yeah," She replied, and thought for a second before going on, "What I mean is that all of you are training us, which puts you in the lead. In a sense though, we should have our own leadership set up now to cover our needs now. It isn't that we don't trust all of you, but do you truly understand the needs of younger vampires."

"That makes sense, even though we would want to lead because we know what needs to be. The truth is that not even the High Council can know what all of you need. We maybe closer, because we don't want to deal with the High Council. But new vampires actually need them in a sense, plus this situation really doesn't help you guys that much."

Pepper then asked, "I don't understand what you mean John?"

Tony came right in with, "Well there is a certain sense that the older you get, the farther you get from your humanity. They say we are the most human of all the vampire races, but even in my kind this is a myth. In fact, and John will like this. In my kinds humanity we actually loose more humanity then most of the other races, and the most inhumane of our kind are usually the most humane."

Paul instantly put his hand up and asked, "I'm sorry Tony, but you lost me on that one."

I put my hand up to stop him as I went one, "Let take killing anyone, whether its a vampire or a human, this isn't a natural act. When we become vampires though we are forced to kill, or die. In a sense this actually kind of shows our own cowardice, but that's for another time. So as we were human we suddenly have to do inhumane stuff, through this we learn to give up our humanity. I also believe that one day we tend to give up so much, that it comes back around to haunt us. This also maybe why its very hard to find a vampire over five hundred years old." I then looked around and had to conclude the truth I was thinking right then, "In fact we might even have to take a page out of our own book here. You see in this situation we are forced into, we as your elders have to force you into our world. A world where our humanity is an abstract idea, rather then a fact. I do have to put it to the elder and see if they see what I do."

I then looked at Naomi and asked, "In so much as what we have to do with these kids, would you think it was possible to learn about humanity?"

She replied, "I really don't know John, in truth I have never really thought about it before. Well in truth I've never thought about it before, because I'm a huntress not a trainer."

I then looked at Tony and he shrugged his shoulders. So I asked, "To be human has always been our end goal, so I ask, could it be wiser to try and be as human as we can?"

He replied, "Well there's no denying that John, we should try to be more like our human cousins."

Kitty then spoke up and said, "We be that which is the start, if we can be no other, then we not be. The fact be in the light of night, that as the dark blinds humans, it has blinded us worse. New means new, and old is dirt. What has been has been tried and lost, what is new has no law to it. The law need be to set is we agreed or is we wrong. That be what the darkness wants, yet we only to the edge of the abyss, we no go over yet."

I can tell you I had to stop and think about what was said, and that last line was real scary. I knew though I had to go on, and try to make sense out of what she said. So I said, "Exactly Kitty. You see everything that has been done in the past is know, what we do here is totally new. There's no precedence for this, so no one can tell us how it will turn out. So in many ways we are flying by the seat of our pants here, this means we may have to change direction in mid stream though. So if we agree that we'll make mistakes, and agree to help when we need change that will be good. We have to understand that in this we will see that darkness come in, but as long as we don't go over the edge we should be ok."

Now you could probably imagine a few added that very last part, I mean her kind where known for their insight, come on. Tony then came in with, "John made a very good point, and even though I'm only a year old, I can already feel my humanity slipping away. So even though the classes will be led by John, Kitty, Naomi, and myself, you can also see that we have to take back our own humanity in the end. Remember that we have learned how to be this way over time, its going to take us some time to learn ourselves. Lastly I can tell you this won't be an easy road, heck just being a vampire isn't an easy road. I would have you look to the kid next to you, and ask yourself what would you do if they didn't come back tomorrow. Why do you ask, well these

Shovelhead's have pushed us into doing things we aren't ready for."

I had to stand after this and go on, "Like we said this isn't an easy life, and having all these Shovelhead's really is complicating things. This is one thing I would have you remember, earlier Caty said they're just humans. In some way we do this to protect ourselves, but to truly protect ourselves we have to also protect what we once were. Most vampires can trace their lineage though this line or that line, but they never go beyond that. Why? Because if they do they have to remember that Jonathan Williamson used to be a normal Dutchman. Or worse off, just a plain old human. All vampires originate from a human, which we all saw with the turning of Cheryl and my new daughter Mary. Then there is the fragility of just being a vampire, I mean what happens if there's no human blood to drink? Old as well as modern vampires tend to look at humans as just so much cattle. The truth of the matter in some circles they don't give a thought of what might happen."

Naomi interjected here, "John perfectly right here, I have seen it all myself. Treating human death as its just a fact of life, when in reality it isn't."

I then went on. "The truth of the matter is that I wish we had this modern age when I was turned. Then those deaths I had to cause wouldn't have to weigh on my mind. Death and destruction is inevitable, but with the new way to feed, and blood bags you can lesson this affect. So in a sense as Tony has voiced many times, we really don't have to kill anymore. With this we now have the option to be better vampires, or at least better vampires hiding as humans."

Tony then sat down as he finished up, "It isn't that we want to kill these guys, its that they won't listen to reason and they force us to do this act. Vampires can easily live in the human world almost like real humans, but never loose the fact that we aren't though. They revel in what they are though, and would make all humans like them. Now you can see why we in the end we have to rid this city of this menace, if not they would make our world unlivable."

Naomi then looked around and said, "If you have any questions we may have to wait till the evening, the sun has already breached the horizon."

Caty then asked, "We can live during the day, why don't we?"

I then replied, "It has to do more with what's enhanced on us. We can see better, smell better, and stuff like that. As all of our kind though, this always works better at night then during the day. As the hunters that we are then, it only makes sense that we go out at night."

Tony then added, "Well and as predators of the human race, they also can't do these things as well as we can."

Naomi then continued, "Well that is if we're hunting humans, right now we're hunting those that would prey on humans. And you can rest assured that's what they're going to do. Yes I also understand that it would be easier to destroy them during the day, but you have to think of the reverse. If we didn't hunt at night, it would be far easier for them to kill us then too."

With that we all then went to our rooms, it took Mary a little longer to get there then me. I then said to her, "I think I know what I did last night and I truly am sorry about that."

She looked at me with a little disdain on her face as she spoke, "Well it hurt a lot. I mean I was just joking at first, but to be just shot down like that. I mean John a woman offers herself to you like that, and you speak to her like shes just some kind of object. Well how would you feel if I talked to you the same way?"

"Not very good, but you do understand, I was really thinking of you, right?"

"Yeah, good thing you have a good friend like Naomi."

"Well I want you to know the facts as my daughter Mary. Our world is a different kind of world then you knew, and I think its because we are so removed from our humanity. Well it's like all of you say kill or die, whereas Naomi and I use the term destroy or destruction. We figure we're already dead anyways, so you can't kill whats already dead. When you are young you cling to your old humanity. Like when you were growing up, and one day you probably said, wow my mom or dad was right, or worse you realize you sound just like them. Well that also happens in this world, as you grow you learn things, some times terrible things. Then one day you come to the realization, wow I'm not a human anymore. Then the barriers that once existed are just gone. Then that four story building that was always your limit in climbing, becomes a ten story building."

"Ok I can fathom that, but what does this have anything to do with what we're talking about?"

"Well when a woman becomes just that a woman, she goes through tremendous changes in her life. I won't go into that though as I'm sure you already know. But what if every time you drank blood your body went back to its original state? You can see what this would do to a pregnant woman's body, and the terrible things it would do to that baby. So at some point a woman realizes that they'll never truly get pregnant again. Some morn the lose of not being able to having a child again, yet then some feel a certain freedom. The latter is technically what I'm trying to protect you from, and maybe give you a little realization of your own."

I looked right in her eyes and said it, "Mary almost any Lord would want to have you, because you belong to my family. You're a very beautiful woman, so that would be an even greater plus. You're just a new vampire, and in 5 years you'll be at your prime state. I think a male vampire will kill to have you at his side. I don't have all the tricks that other do, but they can do things that are beyond my knowledge. So even though you might say never, I say never ever say never. As your father, I do want to be there to help you. So it isn't like I wouldn't like to lay you down with me, and have wild passionate sex with you right now. But to keep this father daughter relationship, I feel its best. This way when you do find that certain guy, that is only there to break your heart. Well one day I'll walk threw the door, and you'll say. 'Oh so and so you remember my daddy The Enforcer. Oh and by the way, for what you did to me, he's really pissed.'"

She did a little giggle as she asked, "Then you really were looking out for me?"

I gave her my biggest smile and a big hug as I replied, "Yes I really was. Oh and the nude thing was also, even though I did want to see what you looked like under all your clothes."

She smacked my chest and said, "I knew that Daddy, a girl can tell."

"Mary," I asked?"

"Yes daddy?"

"I maybe old, but I don't look it. Please don't make me older then what I look." She gave me a look so I added, "Less on the daddy and dad stuff and more on the John stuff."

"Can I say it in private?"

"I guess so, but just we make this your own little thing. I think you might want a room of your own. So as your dad take all the time you want, but just for you own sanity look for another room you like over the next few days."

"Daddy?"

"Yes Mary?"

"You have that backwards, remember you had me find this room for us. So technically I already found my room, so it's your turn to search."

"I guess you're right there. Ok tomorrow I'll look for a new room, and on the next night I'll move out for your sake. But Mary you can come to me, and talk about anything you ever want to talk to me about."

"Even if its really uncomfortable and lady like?"

"I guess so, even though I would think you would want to talk to Cheryl about that stuff."

"I do. I just wanted to see how far I could push you. So should we get ready for bed?"

I leaned over and took in a deep breathe. Then I asked, "Do you smell that?"

She then did the same thing and replied, "Yeah, what is that smell?"

"It's the earth preparing for a new day, it's the smell that tells us we have to find a place to sleep soon. I want you to remember that smell if you ever get stuck in a dark place. Its easy to see the dawn and know its coming, but it's safe to smell it and know your safe."

She smiled and said, "You know a lot of stuff."

I smiled back and said, "That's how I've been able to stay alive for so long. Now lets get ready for bed and rest for the next day."

Then we had done about the same thing we had done the night before. Except this time I didn't have to tell here the best way to sleep. I could see that Mary was going to be a very fast learner. She did ask me why I slept under the bed. I told her that it was so clique that some invading our room would never even think to look under there until it was far to late. She asked if she should lay under there as well. So I went on that if someone did invade our room they would expect one person in it and would start to look. This would cause them to look even though this might be the last place they look. Surprise wouldn't be on our side and that might negate the possibility to save her. She understood and from then on all she had were just simple question and answers. And in about an hour or two we drifted off to our rest.

Chapter 15

<u>Sister Mary Elizabeth</u>

      I didn't sleep well as I woke up with the sun. I liked working with the kids, why did they have to lessen our activities for?

      I mean God said when it was our time to die, no man could stop it, and if you believe in God, everything was possible. This just didn't feel right to me, why in the blessed virgins name were we pulling away from the public. I know Father Micheal said it was for our own safety, but if this was what he wanted he would of told us to be Christ like. I had became a nun so I could face the world, and help those that needed my help, not hide away in a nunnery. Now I just walk to the front porch, and everyone ask, where are you going sister.

      I could hear it from all the kids, not that they would talk about it directly. With all the recent deaths, and us drawing away from the public, they're sure that this part of town has has some kind of terrible evil that is just hanging over it. First we had a couple of home invasions, then those three little girls were just killed right on the street. Worse was that I saw one, and the horror on that young ladies face. Maybe the kids are right, maybe there is a great evil moving around in this area. But then again wasn't that our job to fight against this kind of evil. I had to wonder if any of this was real, were we real? Could it be that I have been deluded all these years, and if I had been then what a waist.

      I then pulled out my old patient blind, these had gone out of date like fifty years ago. But they made the perfect blind to change ones clothes. I then took off my bed things and had to look at myself. I ate like a bird and as of late had been on a soup fast, so why did I have a little ponch? Well I knew that was way wrong to be this superficial, so I quickly put on my shower robe. I knew I wouldn't be the first ones in there, the school nuns had already gotten up, and were probably dressing. I just had to hope that there was some hot water left. I didn't mind cold water, but on a day you were trying to forget your troubles, hot was far better.

I know it was weird to have a communal that was designed to be totally private, but these were. The room was big enough for ten showers, but with the divided sections there were only eight. It was all cider block except for the entry doors in, they were a kind of a golden wood. It really was set up for privacy, I mean the shower head was set close to the doors. Then they were set to spray into the room, so the wood wouldn't get wet. I did have to wonder if that was for us, or to save the wood. I turned on the water to find out that it was at least warm. I then took my robe off and hung it on the single hook. I grabbed the yellow bar of soap, and then walked into the spray.

I allowed myself to drift off, as the warm spray was barely doing its job, when I heard the door open. My eyes popped open, even though I knew no one would ever come into my private shower. Then I heard the Mother superiors voice, "Mary Elizabeth are you in there?"

I replied, "Yes mother, I just stepped into the shower and barely started lathering up. Do you need me for anything?"

I knew the hope in my voice, might have had to much hope for it, as she replied, "No Mary Elizabeth, but I do have good news. Father Micheal says he has a busy day, but he'll see you later if you have the time."

"Good," I replied, then asked, "About what time Mother if I may ask?"

"He said seven, even though he said it might take him till nine, before he can actually see you. But he says that the two of you really need to talk, with the light of things."

"Ok Mother Superior, so what will you have me do today?"

"I'll have to think on that one, but I was thinking the garden. Come to me after your morning prayers."

My Morning prayers, they have been filled with as of late, am I doing the right thing. Those people that say they always get their prayers answered, well I wish he would at least say yes to me. I replied, "Ok Mother, then breakfast. What are we having today?"

"Sister Ignatius is cooking today."

When I first came here I thought she was a wonderful cook, until I found out she only knew how to cook one meal. Oh well I would pick at it, maybe even eat a little, and then have one more day of my fast. "Sounds yummy."

"Sister watch how you say things. We must all do our part, and live the life God gave us."

"I'm sorry Mother, I'll try harder."

"Don't worry sister, even I picked at my breakfast this morning. But we just don't talk about it, but Mary Catherine is making dinner."

Now there was good news, if she hadn't been a nun I'm sure she would have been a chef. Well that perked me up as I asked, "Has she released her menu for tonight?"

"Yep, and she posted it on the door of the kitchen. But I'll let you be surprised for yourself. Now hurry up so you aren't late."

Then she walked out the door. Our mother Superior was a good person, even though she was very old school. Well I knew what I had to do, as I knew I could never measure up to our good Mother. I finished taking my shower, and went to my room. All I had to do was to bide my day, till I got to talk to Father Micheal.

Officer Jimmy Herschel

      I had gotten into work, when I got another phone call. I was sipping on my cup of joe, when I heard him. I knew him well, and knew he would never do drugs, but what he said made me wonder. My partner and I went out to see for ourselves. Apparently the body had been shoved into a bush near an Apartment complex near a park. It had been a security guard that had found the body. He had told that he had made four rounds, and that the body hadn't been there. You always gauge one of them by how well they do their paper work. If its to good they're over zealous, if it seems to be very sloppy then they don't really care. This guys was somewhere in between which means he was the type of security guard you could depend on.

      I looked at the severely decomposed body and asked him, "You said he wasn't here, and if I asked the tenants if there was a god awful smell out here they'll say?"

      "I do have to admit that's how I found him. I mean I know he wasn't there earlier. Plus if he had been I'm sure I would of smelled something that bad."

      Well that was refreshing, by saying that he admitted two things. One he hadn't really been looking that hard, but that he had been doing his rounds which said this was strange. I then went over to the ME staff person after I told him that was all. I then said, "Ok take a good long look at him, and give me what you have as soon as possible."

      He then said something that I felt was strange. "Jimmy this is very strange. I know that his head was taken off with one blow, but here's the strange thing. As decomposed as this body is, you'd think you would have a lot of deflating at the wound. So in a sense when I put bone to bone you should see separation. But look at this."

      He then placed the head to the neck without it touching, but it was clear to see. If he did put the head to the body, it would perfectly match. He then put the head back in the bag and added, "It could be some strange anomaly, so I'll have the doc look at it, and give you his opinion. But I thought you might want to see it."

"Ok thanks, and you do that. Oh plus give me your thoughts on the seen. To me it looked like he was just shoved up there, but I can't imagine someone taking that kind of time, in a well populated part of the city."

He nodded as I move to where my partner was at, I then said, "Jackson this is going to one of those strange ones for us. Who ever did this left a lot of clues, but its like whomever it was really didn't care."

He was a new guy, and prone to for for the worse case scenarios. But I could think that he maybe right as he said it, "Someone that doesn't care what, or whom he kills. Sounds like a mob hit. Well that, or vampires if you if you believe that sort of a thing."

I have to tell you the Mob hit theory sounded good, but I did have to wonder about the vampire thing also. Then a seemingly weirder thing seem to happen, a black limo pulled up, and two guys got out in dark suits. It immediately brought to me the seen from the movie Men in Black. As we stood there watching them walk up, one took out a badge and just said those three letters we hated to hear, "We're with the FBI."

There's never any mistake when you see an FBI badge, even though in a sense it really isn't a real badge anymore. I kind of knew where this was going as the guy said, "We need all your information pertaining to this case."

You may have seen in a lot of cop shows, and that we hated to share information. But since the Murrah Building bombing all our systems share what we have, with anyone that'll listen. So I said, "You know all our books have always been open to all law enforcement bureaus. So once we start putting stuff into our registry, you can look all you want."

The second man then said, "You don't understand, this is a matter of national security. All information will be placed in the NSA security data base, and it has became an FBI case now."

Ok I was pissed now, and wanted something, but I knew these types. They weren't going to say a thing, that's why I quite the FBI, and joined a normal police force. So I just nodded, and handed over all we had, but I knew this wouldn't be the end of it. I did ask though, "Can you tell us anything at all?"

The first guy then said, "Nothing at all."

The second guy added then, "He doesn't mean he has anything to tell you. We just got on the case ourselves, and have as little as you have. But we've received word that this guy is suspected in a string of murders in Los Angeles, and just recently New Orleans."

"Oh shit we have a serial killer on our hands."

I couldn't help to feel kind of strange, when all they did was smile at us. It was like they knew far more then they were saying, and this was far more then just some serial killer. I also knew I wouldn't get anything out of them, so my only recourse was to precede with my own investigation.

Day 4

We got up about the same time, and as we did she just laid there as I got dressed. I said to her, "Ok when you get up remember how to dress. We have to be prepared for anything so try to wear as much leather as possible. Ok meet me in the kitchen."

She then turned to me and placed one leg over the other so she was fully exposed to me and said, "That sounds kinky."

I'll admit I had two thoughts, I'm a man so the first one is the most obvious. But the second one was she knew what we had to do today, and she chooses to mess around now. I thought though if I were frank it might help me out of this unknowable situation. So I said, "Mary even if I wanted to, you know we don't have the time for that.

Now get up, and get dressed." I guess though what I added next really didn't help matters much. "Mary of all the kids you're the most mature of the lot. I know you can handle yourself, and we really do have to go now."

I then left the room without really understanding I really stepped my foot in a huge pile of poop. I was in the kitchen looking to make sure we had blood, before we left, and blood when we came back. As Naomi came into the room asking. "What did you say to Mary? She's crying." I then told her with no mistakes what I said. And she said, "Oh my. You really didn't say that did you?"

I was completely confused so all I could ask was, "What did I say?"

She shook her head and replied, "John saying that in the influx you used, that was like calling her old and reliable. This is not good."

I wanted to take care of this right now, so that's why I stood right up and said. "I'll take care of this right now."

Naomi placed her hand on my chest to stop me as she said, "No John you've done enough damage. Let us girls take care of this now."

With that she grabbed two bags of blood, and was out the door. John knew she was right, but he really wanted to jump up and do something. Exactly what could he do, in these situations he was always just so lost. I knew I had tried to love other vampires, but in my un-life they had always ended it with me. I had to wonder two things in all these relationships though. One why did I have no problem getting a girl, where my problem seemed to come in was keeping them. And if what I had with each girl was really love, why was it so easy to get over. I wasn't known to move on from girl to girl, but I could make the transition so easily though. So the question begged, had I ever really been in love at all? And of course with that question, then what is love anyways? Well that old adage that said, all's fair in love and war. Was it true that a person could be so good at war, and so terrible at love?

Tony came in, and interrupted my train of thought, "Smooth John. I'm not sure what you did. But every lady in the house is converging in on your room."

I had to shake my head, as Joe came in, and said, "Man did you really say Mary was old, and Comfortable?"

"Major faux-pas guy. I know one thing above all else, is you never call a lady old."

"All I know is whatever you did made Caty majorly angry. I went to find out what's up, and she almost bit off my head. It was Naomi that kind of explained it to me."

I asked, "What did she say?"

"Just that, it was like she really didn't want to say more. But that was enough for me to beat feet."

All I could do was shake my head, as Arty came in even more disheveled then the night before. As he sat down he said, "Kitty literally ran out of the room. Anyone know what's up?"

Joe then said, "John may have caused a major faux-pas with Mary."

Tony then added, "There's no may about it."

I saw Paul coming down the hall so I said, "Paul I have blood out for everyone, could you make sure everyone gets some, and they drink it all." I was about to let it lay there, but then I added, "And make sure they're all putting it in the same trash, I forgot to cover that the other night."

Paul looked at me and asked, "Is that important?"

Tony then replied for me, "We can't show that we exist, so you never throw it in the normal trash. So once a week, we collect it all up, and just burn it all, so there isn't any evidence. I bet this house has an incinerator some place."

Joe then said, "Yeah the garage, near the back. I always wondered what that was for."

"It also for, not so fresh kills. When ever you have a vampire that needs to be put down, we don't just destroy him or her. The crew selected to do the job, will also dismember them, and burn every part. This is considered very dishonorable, so there's no pomp or circumstance to this event. So most vampires don't even know about it, unless they take part in it."

I said, "Yeah, when I was young, I was part of a few of them. I can't say I ever had any fun with those, even though some of the elders painted it as fun."

"That kind of figures, elders don't seem to have a good sense of humor, in fact the few I've met, they seem to have a real sick sense of humor."

"Yeah, a few can be funny, but you're right, that most have a pretty sick sense of humor."

Joe asked, "How sick?"

Tony then gave them a serious look as he started the story. "There was this Prince that commanded Chicago, and he invited everyone to a party. He didn't tell anyone about it, but it was because the city was over populated. So once everyone was there, he sent everyone on impossible mission, just to see them die. It was said he only had to destroy a few, but he was having so much fun, he kept going until there were only 6 left.?"

I couldn't believe that story came up again, I had to look at Tony and ask, "Just how old are you?"

"Old enough why?"

"Well almost everyone knows that story isn't true. It wasn't eighty years ago when it was made up, and it surely isn't now."

"Well I've been told that all stories have a basis in truth. So if that isn't the real story, then what is?"

"It did have a basis of truth, about until some idiot got hold of it. Kids the truth is that something did happen back then, and it had nothing to do with most vampires sick humor. A group of six renegade vampires thought they could do better then the human Mob. You see they tried to take over a city, and caused mayhem in their wake. But that is really a story of the High Councils stupidity. You see they sent what they call a Justicar to handle the situation, and gave him the full support of the High Council. When he got there, he saw the only way to handle this problem, was to make those that were in power vampires. After all the dust settled, there were only six left, and they kicked the High Council out of that city. It was the first city, controlled by what we now know as the anarch's. If it wasn't for this one incident, they say they would of never gotten their start. And kids this all happened, during Prohibition and the Depression. Two time periods for there fame in change."

Joe asked then, "John what other changes happened since you became a vampire."

"Well for one thing, we didn't care about guns in general. First they got better, and some of us seen this as a huge change. Then came rapid fire machine pistols, that was a huge break threw. Now a days there are things that can actually horrify a vampire. I mean a weapon that can fire like 2 to 3 thousand rounds a minute. They always had Greek fire, but then the Americans made it very affordable. We always had a problem with our smell, that's one of the good changes, we were able to baths regularly. I guess the biggest change was when they started to bottle blood though. Before that we always had to leave a trail of corpses. Well that, and about the same time, they found out we didn't need to kill. This was a very hard thing for the old to take. For years they had been having to kill, then suddenly they found out they didn't have to be doing this for centuries. We lost a lot of very old vampires over night it seemed."

"Why was that?"

"I think it basically boiled down to conscience. I can't be really 100% sure. I hope those girls hurry up, I need to check them out, and we need to get there early."

Tony then said, "You should of thought of that before you upset Mary."

"Tony even if I didn't upset Mary, it doesn't make those Shovelhead's any less there."

Tony looked down and Paul asked, "When I take up their blood, do you want me to hurry them up?"

I was about ready to nod to Paul, then I thought better of it as I spoke. "No, give the blood to Naomi, and tell her we need to hurry up. Be nice about it, and tell her that if not, we can go tomorrow night. Now go." As he did I then said to the other guys, "Drink up, this is to help you just in case. We might be waiting there for a long time, so don't expect it to last."

Chapter 16

With this the other boys ripped into their bags, as Tony and I used the scissors I had actually placed on the table for everyone. You see when you first drink blood and are young, you receive a high like you're sort of drunk. With age comes understanding that allows you to handle this, kind of like a normal person and a wino. The effect of it being able to heal us lasts for about an hour or so. That's the reason I had them drink the blood before we left, even with the euphoric affect. I to get figured every little bit would help them out. I also knew that I would have to get the facts straight about Tony's age. The rumor he spoke of is almost always dispelled within their first year, and if not then for sure by their fifth year.

Then again I really screwed up too, so maybe his trainer never heard him talk about it. Well I knew for sure this wouldn't be my first screw up, I had to figure there would be many more on the way. This doesn't bod well for his or my leadership skills. I felt like standing and just yelling or hitting something. Hurry up, I didn't mean it, or what the hell seemed like good decisions. Then again with this last screw up, I just might screw that up as well. So all I said was, "Maybe we should do something?"

But then Kitty came in and said, "Firey, Firey hoses are all put out. Grayness now rise and her tempy is all gone. You be more cautious Demon Lord, she very scarlet and still ready to burn."

"So are Mary and I ok?"

"No! No! Nosy! Demon will have to forever give part of him to the scarlet flame."

I couldn't help but shake my head, and I noticed Arty was doing the same thing. I then asked, "I take it you and Arty are doing well in your training?"

Swimmingly was her only response to my question. Everyone nodded and Arty actually blushed. This is when I knew I must of been missing something. Even though I had kind of noticed how rough he looked from before, this was the first time I really looked closely. I had no time to ask the obvious as all the girls came into the room. I then asked, "Mary are you..."

Pepper cut me off with, "Don't talk until shes ready."

Naomi then came in with, "This'll take some time to blow over John, but she knows the importance of the mission, so shes with us. Tonight I talked it over with her, she knows how important it is to sleep with you, but I also explained that tonight is really an over lap night too. So she has opted to take the slight chance, and sleep by herself tonight. So when you get home, you'll have to move to a new room."

"Anything to make things right between us." I looked at her and said, "And if not, I'll still kick the butt of anyone that upsets you."

She covered a giggle with a cough, and she wiped her nose. Kitty then said, "Goodie room by conservatory, plus close to bookies."

I was happy I heard that giggle as I started to talk, "Tony take you group with me, I'll let you out as well as Naomi will let out Kitty's group out. Then we'll move to our sides of the compound, Naomi you take the north and I'll take the south. You guys need to move and hide fast, our groups can easily slide into position so that's no problem. Kitty this is all on you, so we only do anything with your first move. If you decide we've waited long enough, run in the direction of Naomi so she can cover you. Tony when you see this, you do the same with me so we can cover you. Now the blood affect won't last that long, but this is all we can go with, we can't take the chance of them getting any blood. If anyone gets hurt we'll have blood when we get back, try and hold on till then. So any questions?"

No one said anything, I had to wonder if these meetings would always go like this. I would love these days until that one person would wake all these kids up. I then said, "Well then lets get started."

So as everyone moved to the cars, I told the leaders they should check their teams. We all got in the cars and moved to the church. I made a careful visual inspection to make sure everyone were in good positions. They sat for a very long time, I started to wonder why Kitty wasn't calling this off. I knew her kind always had a purpose for everything they did, but I knew it was getting awfully late even for Shovelhead's. Well not for us really, but for Shovelhead's for sure. They always liked to eat early, and this was way past that time, because they loved to go out and torture people. The last time I looked at my watch it was just past midnight, and I thought about calling it off myself. Just as I was about to speak though, a nun came out of a building away from us. She wasn't exactly within there trap though, when three hooded figures seemed to just appear out of no where.

I could barely hear with my vampire hearing, "We were waiting to have some fun tonight. Now look what our lord gave us to play with, a fresh young thing."

All John could think of was oh hell, this is really bad. These bozo's are going to pull us out of our positions, and they even might figure out who we are. I knew I had to act really fast, so I tapped Billy on his shoulder, I had to hoped he could keep up. I could see out of the corner of his eye, that Naomi had did the same thing. With this three shots rang out, and the nun was running. Then I did something that wasn't my normal thing to do, I knew they would focus on me though. So I let out my families sort of roar, and I heard Naomi do the same thing, of course hers was more like a dogs growl. With this a couple of others came to their aid, but seconds later after the three were already destroyed the others decided to run. We went straight after them, and caught and destroyed all we could. As good as our attack was, I was sure one or two got away. I think our attack went so well, because there were actually only four of us involved. Billy, Naomi, me, and Kitty whom had appeared right in their path as they were trying to escape.

As the fight was basically over, I allowed Naomi to direct Billy in an area search. I told Mary and Caty to give her all the help she needed, I also told them to make it snappy. With gun shots, and all this mayhem, I had no idea how fast the police would respond. Then I moved to the others, to see how we had fared. As I got close I saw Tony directing his two to move to my car, but then my head snapped back as I saw Joe kneeling next to a body. As I got closer, I could see that it was the nun, and I knew we were to slow. Then as I got close so my eyes could take in the seen, I saw the blood on her lips. I then said with a little anger in my voice, "Joe what did you do?"

He then looked up at me, and I saw no trace of blood on his lips. He replied, "I thought to heal her John. I read in one of those books that our blood heals, so I fed her some."

I couldn't but show an open sign of relief, as I said, "Oh ok. You did ok Joe, even though we do have to hope that you didn't ghoul her."

John looked at her and wondered why she looked so familiar to him as she moaned, and a voice came from the building she had come from. "Hey you punk kids! I've called the police, so why don't you just run like the cowards you are."

John really didn't have time to think. He just yelled, "MOVE!"

As they all ran to his car, he saw a man that looked like a priest yelling. "YEAH! THAT'S IT! RUN LIKE THE COWARDS YOU ARE! YOU PUNKS NEVER FIGHT LIKE REAL MEN!"

Father Micheal

He didn't feel like he drove off the gang members that were surrounding Sister Mary Elizabeth. He figured he only surprise them, and that it was the actually threat of the police that had done the job. He could see lumps all over the place, and he thought all this death, and destruction for what? He was getting up in years, and moved as fast as he could to her side. He got to her as he just started to hear the sirens, she look terrible with all that blood on her collar. He moved her habit to see no mark, but there was a little blood on her mouth. He feared the worse as she started to move, and he put his hand on her shoulder as he said, "Don't move I fear you may have internal injuries. We don't want you to hurt yourself anymore then you have already."

She then said something to him, but the sirens were to loud for him to hear her. He then stood up, and directed the police to where he stood. The first police officer immediately ran to his aid, he could see the horror on their faces as they realized the victim was a nun. But that didn't slow him down any, as he reached up, and said into his radio. "We need a bus here we have an injured nun."

He heard the operator ask him to repeat what he said, so he did as Mary Elizabeth said in a voice just barely loud enough for him to hear. "I really don't think I'm that hurt. In fact except for a few bruises, I think they just knocked me down."

He pointed his finger and said, "No! We really don't know the extent of your injuries. You're going to the hospital young lady, and that's it. No Debates!"

By this time the ambulance was rounding the corner. They got out, and asked her a series of questions, as he look around. He saw the police covering four bodies close to them, but they had moved down the street as it looked like they also covered four more. Sister Mary Elizabeth was now arguing with the ambulance people. So he turned back to the argument, as the Mother Superior also joined in. She said she didn't think she had been hurt, and the Mother Superior was holding her down. He really felt responsible for what happened to her, and the Mother Superior then said to almost mimic my thoughts. "Father Micheal already feels responsible for you getting hurt, at least make him feel better and go to the hospital, and be checked out."

Sister Mary Elizabeth then said, "Its as much my fault, as it is his. I take all the responsibility for it all, I mean when I walked out I felt something was wrong. So in a sense its really more of my fault. They did seemed to appear out of no where, plus those others came to my aid so quickly. Do you know if Father Micheal thanked them?"

We got into the ambulance with her as we went to the hospital, I explained to her that all I saw were a bunch of thugs, and that I was happy there were some good Samaritans. I did have to doubt that though, because all I saw were thugs to me. The Mother Superior just shrugged her shoulder's, as Sister Mary Elizabeth seemed to drill her also. When she started to help her disrobe, I left the room, and I was immediately confronted by the ladies from the woman's auxiliary. So I had to deal with their complaints, as they also praise the good sister for her courage. Finally they left, and he was all alone as the Mother Superior went with them. She spoke, as he came in and smiled at her, "Those kids, I don't know who they were. But father they really did help me out, even though I also saw them kill without remorse. I think they're on the line that you talked about, even though I've never seen violence like that before."

I could only reply with what I knew, "Yes, I saw all the violence too. At least eight bodies. Sister if these are the people you are talking about, I could not see this kind of violence being good."

She shook her head as she thought and then admitted, "Well to be truthful I actually only saw one stop. His eyes though, I've never seen anything like that in my life."

"Oh was it like complete kindness?"

She had to think as she spoke, he had to think even she didn't believe her words coming out of her mouth. "No Father Micheal." She sighed and went on, "It was like nothing at all, like something was missing. I can't explain it any better then that."

I moved to look directly in her eyes and said, "I believe you looked directly into the eyes of Satan."

She shook her head and in a soft voice said, "I don't think so."

I asked, "Why do you say that?"

"I saw eyes like that once before. They were on the face of a child in a hopeless situation, they changed as soon as she got out of that situation though."

"Satan can manifest in many different ways."

I don't think she really believed me, as she turned on her side to sleep. The doctor said he only wanted to keep an eye on her over night, I did have to wonder exactly what she really saw. I did believe in the Devil, but even I had began to wonder if we caused him to manifest ourselves. I knew all the doubts she was having, I've had all of them too. But I've been a priest so long now.

John

John drove the best he could, as he had been doing this a long time now. He was driving at the top speed of his car, but he knew his reactions were fast enough for this speed. He also knew they didn't actually complete the job which was bad news. He had to talk to the kids, and break this bad news to them, as he was sure they had to go back again. They had killed Shovelhead's, but only one or two were actual vampires. The rest had all been human, and he dearly wished they had caught more of them. He could tell just how fast he was driving, as everyone was white knuckling it. He pulled into the driveway at ninety, and was hitting the brake to come to a stop just within the garage. As he came screeching to a halt, he said, "Get inside now!"

He moved with everyone to he kitchen, he could also see all the smiles. He pointed at chairs as he paced, and waited on Naomi to get in there. As she came in he immediately looked at her for confirmation, and she nodded her head. He then looked around the room, and saw that Kitty was licking blood from her fingers, so he knew she had driven just as fast. He waited for Naomi to join him, he then said in a strong voice, "Everyone take a seat." After they all did as he said he went on, "Ok I only counted maybe one actual vampire. Most of what we killed, were nothing more then those they ghouled to change be changed into vampires. How many did you see Naomi?"

She replied, "Maybe one more, but Billy picked up the sent of one more. Then we had to run, so we couldn't find out what he knows. That don't matter though, even if he doesn't know anything, enough humans got away, where they know of us."

"This is bad, real bad. I hoped we could do this in one trip, but it looks like we'll have to make another trip. We'll have to go with the same trap as we had before, but I don't know if that will even work again. When I said this was bad, that may have been an understatement."

Kitty then said, "Stinky ones don't like even one washed. They be angry, but darkness always tries to conceal the truth, and it be out."

Tony then said in an almost pleading and crying voice, "See man. I knew we should of talked to them. I even know that, they don't like to loose anything or anyone. Now we have a real fight on our hands."

Naomi moved to back hand him, but instead said with anger, "Shut up you fool! They all know the shit has hit the fan, but they don't need you fanning the flames. Boss you know we committed until the end in all this."

John was very happy to see everyone agree with her resolve in this. So he moved away a little as he thought for a moment. John kind of new there would be a few, what ifs, but he continued on, "Well if we're right, then no matter what you think, we have to pay them a visit tomorrow night. We can't just let that neighborhood hanging with such a problem, they need our protection. Even Tony has to admit they'll be looking for blood tomorrow."

Paul then said, "What are we talking about anyways. We just do the same thing, and hope a certain someone doesn't hide behind a tree at the wrong time."

Tony came back with, "Hey I've never been good at hand to hand, plus if you looked three of those guys were hit by bullets from me."

Cheryl then said, "That's not saying much, I pulled the trigger twice."

Andy then interjected, "Hey we all know, do only the right thing when John tells you too. I bet you didn't even pull the trigger until you saw John was involved. I bet you..."

I cut him off with, "ENOUGH!" Everyone's then turned to me and I added, "What anyone did or didn't do isn't on trial here. Ask yourself did Tony shoot, if you can't say he didn't, then just shut up. We have much worse problems then to accusing one another, we have to go back, that's a given, and if we don't work as a team, we all just die. So just remember this, we defend one another, and this defense is to the betterment of everyone.

Tony then interject, "I've always said leave humans to their own fate."

Naomi then asked threw gritted teeth, "You would have this be handle by their own kind to what end. We all know their history, and we know that eventually they will bring in hunters. So you would have us just pull out, and allow the basic possibility of our kids getting hunted down and destroyed like mad dogs. Exactly what kind of a man are you anyways?"

I came in with, "Naomi's right, and even you have to admit that Tony. If we leave them to their fate, they will basically bring some sort of hunters in. The only answer to our problem, is to intensify our kids training, and doubling our effort. Even though I know that the humans can take care of this, Shovelhead's hit like MAC trucks. So they would be forced to look deeper, and that would show them of a least one or two of our kids. With this knowledge, they would even dig deeper, and it is almost preordained that they would find all of us. Tony are you up to showing these newbies the best places to shoot a Shovelhead?"

He replied, "I guess so even though you may have to show me, I'm not that old and I haven't really faced Shovelhead's until now."

"Well that's easy it's just the head. Anything can slow them down, but the head makes them stupid. Naomi when you do your class don't hold back, I know you may hurt them, but in the end it will help them. Kitty try and speak to their special powers, maybe we can light a fire under them. They always say knowledge is power, right now we have a little of both. All they still have is speculation, and assumption. It's not much of an advantage, but its something. Ok, we will give you 30 minutes to get ready, but after that training starts in earnest. Each session will be exactly 60 minutes with only a 5 minute break in between." I then looked everyone in the face as I said the next thing slowly, "Who wants to attend Tony's class first?"

No one spoke, and a few seconds of silence Mary, and Cheryl lifted their hands. He didn't know whether to be relieved or not, but he said, "Ok you two after that you'll go to Naomi. Now who wants to start with Naomi?"

Everyone put up their hands so I pointed at two and said, "You two will have to go to Kitty next. Next of course will be Kitty?"

The response was almost as fast so I pick two and then said, "Ok you two will go to my class after that, and you last two come to my class, and go to Tony next. Well that was fast, we'll try and keep it this way, and only change it if you feel a problem. Ok, and just like yesterday your time will be after this. If you do feel you have problems in certain areas, we expect you to do extra training. If you get hurt you won't be given any extra time. you have to get a blood bag, and have it gone before your next class starts."

Pepper then asked, "Why the blood bags? I mean why not wait until we all get done so we can drink together?"

"Well were kind of doing things in reverse here. A normal day starts that we do, or finish everything at the end of the day. Because of the Shovelhead problem, we have to drink it before we leave. You could ask why don't we just have blood twice a day then? The truth is we have to make our limited blood go long, but I can't just stop it like most houses would. We have to have a little bit of our strength here, so I opted to drink before we face the Shovelhead's, with fresh blood, and possibly fresh healing. You all saw what happened to Joe once he drank that blood on the first day."

With this everyone then left except for Mary and Cheryl. So I added, "Go to the cellar, and Tony will be with you in a little bit."

So with that they both left, so I turned to Tony and spoke, "Assess them, and find out what they're best at. But worse we have to show them how to fight against pain. So take eight blood packs with you, and make it worth their while. This will be the only time I ask you to do something like this, so you know what I want you to do?"

He looked at me with almost sorrow on his face as he said, "They'll hate me."

"Tell them it was my idea. I'm having to move my room anyways, so I can take the pain of them disliking me. I will say to you two thing though Tony. If I ever hear of you not giving 100 % in battle again, I'll make you remember me really well. Plus if you hit on any of these girls while they are in distress, I'll show you your end of your existence."

Chapter 17

      Tony then put his thumb in the air, and almost ran out of the room. John had to wonder if they had done as well as he suspect. Taking so many newbies on a mission like that wasn't a bright idea, he moved to the room where he was doing his level of training. The mission had been done anyways, and they did come out of it smelling like a rose. In the end it hadn't been his choice really, the Shovelhead's had made it for him. He was a little lost in his thoughts as Paul, and Pepper Entered the room. He did acknowledge them, as they sat down and waited up on him. He thought maybe if he was to hurt them also, it might help. If I hurt them it would probably require more then a blood pack, so he quickly ruled that out, because it would keep one good body from the fight. He finally decided that maybe it would be best to to use his hands, and make them pay, but not hurt them. He then lined them up against one another, and set them the correct way. Then came the very first shot, and a scream and whimper. Pepper made a move, but John stepped in front of her and said, "No! You have to get through this, Paul first if not then you can't help Mary. Now do your duty so you can get to her, otherwise we already lost this battle."

      With that they both complied with my order, when ever one looked like they would get the upper hand, I would knock them on their butt. I watched every move, and every influx with all the interest I could. At the end of the class, John only placated them with, "You two did very well, even with the distraction we arranged. You must learn to not allow anyone's screams, even if its your best friend distract you. So this class was a double distraction, as well as a learning tool."

      He did the same with every class, and it did seem that the full eight hours went by fast. When that training session was over, everyone stood in the kitchen as the elders gathered. About half of them were sipping on a blood bags to some degree, and an equal amount were rubbing their behinds. I couldn't stop but help to think, that Tony must of shot them all in the most tender spots, to get his point across. "This session went very well, and with only one mishap."

Naomi then said, "Sorry about that Paul. I didn't think I would hurt you doing that."

Pepper then said with anger in her voice, "What do you mean one mishap? Tony shot us all in the butt on your orders. What was that all about?"

I replied, "It actually served three purposes. Everyone now knows what it feels like to get shot. Everyone had to be taught how not to react when a friend got hurt, and lastly everyone had to see how you would do under fire. You see if you think about it, you all know how to fight through the pain. So even though it was hard on you, not to react, you know they can come threw all of it. If you quite a fight when you're in it, this could cause us to loose the battle. If a bullet flies right by your ear, you won't react to that as much as your opponent. So you can see exactly how important this really was."

Mary then asked, "And I'm suppose I was the first reason for all this?"

I knew she had been the first to be shot, but I had to tell her the truth on this one. "Yes and no. I'm the one that told him to do this, but I left it up to him to pick his first target. Knowing his types deliberate ways, I may should of told him to not choose you for his first target. But where would I have been, if I hadn't really left it up to him. I did hope he would make the right decision in the end though. When, who or where was truly up to him though, but I guess that was my mistake, and water under the bridge now."

Caty with a little anger asked, "And where he shot me that was all up to him?"

Tony looked at her and said, "Sorry again Caty, but you did

move, and so I hit your hip instead. At least it was on the fleshly part, it could have been much worse. I'll only hurt a little while when you sit, in fact almost everyone should b able to sit now."

Mary then came in with, "My arm! Wow it doesn't hurt anymore. You were right when you said we heal really fast."

I came in with, "You see now. I know it might still hurt, but I bet even Caty can sit ok right now. But right now we need to rest, if everyone's done with their extra training hit the rooms. This is your time, now even thought there isn't that much of it. If you need a little help from any of the teachers, feel free to ask us. Paul and Cheryl this is your last night together, so Paul you might want to think about another room. Arty you're with Kitty until she releases you, and by god listen to her carefully."

With that Arty said, "Oh and Joe its good you found that book, Kitty told you about. From what I've seen it'll really help you out."

With this the entire room started to break up, but I went to Caty and said in a low voice. "You may want to keep an eye on Mary, I think she'll be good, but she really needs work."

But I guess I spoke to loud as Mary came back with, "I don't need no damn babysitter!"

I said back with little belief in what I was saying, but I showed it so at least she would see that. "It wasn't about that Mary, but Caty is a better fighter, and I thought she could help you. There's a lot that has happened just this night, Joe will probably stay up late reading that book I heard about. This won't make him that up for tomorrow, so he'll need help himself. This means I'll be distracted with him, which won't be a good thing. This means that not only will you not have a cover, but us elders maybe a little busy. Hey what can I say, I can't rely on just Billy and Naomi with out all of you. I need what will most likely be my best fighters, so you can see why I said that to Caty."

Mary had an embarrassed look on her face as she said, "Oh ok, I can see that." She kind of moved her foot funny as she asked, "I'm one of your best fighters?"

"Well yes. You and Caty, along with Naomi and Billy's abilities are my best. Plus I think that tomorrow we should play on this with special toys. We'll tell you about them tomorrow though. I do believe though Tony, you should give Cheryl and Paul those assault rifles tomorrow."

He replied, "I don't know John. There's so much I haven't covered with them about them yet, we really need a shooting range."

"I hate to say this Tony, because it sounds like I'm beating a drum to death. But I don't think we have the time, and we need to just rely on our basic abilities."

"Ok then, well maybe Paul on the HK-33, and Cheryl will have the Ar-15. I'll take the Walther and give the 38 to Pepper. John I think we should give the Army issue 45 to Joe."

"Ok that sounds good, but by the way how much 9mm ammo do we have? Enough for two thirty round magazines?"

"Probably why?"

"That's part of my surprise. I have an old MAC 10 and a mini UZI, but neither weapon has ammo for them. I thought them with one magazine a piece would be a real big surprise."

He smiled almost ear to ear as he said, "I would say that will be a very big surprise."

"I also have a 32 that I'll give someone, that should allow almost all of us on the ground to have some fire power. I have to think on the rest, maybe go really old school. Naomi that leaves you and Billy the only ones with the barest essentials. Pepper though you have to wear something that guards against blade strikes."

Pepper then asked, "Whats wrong with what I'm wearing?"

I didn't have to field this one as Naomi said, "It's a lovely design, but one slash and you would be looking for a new dress. You really do need to find something that can't be cut so easily. Heck John I'll go around telling everyone of the girls what would be better dress."

I nodded to her, and then said to the boys, "I know you guys don't care if your clothes get torn, but I'm sure you would like torn skin even less. Except for you Joe, with your kind you want freedom of movement is essential. So probably just heavy cloth, but the rest of you should be looking for leather. I thought I made this clear the other day though. Oh Arty wear whatever Kitty says would be best, shes much better at that then I am."

And even though the day was over, John sat there just to see if there were any more questions. I had to wonder if we had done enough for tomorrow, I had to believe that there would be a lot of noses to wipe tomorrow. He had always been older, but he had never really taken up the mantle of an elder. This vampire un-life was a hard life one, but being an elder was proving to be harder then he thought. To be trusted with the destruction of others, had always been a simple thing. To be trusted to help preserve the un-lives of so many, and take on this elder thing was so different. He did have a small thought, that if their original elders had taken them with them he wouldn't be here. And I had in mind that I wasn't a very smart guy, I mean what was I, stupid? Really? No I had to help out, and they have all almost became just like my own kids. Tonight he had to sleep by himself, and had no one to talk to. Then he thought, no I probably wouldn't tell her anyways.

By this time he had his bedroll, and looking for his new room. As he looked he saw the kids doing what kids do. So he had to think what if one of them got dusted, can I even take it? I've lived a long time, and I have had to face my final death so many times. To have to guide others, and in to battle with them facing their own possible final deaths. This was all new to him, I had to wonder if this was the reason why some children attack their very own sires, after creation. That brought around another thought, oh my, what if I'm the first one to be dusted. I could easily live with my final death, but what made me really concern, was the possible vengeance attack. Not many ever really walked away from that kind of attack, maybe I should of told them if any of the elders fell, not to take vengeance for our deaths. Then again that something he never saw that could be controlled, they were all good kids and he didn't want to see any of them die. He had to smile as he could see them at work, and he whispered as he found his new room. "All this work, and not really one complaint."

He looked in the room and thought, this is where the dog house landed me. So he came into the small room, and placed his bedroll on the chair. He never needed much, but for some reason this which was bigger then his normal room, seemed so smaller. He reached up and closed the door with a gentle click. He then whispered again, "No it's much better this way."

He then undressed, and in mere moments he was lying on his back, staring up at the ceiling. He did have to wonder if he went outside, and just dug a hole it might be better. Even tonight, when I was clearly thinking of the battle tomorrow, I was thinking of her. Well he was, and he didn't want her to now that. One thing for sure, even though she is clearly his favorite, he couldn't show it. So in the end, what I said was the right thing to do, she had to know I wasn't playing favorites. As he pulled the sheet over to just cover his private area, he had to wonder why he even bothered. At the same time he thought, man in my old age I'm getting so jaded. In my youth, I would have been trying to get with her no matter what. Here I am though, not being able to see the obvious, twice if I'm right.

It was kind of strange, that as I drifted off to sleep, that her hair turned to this auburn color. Then as we danced nude in the tall grass, her waist got thinner, and even though I would only recall this dream once, she was no longer Mary.

Sister Mary Elizabeth

I saw myself dancing in a gorgeous garden as the sun beat down on me. I knew this was completely different, as I felt like I was eighteen again. I could see how effortless this seemed to be, especially as how self conscious I was at being nude. Nude? But I couldn't help myself, as I tried to cover up. It seemed my mind really didn't want to show anything, and yet my waking body did what it pleased. Well to be totally honest, it did feel kind of freeing, but I was a nun, and we just didn't dream about such things. That's when he appeared, and I move to his naked form. Oh my there's that word again. But I couldn't help myself.

We just danced and danced, as the darkness started to close in. I moved my head back and forth, with a joy I never felt before. I had to wonder exactly what was going on, and why was I nude with this gentlemen. The darkness seemed to pervade my dream, and become an overwhelming force with in it. Then he seemed to just change into smoke, and the darkness became overwhelming to me. I had been scared before in my life, but I had never felt an overwhelming fear like this before. Then the darkness seemed to take shape, and demons seemed to form out of it. The only thing was they looked human, until they opened their mouths, they were full of sharp pointy teeth.

I then turned and ran away from them, and the more I ran the closer they seemed to get. Finally I decided I was through being scared, and turned to confront the darkness. It all seemed to come around me, and I could feel it in areas I've never felt a coldness like this before. I started to scream as I struggled to get free, and the more I struggled the more I seemed to get trapped. Then everything seemed to clear up, until there was nothing but grayness. Then a voice spoke from it, even though I couldn't be sure where it was coming from. The voice said, "This is what happens when you don't make the right choice. All loose it."

I woke up to a start as Father Micheal was shaking me saying, "Sister Mary Elizabeth its only a dream you need to wake up."

My eyes then fluttered open, as I said in a soft voice, "I'm awake Father."

He then backed off saying, "You gave this old man a start

young lady, I've never heard such a loud blood curdling scream before."

He then grabbed his chest as he sat down, and I said, "I'm sorry Father."

"That must have been some terrible dream to let out such a loud scream."

With that the nurse stuck her head in and I said, "I'm sorry just a really bad dream."

She then asked, "How do you feel today?"

"About the same as yesterday, fine enough to go home."

"Well the Doctor comes in usually about 8, and I'm sure he'll sign your discharge orders then."

"Can I get dressed now then?"

"Yes, even though your Mother Superior called, and said shes bring you a clean Whipple."

"Did she say whether she was on her way?"

"She was just leaving if I understood her correctly."

"Well her, on her way, is usually different then most peoples on their way. That probably means, after she puts out like a hundred fires first."

Father Micheal smiled as he said, "Sister Mary Martha likes to keep herself busy, doesn't she?"

I had to smile back at him, as I nodded to him. Then we had a little chuckle and I said, "We are so bad."

"Would you like to tell me about your dream?"

"I would, but after I reason through it. The last line though was a little strange though."

"What was that?"

"Well I heard a voice say; This is what happens when you don't make the right choice. All loose it."

"All loose what?"

"I don't know, that's when you woke me. But it was an awful dream with demons and stuff like that. I'm not sure, but I think it had to do with love."

"Maybe its because you're thinking of leaving your order. You know nun's are considered to be the brides of Christ."

"Well because of what we were doing before..." I let my voice trail off, as I realized that I probably shouldn't tell him I was running around in a garden with, if that was Christ, in a very compromising position. I then said so he would stop staring at me, "Let me figure this out. I don't think it was Christ given, but I do think it has something to do with my decision to leave my order."

He nodded his head, and we then talked about just normal things, and just like we figured Mother Superior finally did arrive with my clothes. I knew I only took a shower yesterday, but I wanted to take advantage of a steamy shower. So I was very grateful she brought me under things as well, this did allow me to think about the other night. Added with the strange dream, I just had I had to figure someone was telling me something big time. I just wish I could figure it out, for myself, and I knew the the good Father and Mother Superior would convince me it was Jesus telling me to stay with the church. As I reasoned a few things, one was this dream was definitely not from Christ. Another thing was that the thing taken away, I think though, did have something to do with Christ though. Lastly this was the biggest decision of my life, and I think everything was telling me to go with what I had been thinking.

I know that a lot of people would say they were disappointed in me, but I had to think if I didn't do this, I would be just as disappointed in myself. Something did bother me about my reoccurring vision of what I saw last night, one the emptiness I saw in his eyes, like everything in his life really didn't matter anymore. What really got to me was after he did whatever he did to me, he smiled at me. Wasn't it only Satan the enemy that had pointy teeth, but this kind gentlemen had the biggest pointy teeth. So once I was ready, and convinced in what I was going to do, I just put that down to an over active imagination.

So this was it, this was the last day of me being a nun, and boy was it ever right on that one.

Chapter 18

Day 5

     In all that has been said, a day of destiny always seems to be different then any other. It can be the longest day, or a day that seems to pass extremely fast. In a lot of ways you could say that it is just another day. Well I guess that's really true though, most of the time you really don't know it was a day of destiny until it has past. In fact some are only known by those that haven't lived through them.

     I can say that this was the longest day I had ever spent, but at least I could feel dusk fast approaching. I knew I would have to suck done a juice bag, no matter what to just make it threw the day. Heck it wasn't like vampires really had to sleep. I remember going two weeks once without a drop of blood or sleep. After that though, I thought I would never quench my thirst. I made my way down to the kitchen, and avoided all the little sun light traps that had set up. It wasn't that I couldn't take a few rays of sun light, but I thought it might be prudent just this once. I then went to the refrigerator and got out a blood bag, the new vampires started calling them juice bags. It does seem to be a fitting name for them, once you realize what they're referencing. I used the scissors that were there, and then sucked it down. I then heard a slight cry of pain, "Oh man! Oh man!"

     So realizing who it was I heard, "Run in here Joe." Joe then came running into the room, and John could instantly see the gray spots with just a hint of blackness here and there. "That's what the sun does to us when we're low on blood. Are you ok though?"

     Joe shook himself off and asked, "So it does, and it kind of hurts like your whole body has fallen asleep. I guess you couldn't sleep either though."

I didn't want to worry him, but I was a bit concerned that he was up so early. "No not really, just couldn't stay asleep. Why are you up so early?"

"Oh I just finished the first chapter in the book Kitty found for me. It was a little confusing, but I think I may have started to understand a few things. It keeps talking about realization, I'm not sure what that means. I feel a little wobbly, so I thought I would get a blood bag."

I had to look sternly at him and said, "I wanted you to learn what was in that book Joe, but I didn't want you to loose any sleep over it. Well at least for now, you can help yourself with a juice bag. Go get yourself one, but we must remember to try and conserve it in the end."

Joe moved to the fridge, and with a questioning tone asked, "Did you just call this a juice bag?"

"I guess I did, the new kids use to call them that. I guess I got in the habit of calling them that also."

Joe then pointed at the juice bag near me, and asked, "Are you the exception to us conserving our blood?"

I replied, "I said I couldn't stay asleep, I never said I actually got any."

"Oh ok, well then I can understand that. So why didn't you sleep?"

"I don't know what the problem is. I mean I usually don't sleep well, but I have always been able to sleep a little while. I have no idea why I couldn't at least drop off for a few minutes."

"Hey I understand, you probably had Mary on your mind."

As I thought about it, I suddenly remembered actually falling asleep and waking up. Then it came to me, that I actually had a dream. This is very strange, because I've never ever heard of a vampire dreaming. I had no idea if this was a good thing or a bad thing though, heck I couldn't even remember what I dreamed. Only that I had, which to me was weird. So I just said, "Yeah. Who can figure out women, I seem to have had problems with them all my un-life. Mary may have a point, but all shes going to do was get younger, and shes worried about her age. You'd think they would grab hold of that, and just drop their age, but I met a vampire almost 600 years old, and she still wouldn't tell anyone her age."

"Yeah go figure. Us guys never worry about such things."

"Well not all guys, I have met a few very vane guys. Heck some were way older then me, well I guess it really takes all."

"How old are you exactly anyways?"

"I would love to tell you Joe, but all of you're very young. I'm not saying that it will happen, because it takes someone with the ability like Paul or Cheryl. But certain vampires have ways of pulling stuff from you guys minds, since you're so young. Plus if you have like one digging, you might have two or ten, and right now we need a few secrets. And well...never mind."

"You can tell me John."

I directed him to come close, as I said in a whisper, "They may dig out how I truly feel about Mary. I can tell you, I've had a hard time resisting her, the other night I did think of making love to her. Joe I saw shes a perfect ten in every way, it took a lot to keep it all business. In this type of situation, I figured it was best if anyone tried to read her mind, they only saw me reject her. If they saw I had feelings for her, they might try and use her, or worse get to her to get to me. I know its hard to crack you kinds brain, and I figure they maybe looking for other stuff, once they realize what you are. And Joe considering the implications of this, you say one thing to her, it could cause danger to everyone. Since this is a highly confidential statement, I may also rip your heart out."

Joe whispered back to me, "The first woman I ever saw nude was Kitty, the other day. Their room is directly across from me, and she thinks of nothing walking around with nothing on. I usually clear my voice, and Arty will get up and shut the door. But to me shes the most perfect woman I ever saw, not that I have much to go by. Then to see Caty last night, well not fully nude. I saw a little bit of breast, and they seemed so perfect and round. and all in less than a week. I could die and go to heaven, except for one thing." Then he used a little louder voice, "Man this has been a real show, but I heard its never the same until you test it out." He put his arms behind his head and added, "I'm just waiting for it to be my time is all."

I couldn't believe how young he sounded, so I said, "Yeah, but you'll learn Joe. It isn't that in the end. As you get older and go other places, you'll see things you won't believe at first. These things will pale in comparison to these days."

His eyes got wide as he asked, "What do you mean?"

"Well think about it Joe? Going into a house where no one wears a stitch of clothing. They make it so everyone has to be like this, human and vampire alike. You watch the gorgeous human women trying to match the vampire women, which they'll never do. You see jiggling butts and breasts every where. A young vampire can't help but walk in and get a hard one, but to an older vampire its just more of the same. Then you have the day when vampire women realizes they can't get pregnant, and they treat sex as just an act or a thing, and it loses all meaning to it. So after awhile you look around, and get excited about even the smallest piece of clothing worn. In the end sex and nudity just becomes a thing, and most of us become jaded to that."

He looked at me like he was really curious as he asked, "You've seen a lot in your life haven't you? But has it always been like that? I mean has the vampire society always been that way I mean?"

"Yeah, I guess so. Kitty is a prime example of that. This is just new to you and Arty, but its all just more of the same to her. One of the rarest things you'll ever see in this un-life, is a lady over a thousand years old. I actually met one that was over two thousand. She was so set in her ways, and loved everything to blow in the wind, she may have hurt Arty for closing the door. Like Kitty she looked way younger then what she was, and Joe she truly was a perfect ten. The only thing that moved her down that list of attractive people, was the fact that she knew how beautiful she was, and used it as a weapon."

Joe had a surprised look on his face as he asked, "Do you mean we could actually live past 600 years old? I mean I have always been told we die around that age."

I came back with, "Yeah, and yes." But then I thought maybe I should explain better, "They say we can only live to that age, because its rare for a vampire to get past our own depression. There's nothing in the rule book that doesn't say we can't live forever. She was rumored to know her beauty way back when she was created, and the one thing that keeps her alive now, is knowing shes the most beautiful woman on earth. So I think you need a reason why to live that long. I can tell you Joe you would get tired of her court real fast, except when she goes into public they're nude twenty four, seven, and when they do come out they wear the barest of clothing."

I knew he didn't get it, when he came back a little excitedly, "You mean she was nude in front of you, all the time, and were able to resist her. I mean without at least jumping her bones, I mean?"

John knew he wasn't getting through to him. So he just went with what felt right, "You see kid, you haven't realized this, but you just can't go jumping a woman's bones, so to speak. That isn't really the smart thing to do, and in the vampire world, that's just plain stupid. They say about my breed, that we are plain born killers. So what if she was one of my family? Well you've just gone to your final death. Then they may try and find out, if they may have actually liked you in the end. If you have questions about our way of being intimate, that is far more important then having sex. You have to learn control, so you can realize when a woman wants you, and doesn't. If you don't, she just may show you what you don't want to see, like maybe whats left of your heart. There are many that may use their whiles to get to you, so they don't have to worry about you. Plus with age comes importance, if you do something wrong, they may not to even want to get their hands dirty. So you might not even know why this guy is ripping your head off. In this world we have enough to worry about, the local leader and exactly what to call him. Then you have the Sheriff under his control usually, there are the few whom don't bow to the prince though. Let alone the Shovelhead's like we're facing now, you have these very sexy Chinese vampires that technically aren't. All in all you have far more to worry about, then getting some in the end. Then again you are very young."

"What are those last things? I mean the Sheriff I may understand. The prince in this day and age, why would he call himself that? And why are vampires not?"

"Well the gin, or as you may know them as genie, are demons actually, oriental demons. Their actions have been seen as almost like vampires, so the European side of things have just named them vampires to be done with it. The Sheriff is usually set up in an area to keep the justice, but some bend their will to serve the prince. And the Prince or Princess's had more to do with Europe then America. Here they name their leadership whatever seems more correct, then those titles. It's just that it is such and old title, and the eldest of vampires still tend to use it."

Right about then they could hear everyone else stirring, so John quickly when to his car to get his extras, and was back before anyone really got into the room. He knew well before the sun has set, because he could feel it as usual. So they finished their juice bags, and directed everyone else to get one too. Joe had also left and came back with a padded jacket, with no arms. John told him that was perfect. Kitty though had been there just as John got back, he knew he didn't have to say anything to her. She had put on turquoise and a pink dye in her almost white hair. She wore a white leather jump suit that seemed to matched her hair color. John wasn't about to ask how she got it that color, plus he knew all the boys would stare as it was very form fitting. Pretty good for her kind.

Pepper then burst in, with Caty close on her tail. I couldn't believe how short her dress was, but she wore a leather jacket just a little longer. Caty was in a short skirt also, but it was leather along with her just a little darker red jacket. They almost matched perfectly, the boots were a little off setting though. They were those kind that had a heel, but really didn't, and were about six or eight inches at the heel. Really clunky was all I could think. Pepper had high heels, but they were more like golden sandals. Arty wasn't far behind them, and he had on a really good Billy idol look going, which match him really well. I could see if he made that same sneer, he would be mistaken for him. Even though they're were a few things that kind of reminded me of that bondage stuff. Naomi was next into the room and she was in her normal suit like always, but Billy came right behind her, and I noticed that he seemed the same. Then I noticed the leather pants, and with the Army jacket, I figured it would be enough.

Paul then came in, and he had on a gray suit, I was about to say something. Then I saw a slight glint off it, and knew this gray suit was made of leather. Just a moment behind him came Cheryl and Tony. He look the same as always, but he had added a loose fitting leather jacket. Cheryl had on knee high black boots, with a knee length black leather skirt, and a cream colored blouse. Over all of this was a long black leather jacket, that I could see when done up would look like a suit jacket. The last person that came in was Mary, and I couldn't believe she had on a school girl outfit. Ok maybe not exactly a school girl outfit, they didn't wear thigh high boots. She had the wool skirt, you know with a plaid design. With the white button up shirt, and sweater tied around her waist.

She saw me looking at her and she said, "This was Naomi's idea."

I then asked, "It might be a good one. But where's your leather?"

She then lifted her shirt to show the leather thing just below. And she said, "Everything under my clothes are leather. Naomi said that since I like to wear leather undies, that just in case we need it I could go out to look around, and just be seen as a late day student. This way if needed, we can take a gauge of what's going on, and maybe move sooner today."

I can't say I was very happy about it, but I had to admit it was a good idea. So I went on, "Ok here's my UZI and MAC 10, one has like 7 bullets in it, the other has like 2." Tony and Kitty took out the magazines and started to load, I took out the Beretta I was using, and handed it to Mary. "Use this just in case you need it, Tony give Caty that 38."

Mary instantly came back with, "John I can't take your gun away from you."

I then pulled out what I had in my other holster, and set it down on the table. And said, "I decided it might be best to use this big boy."

Tony instantly asked, "Oh wow is that a Desert Eagle?"

I replied as I put it back, "Not any Desert Eagle, but the six shot 50 caliber Desert Eagle."

"I gave Joe that Army issue 45, and told him just aim for center mass. With those two, we should be setting a few of them on their butts."

I then lifted up my tire iron and said, "My other two weapons are far to big, even for me to use with a pistol. They gave me an idea, in my early days this, or a baseball bat came in handy."

Paul then said, "Hey, I know where there's a baseball bat."

"Good, go get it." He turned and sprinted out of the room, and then I handed it to Cheryl. Then I said, "Keep it next to you, if someone gets to close, just hit them over the head, and keep hitting till one of us can rescue you." I then said, "As soon as Paul gets back were on the move. We can't give them any time what so ever. Naomi I saw yesterday we were to close to Kitty, and not in place to really react. We'll both move a bout 50 feet to our right, this should give us enough room to react. Now we have to try to contain them today, if they show. Can't say that they will though, but even losing a few vampires says they will want revenge." Paul came into the room, and I then said, "Ok lets go. Anyone's that not drank to bad."

    I then moved my hand toward the cars, and we all moved like clock work, I saw this as a good sign. I was glad it was a distance away, but yet not really that far. We parked the street over from the direction they came from last time. We figured if something went wrong, we could fight to the cars, and at least take some with us. Of course this was just in case the worst case scenario happened, we moved carefully as we made sure Tony was in place first. Naomi then moved off with Kitty trailing me, as soon as I was sure all my guys were in place, she moved off with her two. I knew no one except two had ever seen what Arty and Kitty could do, so we all watch Kitty hide Mary first, then she got Arty in place, and he seemed to slowly fade into the back ground. Finally when she was satisfied, she just seemed to phase out. I knew she really wasn't invisible, but that would take far to long to explain that, and would probably give everyone a headache.

    Now we were set, and whatever came would come. But in all this I had not figured for one thing, and that was the extra police patrols. Within an hour I saw three cars go by, and I knew as long as there was that strong of a police presence, that they might not show. I did have to worry that they may have saw us also, as they are trained to observe, the police not the Shovelhead's. After the third car, I was convinced we were hidden well enough. Not that we weren't well hidden, I guess it was just all the waiting, this does make kids very restless. Finally there came a time, after I saw a police car go by, a lone figure came out, and looked every where. Then he moved over to where we were set, and started to look around. I was very glad that he wasn't very good at this at all.

Then he lifted his hand to his face, and made the worst crow call I had ever heard. With this three other came out, and moved around the tree where I knew Kitty was at. As they moved around the tree, and one was actually standing with his back to Mary. I watched as the lone figure move out to the street, and again looked around. Finally he lifted his fingers up to his mouth, and pretended to whistle, well or just couldn't. Man what kind of vampire was this guy anyway, but six more appeared, and stood right in front of Tony's firing line, they only gave him maybe ten or twenty feet. I could see all except one had snub nose pistols, that one I think had a TEC 9.

With this the guy came to the center of the street, and moved back and forth really jerky. Then he finally whistled for real, and another 6 came out, and I knew we maybe in trouble. We were only twelve, and they now had sixteen, and as soon as the six technically cut off our exit, the first one made three whistle blasts. Of course 6 more showed up, and as soon as the came into the circle, I knew who was the leader. He pointed to the tree, and the first three turned. One of the three then said, "Hey what are you doing here?"

With this came a gun blast, and I knew to move, so I direct Joe toward Mary ,as I swung up toward the front. I saw Billy had barely a lead on me, as one of the three's head fell off his shoulder's. Arty then appeared, and let loose with his MAC 10, and all hell broke loose. My pistol was instantly out, and I targeted the leader, with a deafening blast his head almost disappeared. I could hear Kitty's UZI now sounding off, and what sounded like high velocity rounds going off. So I knew Tony was engaging also, but I didn't have time to think. I made it to the leader, with two more shots, and I severed what was left of his head. I could see a person get in trouble like Pepper, but then Caty appeared, and took the guy out. All this barely registered with me, as I wanted to catch them all.

I knew Naomi was close to me, as I saw from the darkness a hand come down with a clang on one of the Shovelhead's. When I came close, I saw Cheryl standing there with her crowbar in her hand. I then took his head off, and she said in a small voice, "We did good huh?"

I had to wonder what she was talking about, as I turned and saw all the Shovelhead's lying on the ground, or trying to crawl away. I couldn't believe it, it had gone so fast. I whispered back, "Apparently we did."

I then started to bark orders, "Make sure no one's head is connected to their bodies. Naomi you know what you and Billy have to do, but make if fast the police will be here quickly." She nodded to me and was off, then I said, "Tony cover us and move as soon as you feel free."

I didn't see or hear him, but I figured he knew what I meant. So I moved in to see that Pepper had been hurt, so I asked, "How bad is she?"

She replied, "It hurts like hell, but I think I can make it home."

I then direct Mary to me and said, "Get Pepper to Naomi's Jeep."

With this Mary put her on her shoulder, and started to walk off. I looked at Kitty and she said, "Demon Lord we have no more smelly ones here."

I then said, "Good, everyone move." Then I added for good measure, "That means you too Tony."

Chapter 19

With this we caught up with Mary, so I helped with Pepper. I watched as Billy and Naomi past us on either side, and by this time Cheryl and Paul had caught up with us. I then said, "When we get to the house, we'll do a weapons check. Tony and I'll show you how to clean your weapons." I then looked around and added, "He better hurry up on his last sweep, we can't be caught waiting for him."

Paul then asked, "Who John?"

"Tony, I figured he was doing a covering sweep."

"Oh he isn't back there, he took off as the battle started. He was amazing though, he would take aim with one gun and shoot, then run and do it again. I think he was trying to keep those guys with guns off balance. I lost him when he entered the area, where you came from."

Cheryl then said, "Yeah, I saw him too, he was moving this way and that. But then suddenly he just stopped, and seemed to just disappear."

Oh great, this was exactly what I needed as we got close to the cars. I was relieved to see him, as we got close to the cars though, but then I had to wonder why he left his charges in the middle of battle. Naomi was at the cars right after Billy, and I knew this because Billy immediately said in a loud voice. "Man John's going to kill you dude."

With his comment, came Naomi said right away, "You idiot we don't have time for this, just get into the damned Jeep."

I moved to see what was going on, and I saw a gorgeous auburn haired girl on his lap. I pointed my finger at him and said, "When we get home, you go right to the council room." I knew everyone knew I was angry, so I decided to go with my original plan. "Naomi we go different directions, but they may think that we'll speed tonight, so drive as normally as possible."

She then said to me ok, and we both drove off. I could hear the first police car just as I got to the end of the street, so I did wonder if we would make it home.

Father Micheal

I didn't expect all this trouble today at all. I had expected the police of course, but not those FBI men, and certainly not the monseigneur. Plus he wanted to discuss every little aspect of what went on today, I mean last night. Then you have the entire inner council wanting to talk to me, where were they when we first suspect this to be going on. I so wanted to get to Sister Mary Elizabeth before now. She was a fine character of what it meant to be a good Catholic, she sat across from my chair as I slowly moved to my chair. My right leg had always been bad, but everything I had to do today made it really sore. After I made it to the seat I spoke to her, "Sister Mary Elizabeth I wish you would reconsider this decision. We need many more people like you doing the work for God."

She looked away from me and said, "I wish I could believe you Father, but everyone is saying be patient, and my soul is saying I need to be out there doing something."

I had to smile at her as I said, "Gods work takes time, look at how long and patient the Church has been."

She looked me in the eyes and said, "My dream spoke right to my soul Father. I thought about it and if you think about it, it showed me that the entire world was going to the Devil. Well at first it was very pleasant, and then it turned toward the Devil. I guess this could be explained away, if not for the warning. This is what happens when you don't make the right choice. All loose it. I have to think it is this choice, and it has to be made."

"I think all Gods choices are deeper then that, but I respect your decision. In fact I've seen how the Bible has layers upon layers, so if it is God given, I think it may change over time. This is why I think you should at least stay one more night, so I can talk to you farther on this subject."

She thought about it, and finally said, "Ok, I'll tell the ladies to pick me up around noon, and stay so we can talk farther on this."

"Sister Mary Elizabeth I think you have made a wise decision. Tomorrow you'll see that it'll be better to stay here, and we'll have rest so we can talk longer on it."

I stiffly got up with a little moan as she asked, "Father do you need help?"

I smiled and replied, "No with all the extra movement, the old club leg isn't working so well tonight. Don't worry though, I'll put some of the cream the doctor gave me an it, and I'll be brand new in the morning."

I opened the door and allowed her to leave, then my strength got the best of me after I closed the door. I had to drag myself to the door way chair. As my behind hit the chair I heard a loud bang, I tried to move to the door. Then I heard the machine gun, and my worry grew for her, because I knew she was in the middle of that. I got my cane and worked my way to the phone, and dialed the number. Then a young man answered and I said, "Detective Hershel this is an emergency."

John

Since I had told Naomi to go a different way, I had no idea how her progress was going. As I pulled into the driveway, I was relieved that we actually didn't see any police. I was also happy to see that Naomi's was parked in the garage, I could see that everyone had a little blood here and there. So I parked, "As soon as the bathrooms are open, get a shower. No Baths, just showers, clean as best as you can. Also make it fast, we haven't the time for anything else. I'm sure Naomi has told everyone to meet in the Dining room, but just in case remind the others. Naomi, Kitty, and I will be there as soon as possible. Billy make sure all the garage doors are shut, see everyone once we get cleaned up."

I would normally end it with lets move, but they were all already moving. Naomi met me at the door and said, "I have Tony restricted to his room, and I sent a kid to every bathroom. I told them we had to do a debriefing, and to stay in the meeting room until we are ready. But I also added since this is only a debriefing, its really their time until we get there."

I nodded my head and said, "Kids I agree with Naomi, so even though we want you in their, its still your time until we get in there. Once everything is done, give all the guns too Tony, so he can look at our ammo problem. Not until we get done, so keep all your guns with you, on safe. If I hear one pop of a bullet going off, I'll stick my size 10 up your butt, got it! Ok I guess it's show time." I spoke in a louder voice, "Hey Joe, can you come with us?"

He nodded yes, and we all started the long walk up to Tony's room. As we walked up the steps Naomi, and I explained why we wanted him. The stories were thick on how neutrality, and justice was almost a feat and honor to his family. I went through the entire litany, about how they had great power, and with this power they had to instill justice. Naomi did her little bit to, and I had to believe that she thought it was as much hog wash, as I did. In a way though, this helped Joe though, it technically gave him an insight into his family. Even though neither Naomi or I told him just how young the true litany was, to his family. Let just say before that, they were more known for their own darkness.

We didn't have long though, Tony's room was on the third floor, but it wasn't that much of a walk. We got there and I knock, and he told us to come in. We all came in, and moved to the bed where the body was lying. He had her head poised on his lap, and looked at us like he was going to loose it any second. I then asked him, "Do you know the law about making a new child?"

He nodded his head as he replied, "I know, but I had two things against me at the time. One I could feel the life traveling out of her fast, plus I knew you were all involved, and I didn't think you would have the chance to say yes or no."

Naomi then asked, "And what about her, since you didn't asked. What if she rejects this un-life?"

"I heard what John said, so I figured we would just write a new rule on that one. I knew it was stupid to trust in fate, put her pull was so strong."

Kitty jumped on him, with her razor blade draw and said, "Me know the fates as a daughter, is you making fun of them, or is the Great Harlequin going to have to..."

I stopped her there as I asked, "What do you mean, her pull was to strong?"

His eyes were pleading, as he tried to explain himself, "When I saw her, I almost just ran by her, but then I had this huge draw, and really didn't know what was going on. I knew when I saw her, I should just let her die. John I have never felt a draw like that before."

"Would you call this draw, like the normal draw we have for human blood?"

"No John. I mean I really desired her blood, there's no doubt there. But this was more, even deeper then that. I hate to say this, because on one hand it's the Shovelhead's that talk like this. It's was like my dead humanity inside me was screaming out to her. Damn I know I sound like a moron, but that's my only excuse."

"Well what do you two think?"

Naomi spoke the plain honest truth, "Well his kind are closer to their humanity then any other."

"But is that any excuse really?"

She shook her head, then Kitty said as she pointed her razor at him. "He no good with this and that, but nearing the reality of the kiddies he be goodie. I speakie this one Blue Nasty Boy. But you makey of the Great Harlequin again and Kitty give you extra smile."

Naomi then said, "I maybe agreeing with her right now, if I got it right. We are only four, if we give him his final death, we'll be down to three. He has the way and re-pour with the kids, and that could help us in certain situations. Also like Kitty, I don't do this often Tony, so be glad about what I'm saying here."

I walked to the door, and then back thinking. Finally I realized that a simple question may also remove it from my hands. So I asked, "Tony exactly how old are you?"

Naomi snapped back with, "John! You know that isn't right?"

I put up my hand and said, "I know, but I have a reason why I asked, and it may relieve us of the pressure. If he has the re-pour with the kids, you say he does, it might save him. So Tony as a vampire how old are you?"

He looked up me, with remorse in his eyes, as he said, "When your guys made me an elder, I was so proud I didn't want to correct you. I'm far to young to be an elder though, I was made a vampire only a year and a half ago. Even my degeneration is happening slowly, I say I'm 28, but I was turned when I was 29 and basically still look it. It's like that switch that's turn on inside all vampires, wasn't in me. I mean John my type are said to have invented that switch."

I put my hand on his shoulder and said, "Hey Tony don't worry about it. First we are in a need for good trainers, and you've proven to be good. To be safe we won't call you an elder anymore, but also to be safe with the kids for now, we won't tell them till their training is done. Joe I want you not to tell anyone about this, but as your kind, you know why you're here. So what I need is for you to hear his case, and present it to the kids as best as you can. Tony we aren't going to tell the kids this either, but technically this is a case of ignorance. So you have two things to get bye."

Naomi then asked, "Two things?"

I pointed at the gorgeous lady lying on Tony's lap, and asked, "Tony, I take when you changed her, you didn't do it the right way, and she wasn't in the state to answer questions. Right?"

He replied, "No John. In fact, I think she was fighting to just hold onto life."

"So as our way, she still gets that choice, and that alone could end your life, even though I'm hoping not. We really need you. If you get past that one, you have the kids. If everyone's correct, then that should be a shoe in. So I guess we'll leave you to talk to Joe. Hey we'll send Pepper back to get her some new clothes, if she completes the change. Now I think we should go see if the showers are free. Joe you can be late for the first part of the meeting, so you can get your shower."

He nodded and we all left, then Naomi came close and said in a low voice, so only Kitty and I could hear. "Sorry about that John, I forgot about that little fact. By the way, you know I'm not old enough to be an elder. Too right?"

I smile at Kitty, and she nodded her head, so I whispered back. "We've known for a long time Naomi. We haven't said anything, because of just how good you are. Besides who else could possibly know, you aren't an elder except us, right?"

As we walked here came Pepper, obviously wearing nothing but a towel. Naomi then said, "Child have you no modesty?" She waved her hand for her to come over, and said two thing. "The new girl is a mess, and needs new clothes, make sure she has new ones, and she'll wear them. She seems a like conservative to me, and child you need to drink that blood, if you expect to heal. In fact if you have, and that's how its healing, Tell Paul I say you can have another pack."

They kept talking, but about midway I changed direction, and as we got close to another bathroom, Kitty stayed there. I looked at my shirt, and only saw spray, so I went to my room, and got a new shirt, but knew this one could be cleaned. From the night before, I had used up almost all my shirts. I decided just perchance that maybe Pepper had taken care of me. So I opened the closet, and there were seven shirts there with a note. I pulled the note out, and read it, but it didn't surprise me much. It read;

John

Kitty came to me, and told me you would be in need of these soon. There were tons in your size, strange that the boys wear weird sizes. Well except for Billy, he wears your size, but he prefers T-shirts. Dang, I just started this and I'm already babbling. Well anyways here ya go. Pepper

Well how could she not know, Kitty's kind seem to know a lot of unknown things. When it came to shirts I only wore yellow, red, or blue, even though I did go for the darker trends. I looked at the shirts, and I was torn between the orange and purple. I took the purple, because it was much darker, then I pulled out my soap. It may sound funny, but I really like the feel of real lye soap. The only problem was that, I had a time getting the paper off it. That's how I usually wrapped it up, then I made my way to the bathroom closes to my room. Since it was in use, I waited on the chair just outside, I didn't have to wait long. As Billy came out, I saw him carrying his clothes with his towel barely around him. I then put my arms out and said, "Give me those, and do up your towel better. Billy I can see you didn't get all the blood out of your leather. Come to me after the meeting and I'll give you...Oh heck I have time."

I gave him his clothes back, and pulled out my knife. With it I cut a small piece off my bar off and said, "Rub this on there and once you have it soaped up just wash it off. Now you'll have to wait till it dries, because you want to apply that dry also. Only use water when you're sure you have all the spots covered."

Billy replied, "Thanks man. I'll do that."

Then he ran off with his stuff, and small piece of lye. I barely got the door closed, as I heard a girl scream, and say something like. "Arty your towel!"

I could try and tell you who it was, but that would be truly guess work. In fact, I could go into detail about my shower. Like how I got undressed, and how I got dressed. But really that's for a later time in the story, because it has real meaning then. I will say that getting undressed, and dressed I probably did all the wrong things. I mean a friend of mine once told me, I should tuck my shirt in before I put on my pants. And after doing what he told me to do, he basically told me I had done it all wrong. I do believe he was, what you would call the proverbial gay vampire, not that there's anything wrong with gays. I'm just not that way, plus at a later date, we would find out one of our own was gay also. He kind of broke her heart though, and in the way he beat himself up, his too.

Anyways I came down the stairs, and met Kitty and Naomi outside the door to a room, with a lot of talking. I took a chair and set it down for Kitty, and Naomi got her own. We all sat together and waited for the room to die down. After it did I said, "Come over, and sit like you want in a semi-circle."

I watched as they all did what I asked, and we were getting smiles from everyone. Then they all got quiet and I spoke, "Now in a debriefing one usually speaks to the entire groups about the mission. But even though Kitty is who kicked it off, we had no real over all leader, so I felt we could handle this like, I believe families would. So I'll start. Billy you were part of my team, and I saw you moving like a madman. Whenever someone needed help, you seemed to be there. Of course we were on the move, so I can't say all you actions were right. But from what I saw you did very well."

I turned my attention to Mary and said, "Mary I can't say your first reaction was the right thing, we only use guns to throw people off balance. But after Arty did what he did, and completely caught his attention, your next thing was spot on. I'm sure Kitty has already told you how good you were Arty, but from me Arty spot on. You may have helped my daughter save herself. Caty I saw you young lady, I know you were having problems keeping up with Naomi. But then I saw this sudden realization, young lady did you find your speed?"

She gave me a shy smile as she replied, "I think so John. I was whizzing from here to there in like a second. At times I thought it may have been faster then that John."

"Very good." I could tell you everything I said, but I think you get the gist of what I was doing here. Naomi and Kitty did the same thing, and by the end of this little bit, I think we had them all smiling. We let Naomi go last, so she could say the next thing. She then said, "Young people, now for the fight we had, we won a battle, but we still have a war to win. I think John will agree with me, that this level of attack was unplanned and unsuccessful. No Shovelhead leader would ever had let this go without a back up plan, I can't say that they don't, but from Billy's and my fast search we found no other smells." She then turned to me and said, "Give them the worse case scenario John."

I stood up and smiled at all of them before starting, "We did this to try and stop what could have actually already been put in the works. I say it this way, because we just don't know really. So for right now, we have to get ready and try and find the rest of the Shovelhead's. Along the way, we have to hope they didn't contact any hunters, if they did someone may have an unwanted surprise some night. This wasn't a clean operation, like our society usually likes, so we might have High Council guests also. Plus whatever we left behind, maybe cause for the local police to look for us."

I then looked at Paul and said, "If your sire were alive, he may have had in roads to help us here, even though your kind are the catch all for everything. In the human world though, your kind has an easier time with higher up individuals. To tell you the truth, Tony and Pepper have a better time with that, but their kind usually don't pay much attention to city officials. It is kind of weird though, I mean even Joe's kind are always known to have followers, like Tony and Pepper's kind. But again they don't pay attention to having followers, like Joe's group does. Anyways I think we may have saved ourselves some trouble here, but we really have no way of knowing."

I turned to Kitty and asked, "You got anything to add Hun?"

She replied, "No Demon Lord cover all bases with red paint."

Chapter 20

Caty started to ask a question, but right then Joe came into the room and said. "John, we're ready. She's been awake now almost forty minutes, and Tony and I have been talking to her."

I then said, "Ok Joe. Everyone we have a few things to take care of, put your seats in two straight rows. Not columns Arty, rows are the across the room not the long way."

And with that and a little loud noise the room came together. While they did that I also set out three chairs for them. Then after everyone was seated I said, "Ok guys. This is Joe's first time, and Tony's first child, so give them the respect they deserve."

Then I sat down, and Joe came into the room. He then said, "Ok as the only member of my family, I call this meeting to order." Arty made a sound, and all the elders in the room glared at him. Joe could see that our glaring worked, so he went on, "I have the pleasure of introducing a new sire to out group. Tony would you come in here, and introduce your new child."

Tony came in with the beautiful young lady on his arm. I have to admit he looked a little nervous as he spoke. "I fear what I must tell you now, but our way is our way." Ok I'll admit it, I was like what the heck right then. "She has walked her life as an individual that is different then most, at least those that have come into this life." I was really getting curious now. "In her human existence she was know as Sister Mary Elizabeth."

Ok that knocked me over like getting hit by a baseball bat, my reaction was immediate, and I was moving toward the door. Naomi was vamping out, and swirling around like a rabid dog. Kitty was hissing like a cat that had just seen the same rabid dog. Tony put his hands up and yelled, "NO COME BACK. IT ISN'T WHAT YOU THINK!" He then placed himself in between her and me. I knew he had to know I could tear him apart as he said, "SHE WAS IN THE WRONG PLACE AT THE WRONG TIME! SHE'S NOT AN AGENT OF THE CHURCH!"

I couldn't believe his mock-see, and she didn't look like a threat. So I stopped myself instead of just ripping right through him, I looked at the other two and said, "We give him just five minutes to explain himself, then we go from there."

Then we all sat down as he went on. "Like I said she was just in the wrong spot at the wrong time, but if you know vampirism, you know how unique this is, so I'll allow her to explain. I like you didn't know what she was, and she wasn't exactly wearing those nun clothes. So in a sense, I'm not to blame for that either. I asked her what she wants to be called. At first she opted for Mary, but I explained we already had a Mary in our midst. So she rethought about it, and opted for Elizabeth. So may I now introduce you to my child, named Beth for short."

Joe stood up and said, "I'm sorry about this John, but after we talked awhile, we decided it was best to go through with this." He then turned and said, "Beth since this un-life has been thrust upon yourself, and we never ever do that, you have the choice of death or this un-life now. I know you were having trouble deciding, and if you're still having trouble, you can delay your decision."

She nodded as she stood up, and started to talk with the most musical voice I had ever heard. "That was very true, until I got into this room. I see so many young faces, and since only three reacted to me poorly, I figure only three of you are of the older variety. You see I became a nun to help people, but that never really happened. I was content to help the kids, then all this trouble happened at the Convent, and I thought what a good time to help. Instead of doing what I thought we should do, they pulled all of us back into the convent. To be truthful I couldn't see why we feared these terrible people, more then we feared God."

She looked down at her hands, and said as she lifted them up as an example. "These were meant for more then just burying them in dirt, so I had to make a decision. I knew good people that thought like I did, but weren't ready to just do what God called us to do. I won't lie to you, it was a very hard decision, but the other night made my mind up. By the way Joe, thank you for saving my life."

I think we were all surprised at her admittance, but none as surprised as Joe. "They were calling all of you evil, but I couldn't see how evil could do such a kind act. So I knew what to do, and I left the faith to go to an intern school. I was do to leave the next morning, tomorrow I guess. So when I was actually turned, as Tony told me, I had left the life of being a nun. So in truth, I think the title of sister no longer applied."

I interrupted her with, "So technically, when Tony got to you, you weren't actually a nun."

"Please don't interrupt me, if I only have 5 minutes to prove myself."

"Oh I'm sorry."

Ok I don't know if you ever got corrected by a nun, but right then I had been served, and knew this would be a woman to deal with. "Yes I wasn't one anymore, so you're correct. Truly I didn't know where my path would take me, until I saw these children, and my heart went out to them. So my answer is yes, I except this un-life."

All I could think right then was, ah hell. Joe stood up and said, "What Tony did was illegal, and for this he has to be judged. Normally this would be handled by the elders, but they found a reason for special dis-compensation. So instead of being tried by them, he'll be tried by the entire house. First he gets to say his case, so I'll sit down, and let him talk."

As he rose, I put up my hand and asked, "Joe may I ask Beth a few questions first?"

He nodded his head, so I turned to her and asked, "You don't have to get up, I just want to ask some general question if that's alright?"

She replied, "You may ask what you want?"

"Did Tony tell you what we live off?"

"Yes, even though as a kid, I already knew that."

"Did he tell you, whom attacked the Cathedral, and that technically we're still not out of the wood yet?"

"He did tell me about those awful things that attacked us yea, but about the other part, no. Even though I have to admit, I did feel I wasn't done with them."

Naomi asked before I could, "And did Tony also tell you that we may have to destroy many more? And that with this kind of fight, that means everyone has to put there own two cents into the battle?"

"No he did not. But I have always believed in pulling my own weight."

Both Naomi and I asked almost at the same time, "You do know this means destroying those thing, which in your human existence means killing?"

"Oh I see where this is coming from. The Commandment thou shall not kill. Well in recent years, they found out that that had been mistranslated, and it should read. Thou shall not commit murder."

Caty was very fast with, "Isn't murdering and killing the same thing?"

"No actually murder is a wanton act. If you commit murder, you have thought about it, and in some way planned it. Whereas killing is a general act, and yes murder is killing, but killing isn't necessarily murder. If you kill someone by mistake, its killing not murder. Just like if someone is going to kill you, but you kill him in self defense. Technically that isn't murder either. And with the blood issue, killing an animal wouldn't be murder, especially because we just do it to survive. So as long as I take the blood, with only survival in mind, then I'm not technically murdering. Even though with what Tony told me, that might never actually be an issue. Now does that answer the questions for now."

I knew I had to have like a million more, but right at the moment, I couldn't think of one. It was a good thing Mary was there, as she asked, "What about your change, did he explain to you the three days after your change?"

"Well he did, and it is unsettling to me. As an unmarried woman, I know I have to do this. I have told him, I will absolutely would not be undressing in front of him. And only when I found a good man to marry, will I allow him to see me nude."

She was the most beautiful of her kind I had ever seen, so I had to wonder exactly how long she would be keeping that promise. I did admire her beliefs, and how she just stuck right to them, through thick and thin. I had to wonder though what would happen if her values were tested in a bad way. Not all that become vampires, are suited for being vampires, and right now, that was a big question mark over her head.

Anyways Tony went on from there, and explained everything, and even said a few things I didn't know. As one of the three elders, I would always vote last in a house vote. Naomi had been correct, and he was very popular in the house, so we never had to vote. I didn't give them a break for the day, I had decided to go on with our training. I think every teacher took extra time with Beth, as she was really new with all of this.

And when it came to the end of the day, I let out a real sigh of relief, because I figured we had really dodged a bullet there. Just before bed time, I explained to everyone what I had told Mary, about why we were going nude. I also added that even though I wouldn't force Beth to do that, in the room with Tony. I did eventually expect her to do that, in her own room, which Paul pointed out we were running out of.

You see we were now thirteen, and with two groups bunking together, that only left one out of twelve rooms. So we only had room for one more. It's kind of funny how things can change so quickly, like all the rooms being filled by the very next day. I guess the worse thing about our next visitor, is it was as much my fault, as it would be the person that invites him. Like I always say in this life, stranger things have happened.

Day 6

My sleep was truly uneventful, when I rose in my lonely room it seemed like any other day. Everything had changed in the blink of an eye. First the kids had gotten through a great test with flying color. Next they had an unprecedented new arrival, that the vampire world had never seen. I allowed the thoughts go through my mind, I knew I really couldn't tell the vampire world of the new literal new enlightenment. Plus they had to cover the basics of the vampire world with all the kids, and what a good time with the new arrival. There was something else a total newness to everything, I had to wonder if they should start to change things up.

I finally gave a big sigh, and got up, because it was clear I wasn't going to solve this by myself. I got dressed really fast, and went down to the kitchen. I didn't have to long to wait, because everyone was already up. Tony had joined me, and I said to him, "We have to train just like normal, but I feel we have to do more for the kids though."

He nodded his head and said, "I think we have to give them more anatomy to do their own thing, I just haven't a clue how to do that."

I saw Naomi down the hall and asked, "Naomi can you come here?"

She came in and asked, "Whats going on?"

I prompted Tony to speak so he said, "I was telling we have to give the kids more anatomy. The only problem is, I really don't know what to do?"

I added to that, "I know we have to still do our normal training too, and that we must do more for the kids. What should we really do as, we can't technically give them total anatomy."

"Hmm." She said. Then she looked away and said, "You know my kind, and we aren't much into new thing. John this might be a time to try the great experiment, and before you say anything, I know it failed in every city it was tried in. Like you said though, this is a different situation, and just maybe they have enough freedom,where it could actually work."

Tony then interject, "You know it'll piss the old farts off to no end?"

Well that was enough for me, and I said, "Heck you know my kind, anything that seems like anti-establishment, I'm all for it. If we're going to do this, we have to do it on a two way basis. So I would suggest we use the old offices, and let them decide what they're going to call them, and stick with the making up rules as we go along."

"Well then, maybe we should discuss this final death as the punishment for everything?"

I looked at Naomi and said, "Well it couldn't hurt really, plus we could discuss the only two choices to humans, as being invited to join a house or death thing too."

Naomi nodded her head as she added though, "We may need to

add, why the final death is our major punishment, but I do think it has to be discussed yes."

"Ok, lets go get the kids for a fast meeting, then I was thinking a field trip to show them how to get the small sip. Finally back here for a good training round. Does that sound like a good idea?"

With their nods, we all moved through the house, telling all the kids we were going to have a meeting. They all grumbled as they made it to the dinning room, saying things like, we just had one last night, and why do we have to have so many darn meetings. Kitty joined us as everyone got seated, and as we stood it came to me now to start this one off.

So I said what was obvious, "Ok guys, in a house like this, its normally run by those that own it. You all know whomever that was, has gone away, and most likely met their final death. In this case it would go to their child, but here's the problem with that. Do any of you know who was the child of the owner?"

I waited for someone to answer, and when enough silence went by, I spoke. "I didn't think so. So this is what we came up with. The original six of you are joint owners, and the three recently made vampires were all born here. This makes all of you owners of this house, but nine leaders would be shear chaos, which isn't a good thing. Before I suggest what the elders are thinking, I want to introduce one thing. In a city they have a neutral party, that even though he doesn't govern over anything, he is in away the judge over everything. He has many titles, but the most used title is a judge. So I would like to nominate Joe, as the judge over this city. Will anyone second this decision?"

I was so happy to see everyone's hands go up, but before I could pick anyone Naomi said, "I second the nomination."

"Good. Does anyone want to try, and run against him, because Naomi and I saying we back him is a huge endorsement."

No one spoke, and I moved to Joe and shook his hand, and said, "We could hold a vote, but since one vote would mean you have the office, and I know you have mine. So congratulations Joe."

After I said that, everyone patted him on the back, or kissed him on the cheek. I then moved on with, "Ok the house leader is given the honorary title of royalty, like Duke, Baron, or Prince. We'll use just one title, and call that figure the Prince or Princess. Remember though we're only using the title for now, as we said this is a new thing, and we are rewriting the rules as we go along. So since we are the elders, we will over see it, but as we aren't true residence, we can't be nominated."

Naomi leaned over, and whispered to me, "Oh that's why you went with that instead of city Prince."

I winked at her, at the same time Pepper said, "I nominate Caty. She can get pretty angry, but I think she would make a good Princess."

With that Billy said, "And I nominate Paul. He's not much in a fight, but he's a huge rules lawyer. Especially when you're playing Monopoly."

I didn't know if that was a very good reason, but then again I have seen some pretty strange reasoning in all things vampire. So I just asked, "Does anyone second these nominations?"

Cheryl seconded Caty and Arty seconded Paul, even though with his second, I had to think it was a big joke with the two of them. I then said, "Because we don't want any hurt feelings. Cheryl get some paper, and pencils or pens, because we have a couple things to vote on, only use part of the paper. Tony collect up the ballets, and we'll count them, only if there's a draw will we vote."

Beth then spoke, "John that's not fair. I don't know any of these kids, and I know I'll vote even if its a none vote. All votes should be counted together, then told in one final call. Then if there is a tie, that one person should be held out in the end, and that one person should be the only person counting. Since Joe is now your judge, I would say he should be that person. After all isn't a judge suppose to be neutral in all things."

Ok I had to admit she had a point, so I just said, "She has a point, so I think we should have Joe do it all. Plus for people like Beth, we should have a neutral vote. She's right, she really doesn't know the kids."

I then put my hand out and said, "I'll tell you what us elders came up with, as we go along."

He got to the front, and asked Cheryl to do that for him, and that Pepper should help her. Now at the time, I didn't think just how sexist that was. He went on, and when all the votes were cast, there were six neutral votes, two votes for Paul, and four votes for Caty. I knew my vote was neutral, it wasn't that I didn't have a choice, it was I didn't want to show favoritism toward Caty.

Then I explained about the office of the sheriff, and how he, whomever they were, couldn't show favoritism toward the Princess, or the judge. Then I went into the judges job of making sure that all the laws are followed. Then about how he was supposed to be just, and yet blind to everything save the law. Then I got into the Princess, and how they are supposed to be the leading example of the law. Then to the part where she was supposed to help everyone, follow the law through her example. Finally I went into the fact that the sheriff was the enforcement of each of these two's will in the end, but I also explained that it wasn't like what we know as a wild west sheriff.

After that I allowed Joe to take it over, and Billy and Mary were picked. I went ahead and voted for her, well because I was proud of her. When the vote was read there were four neutral votes. One vote for Mary, and seven for Billy. Billy had won, but I thought it was weird that the only vote she received was from me, she hadn't even voted for herself. Of course I knew there was only one person I could ask, and I wasn't about ready to embarrass her in front of every body.

Then I got up, and went over the final death law, and why

maybe it should be banished for this house. I knew I had to give both sides of it, so I also went over the fact that when a vampire that wants to commit crimes, you don't have much in the way of punishment. Naomi then went into why some times the punishment was to harsh, and at times why the punishment was very fitting. I asked that we either keep this law, or just get rid of it. Beth was the point of reason again, and said that maybe we should just say decision pending upon knowledge that a law is broken. I wasn't surprised that the vote almost went overwhelmingly toward what she had said. I figured this was a good thing, so I then moved onto the last part of business.

So we talked about what had happened between Cheryl, and Paul. Then I added what happened in between Beth, and Paul. Then I went round, and round about how we ended up forgiving them for what they did. But how the law was meant to protect the humans from others, not for what had actually happened. And finally how I actually agreed with the law, because even though normal vampire don't remember they were human, we needed to. After all if we didn't, we were nothing but the monsters, humans thought we were. I loved that Beth was really getting into this, as she added that the basis for us was humanity anyways. That having the attitude of normal vampires was wrong, when they are the source of what we are. Finally she went into the fact that this would also protect everyone's parent. And even if they might of done you wrong, they were still in essence your parents.

After this everyone got real quiet, as they cast there ballet. I know everyone of the elders would vote neutrally, but I figured a few would vote the other way. I was surprised that there was only one vote for the other way. With three neutral votes that made and overwhelming eight votes to keep the rule intact.

Chapter 21

I did think this was a good time to discuss the six basic laws, but the time said it was better if we went out training. So once everything was done, I stood up and said, "Ok so now we now who's running the show. Of course out in the field, like when we have to battle the Shovelhead's, we will still be the elders. In house this will be set on all of you now, even though we'll give up our positions slowly, to all of you. Now for today, I thought we would get in our normal teams, and show you haw to get blood with the little taste. This is really good at a time like this, when we're trying to conserve blood. Beth I think you can appreciated this also. You see we found out about three or four hundred years ago, we could do certain things, so we don't have to kill our prey."

"We can gain control of a humans mind, and whisper to them. The usual thing we whisper to them is, this isn't happening to you. Once you think you have enough, and this is well before you're full, you let them go. Now if it were that simple though, we would have been doing this for a long time. It does sound a lot easier then what it is, now you must first bite part of the inside of your mouth. Next you need to apply it to your victims wound, and get the blood off before it mixes to much with their blood. They can fight off what our blood will do to them, and normally it'll just make them really sick. Now when you leave them, you can't release their minds until they can't see you. Once all these things have been achieved, you have succeeded in taking what we call a little sip. I will admit that it would take in between eight, to ten victims to achieve not being hungry."

"We suggest though you use this just as a replacement to our normal drink, now a normal drink is to empty a humans body, or about four pints a night. You have all heard me say though, why kill a human when you can take a little drink. I can tell you at one time, it was very easy to hunt our kind, because of all the bodies we left behind. This all seemed to change, with the first advent of donor groups, that were dedicated to just vampire. In the 1860's they made it even easier, with the advent of the Red Cross. What they use to do for us, they don't anymore since the Vatican discovered we were using them for our blood source. The good thing is that the Red Cross administration of our blood source, has gotten easier since its been taken over by the bureaucrats. So what the Vatican tried to take away from us, just made it easier for us to get blood."

I had to shake my head right then and said, "I'm sorry for the history lesson. Anyways we want to show you the small drink, then you can feed yourself without worry. Now ant questions?"

Beth then asked, "Who do I go with, since technically I don't have a group?"

I looked at Tony and asked, "She's your kid Tony, do you want her to go with you and Naomi? Or would you prefer her to go with Kitty and me?"

He replied to that, "This is her first night and everything. I know we can be separated like about two hours, but we really don't know how long this will take. So for now I think she should go with me and Naomi."

I nodded to him and said, "Well there ya go. Ok lets move out."

We all moved to the cars, I knew I had just enough gas to get to where I wanted to go, and get back. My car turned over in that low familiar growl, I always had to wonder why no one else couldn't tell this was my car. We then moved to the area down town where I had seen all the light, I knew wherever there were lights there were shadows. This part of this city didn't disappoint me at all, you could look every direction, and see those amber lights, which really helped us out. Yeah, I know they are supposed to make it easier to see for humans, but whatever was good for humans, was ten fold for us. As we walked down the street with Kitty, and our four kids.

I said, "Look around, and see potential targets. I'm not telling to go to any of them, just watch what they do. When you see someone approach a darkened area, that is a chance for a free dinner. Really think about it though. How long could you eat before someone would investigate. Stealth is a good way to get an easy lunch, as long as you're sure you won't be interrupted. Remember the place you select for your small drink, has to seem as normal as possible. In a dark bar you could make yourself look like you're making out, but then you have to control all the noises. I can guarantee one whimper, and the bouncer will be wanting to kick you out of the bar."

Mary asked, "Could we just seduce a guy on the street?"

"You could, and we have a special knack for this, because of how strong we are. For a weaker vampire, this could be a problem, especially if he chooses to fight back. One macho guy with his friends near, could break your day, even though in a bar fight we do have the upper hand. There is a way around this, allow them to look you in the eyes. Some say that it feels like a pull, but once you have him, you can start to talk to him. If he at first resists you, then move onto the next guy. Mary we aren't as good at this as Paul or Joe here would be, where they came usually grab the first mind, see it may take us four or five for us to find a mind vulnerable enough for this. Kitty will you show them your favorite technique you use?"

She nodded, and walked off like a little girl. She approached a young man, and you could see she already had him interested. I whispered to the group, "Remember shes had year of experience at this, so don't expect to be as good as her."

With in minutes, she had him hanging all over her. I could see she was careful to place his hands on her. So I then whispered to them, "See how she keeps control of the situation. The guy may think he just hit the jack pot, but shes controlling her every move."

She then moved him in a way so that everyone could see, as she used her finger nail to cause a wound. Then he started to quiver with her touch, seconds later she took her first drink. I then whispered, "Now she'll use her tongue and teeth to open the wound more, so it will be free flowing. You have all drank blood bags at the house, she'll only drink about half that much blood."

And just like that, she started to back away, and I moved the group along, so once we got moving, she could freely rejoined the group. Once I was sure we were out of ear shot of her victim, I said, "Four this exercise, we'll give this to Mary and Billy. You two should be good at the next one, that's why I'm giving it to Arty, which is kind of unfair, and Joe because he shouldn't be so good at this either. We may have made a mistake Kitty, like replaced Billy with Pepper. Well we're all just people, and we make mistakes. Well anyways, Arty will probably be good at this, sorry Joe for not so much a comparison partner."

I think we must of left the neighborhood we were in, because there were a lot more shadows here. So we crossed the street, and started back, I then used stealth to get a little drink. When I came back I then asked, "Did you see what I did there?"

Mary then said, "John, Kitty was drilling us just like you were. I think we may have this."

"Ok then, we'll go to that convenience store. Kitty will take one side of the street, and I the other. You have until we get to where we got victim number one. With me will be Arty and Joe, Joe I think for your sake you'll go first for my group. You other two will figure it out with Kitty, we'll watch you closely the first time. Then we'll tell you what you did wrong, but for your second time you'll be on your own. Don't get me wrong we'll be watching, you just won't see us."

Then we did exactly like we said we would, and we made a complete round. I then told Joe what he could have done better, and what was wrong, and how to improve it. I was surprised at how many mistakes Arty had made, I mean I was right, and he was much better at it then Joe. So I did the same with him, as I did with Joe. Kitty had said she thought it would be better to do this separately, so we weren't influenced by the other elder. I wasn't so sure about that, but I really didn't see a problem with that either. So I agreed with her, but what I didn't tell them, is that their second round was more free form, so Kitty and I could get our second drink.

But at least we kind of knew how to handle all this. When they were coming to the car we both folded our arms, and gave them a flat look. With this they all told us where they could make more improvements, I knew we had both been around long enough, to know this old trick would work. Just like a good vampire elder, we both told our group not to do it again, and to be more careful next time. To be truthful, I didn't know if this was a good teaching tool, but it did seem to work every time. Plus it wasn't as if they weren't going to get more blood at the house.

We then moved off the main fair to a side road called Lincoln. I found a parking lot as we got out and I said, "I want to talk about two things here. First you just had your first drink from an open vain, and I want to hear your thoughts. Secondly yesterday while you fought, I want to know any unusual feelings you had. Arty I think we'll start with you, when you're done, just give it to the next kid. If you want to hear what we think ask us, but right now, we just want you to share your feelings."

Arty then said, "Well I can tell you, I was scared as all get out. I was like I don't think I can do this, and I maybe sick. Then the blood started to flow, and it was like, I don't know. Oh like a State fair corn dog, not the taste really, but just the goodness of it. I guess the blood tasted like well blood, but different, jeesh this is hard to explain. Well I got really light headed, and it seemed to fill my body up both times, in fact I kind of looked forward to it the second time. Anyways about yesterday, I was standing there, and Kitty said to just let all of it go. I whispered what she meant, and she said, 'No thinky, let goey and just being.' I figured she meant don't think, and just let go of everything. I was still having trouble, then she kissed me as she petted my hair. All of a sudden I just felt this release, and she then whispered, 'Good young man just go with that.' I knew I must have been doing it right, because it really felt weird. It stopped when I saw that guy about ready to swing at Mary, I knew I couldn't get to her, but the guy was completely distracted, so I took off his head. Well then I couldn't get that feeling back, so I just opened up with that MAC 10."

He then nodded to Joe. He then said, "You got that straight, and you telling me I wasn't as good as Arty made me terrified. Once I had that blood in my mouth, it was fantastic. He did pretty good describing the feeling, but truthfully I wouldn't know what to say either. Well in battle I was trying to do exactly like the books said. I was sure I wasn't getting it though, because it said it should be like second nature to me. Then I saw that one guy look straight at me, and he was like going straight for me. I think he would of made it, until suddenly he just stopped, and had this really terrified look on his face. I felt something so I held onto it, Mary had taken his head, so I moved my vision onto the last guy standing, and did the same thing. Naomi then got him, and I can't be sure, but I think your one swipe caused him to blow up."

I then said, "I knew that last one was to easy to kill. Joe the reason why Naomi, and my kind don't like your kind, is because you rob us of our kills. For our sake and the sake of the house, this isn't a bad thing, it's a good thing. Mary you should do next."

Mary had a shy smile, "I'm like these guys, even though I also had a worry that I may have not been able to stop. That fear carried over when I tasted the blood, but I think I have a way to describe it. To women its like chocolate, I say to women, because I can't guess chocolate is the same to guys. I know that its the worse thing for us, and yet we crave the taste of chocolate. Now I am talking about real chocolate. Most chocolate is good, but the less paraffin it has in, the better it is to us. It's like it melts right threw you, and going through everyone of our pours. As I have always said, which I can't tell you where I heard this first. But anything that good, in the long run, has to always be bad for you, in the end."

She then kind of gave me a sorry look, as she said, "When we were fighting, I was doing the best I could do. When that guy looked right at me, and said what he did, I kind of panic, and just pulled the trigger. I think I pulled the trigger way more then I should of, and I stuck them way less then I should of. As we fought, I did seem to catch onto a rhythm, and just moved with the flow. There was a time when I seemed to be moving without thought, and my blows were more like automatic strikes, then of my own. Strange feelings, and all that, I can't say I had any of those at all."

Joe then asked, "John is it possible for someone to be using their special abilities, and not realize it?"

I nodded as I replied, "Yes it is, Kitty is a perfect example of that. She may have had to realize her abilities, but in truth, it for them, is always there. So even though they have to realize it, they never know that, because it all, just seems more of the same."

Billy then spoke up saying, "Hey I can say the blood was good, just like everyone else. But did anyone else have a problem as soon as they started to drink?"

"Tell us about it Billy?"

"Well I started to drink, and Naomi told me to watch myself when I did that. I was aware of what was going on before hand, but it was like everything was shifting between a strange red glow and normal vision. Plus saying it was good, really doesn't cover what it was doing to me. I mean I was torn between just drinking, and ripping their throat out. I've never had that many problems stopping doing anything before, it was like, if I didn't rip myself from that, I was never going to stop. John I'm not sure that drinking fresh blood is so smart for me."

Kitty then said, "Oh poor Wildman, just now knowing the beast within."

I knew what she was saying, but I wasn't sure he already knew. So I said, "There's something we like to call the beast within. It's an easy thing to control, but not for all of us. There's another term we use called, being close to the beast. Billy your kind, like my kind, are very close to the beast. When you do your whole, almost turning into a cave man, that's how you show it outwardly. With us its our anger issues, over time I have learned how to control mine. Think about this, you get in an argument with us, and we loose it. Not like any other vampire. We will suddenly rip your head off your shoulder's without knowing what we did, but everything that's bad about us, can be used for the better. This is another reason why you should be with Naomi. I can control you, but my ways could really hurt you. Now can you go on about the fight yesterday."

"To tell you the truth, I can't explain it. I suddenly fell over the edge, once I was there I felt things inside me well up. I could see, and now know what I did to them, but all I could think at the time was how wonderful the flesh and blood felt on my hands. I think in many of those I destroyed, it was really over kill. In a lot of ways, what Mary said I saw myself doing things in that manor as well. John when I took my shower, I was pulling small bits of meat from my teeth. I wasn't well, but some parts of me, well really didn't want to clean the stuff in my teeth, you know all the gore."

I then said, "Very good, I want you to take what you learned, and move on with it. I know some of it can be frightening, and then some of it can also be thrilling. This is what we are, even though we never have to bow to the beast, it's still part of us all. Kitty and I are older, so we have had time to learn this. It takes time to get to where we are, but you'll all get there one day. Know that even though we are older, we still have these issues too. Through our training, we have learned to deal with it though. Ok, I think that's enough for one night, lets go home."

Then we all piled into the car and drove back home. We got home with a lot of time, so I said to them, "Ok, everyone go and do a little training. We'll get back to normal training tomorrow, even though I'm not sure where we're going. Billy run around the area, and see how things are. Mary and Arty since Naomi is here, make sure the garage is completely sealed up. Well except for the side door, Joe make sure all the trash has been burnt."

Then we, that would be Kitty and I, walked in to the house. I heard Naomi talking, before I saw her, I think her, and Tony were doing the same thing, I had already done. As we passed by I said, "If you need me Naomi, I'll be in the Living Room."

The living room seemed a lot smaller, then you would have thought in a house this large. The floor was made up of dark wood, the lower half of the walls seemed to be made of the same wood. It also had a lighter wood trim on the base boards, wall separation molding, and crown molding. The wall paper that seemed to cover the rest of the wall, was a paisley style of a light red and black. All the furniture seemed tightly fit in this room, but it all seemed to match the walls. I mean the cloth, matched the cloth, and the wooden parts, match the wood, even though some of the wood had an almost reddish hue to it.

I had nothing to do, so I just kicked up my feet, and laid back a bit. I had barely sat, when a slight tapping came at the front door. Since no vampire in their right mind would ever use the front door, I was instantly on alert. I moved to the large front peep hole to check out whom it was, I was surprised to see a scraggly old man standing there looking away, as if he had a secret to hide. I cracked the door and asked, "May I help you?"

He smiled at me and said, "Yeah buddy. I'm here to see the sister."

I had no idea who he was talking about, so I said, "Friend I can assure you your sister isn't here."

"Not my sister. The good sister, oh her name is Sister Mary Elizabeth."

I turned my head and asked, "Beth do you know this guy at the front door?"

She came into the room and asked, "Is that you Sammy?"

Sammy replied, "Yeah sister. I got a lot more then I thought, so

I have Johnny down the street waiting on me sister."

She came to the door, and I stay real close to her, as I looked every direction. She then asked, "Sammy what do I owe you for this?"

"Nothing much sister, maybe enough for a bottle. Don't worry sister, no one was around, so we didn't have to make any promises."

"Sammy I don't see anything, where is it?"

He smiled at her and replied, "We weren't sure this was the house, so we hid it in the bushes right there."

He then pointed to a bush near the porch, as Beth asked, "John do you have enough, to get them a bottle?"

I can tell you, I was confused right then, and there as I asked, "How much does a bottle go for these days?"

The Guy Sammy replied, "I can get a cheap one for a ten spot, but if you could spare a twenty that would go a long way."

That was the hardest thing I ever did, yeah I had the money, but it was so tight right then. I did give him the twenty he asked for, then the two of us were down the steps, as Beth was dragging the white boxes out from under the bushes. With what Sammy said next, I was finally clued in on what they were. "I know you religious types like your strange food, but that's an awful lot of blood."

Beth's eyes met mine, and she gave me a little smile, as she said, "Remember Sammy, I was telling you I was showing the kids how to do some Turkish food? Even though what we are starting with technically isn't actually Turkish, it is known as one of their biggest enemies foods. Kind of like that blood sausage, the Sister Mary Alisha likes so much."

Ok to say I was impressed how Beth was handling this, would have been an understatement. Sammy seemed to be satisfied with her explanation, and was walking away. I moved to help Beth out, and we moved the three styrofoam containers into the house. As we came in, I made sure the front door was locked again. Finally we moved into the kitchen, and I asked, "Pepper, Billy, and Paul would you do your thing with our new supply of blood?"

They were all in there within just a moment, so I went on with, "Beth, Naomi, and I need to talk to you, in the living room really quickly."

Chapter 22

As we all sat down, I knew that this wasn't her mistake, because she hadn't been around long enough. I then started with, "What you did was out of the ordinary to say the least, and to tell you the truth, I don't see anything wrong with it. But we have a kind of unusual thing about our kind. Now bear with me, as I tell you this. You see vampires are supposed to give hospitality to any vampire that wants it, at the same time a vampire is supposed to respect anything that has to do with your territory. All this generally doesn't apply to humans though, but is also applied for our own safety per-say. So if a human comes over he is expected to respect our sanctity of our house. Normally I wouldn't have checked the peep hole, like I did, normally I would of ran around the house, and confronted them on the stairs."

I gave a good smile with a nod, and continued on, "You can see how that wouldn't go well for a human? Next time you want to do something like this, I think maybe you should tell them to come to the back door."

Naomi then added, "Yes, and tell someone, so we just won't off them."

Beth asked, "You wouldn't just do that, would you?"

Naomi replied with a smile, "We try not to, but it has happened."

Then I added to that, "Beth this life is a hard lone. Things have changed greatly in the past hundred years. Whereas somethings have gotten much better, other things have gotten much worse though. We can resist a whole lot of damage, there are things that have stayed the same. Then you have those thing that used to deal small amounts of damage, that can now do huge amounts of the same damage. In the end it is more about trying to stay away from things that do that much damage, well that, and the sure longing of depression, which some times takes over vampires."

She looked at me and asked, "What do you mean?"

Naomi took it from there, "When you see a weapon that you could resist the pain from before, that at first doubled or tripled in their damage rate. Well in a sense this country has totally change that, like a weapon the can shoot two to three thousand rounds a minute. When I was born, they had a gun that could only fire two to three hundred rounds a minute. Now I'm just talking about guns, but the thing they've done with explosives, are beyond what normal humans could possibly believe, until they see it for themselves. Then you have so many..."

Beth cut her off with, "That's not what I was asking. What I meant was, what do you mean, by the sure longing of depression?"

"Oh that. Well we can live for as long as we can stay alive, which means probably thousands of years. Like John said, this is a hard life, and it does take getting use to. So if you live more then fifty years, they think you're doing fairly well, but usually the real turning point is about a hundred year. I say about, because the realization comes to our kind in different ways. It does eventually though come to us all, and usually its around the time you realize that everyone you knew is dead. Even this though is subjective though, some decided to just stop after a couple of hundred years. In general we usually say though, that if you make it to six hundred years, that's a long life."

Naomi looked around, and saw that everyone was now crowded into the small kitchen. But she went on, "I don't know exactly how, but most that make it to six hundred years, say they found away to survive that long. There have been rumors, that there are these thirteen original vampires, that have survived over countless generation. I have and don't know anyone that has ever met one before, so they just might be a myth. I have met a few people that say they have met vampires around a thousand years old. I have heard rumors myself of a rare few that have seen a few a couple of grand in years old. Then again I have never met these guys either."

I then interject, "I met one that was two thousand years old, even though in truth she just suggested it. Remember if you meet an elder of any age, they don't like to talk about their age. I will say that age equates power, so watch your step around one. And for you girls, I'll tell you they like to take what they want, which even means young vampire women. I've heard this saying once that went like this; There's nothing that is closer to God, then a General on a battle field. When you see an elder, just remember this saying, and it might help you save your unlife."

Tony then asked, "Even someone like Beth, John?"

"Hey anyone Tony, they don't know the proper bounds, like this modern generation of vampires."

He sighed and said, "I didn't want Beth to know this, but I think shes different then a normal vampire of my family."

"How so," I asked?

"Well I can't be sure yet, but her transformation will give you insight to what I mean. When I looked down at her, and she was dying there right in front of me. She had really short hair, almost like it had been chopped off. Her skin had a pinkish hue, and her cheeks, and lips were that kind of orangery pink color. Then I felt the pull from her, and knew she had to live, I can't explain that part. So I sliced one wrist, and ran her to Naomi's jeep, half expecting her to die. When I got there though, there was an immediate change in her. I wasn't sure I had given her enough blood, so I cut my other arm, and fed her from that one. A few seconds after that, I noticed she was rapidly changing, so once she was past that point, I decided to do the final step, and cut my neck, and let her feed. With this though, she seemed to change immediately, from what I described to you, to what you see now."

I had to look at him as Naomi asked, "Why in sweet Jesus, did you not tell us this before?"

I just shook my head, as Kitty actually spoke up, "Blue Suave One looking to protect beauty, that all shiny and sweet and everything nice. He knew the wind blows, and change be on the wind. Old is new and new is old. Those that are dark see nothing, but darker change, the new see lighter change. They all fear the new shiny marble, in the end. They see, but they are blind to the light. The light that come into the world, not for only you, but for all the people."

Ok, I kind of understood what she meant, but one thing was that some times, what they say can literally change over night. I had a good friend explain it to me once, but she was a lot like Kitty, and I had problems understanding her at times too. What she said was that the streams of time are already there, and they only kind of pick up on them. They can see the past, as well as the future, even though they aren't, what you would call fortune tellers. The reason why that is, that the flow of time can be changed by a sudden event. Of course I asked her if time, is flowing, then would the sudden events already be set in the flow of time. Well she had no real answer for that question.

I can't say I was having a long train of thought, but it was Beth that pulled me out of it with, "Earth to John? Is anyone in there?"

I very intelligently asked, "What?"

"I was asking with all this talk about family, exactly what does that mean?"

"Well that's really not that hard to explain. You heard Naomi talk about the thirteen originals? Well they were separated into the different clans, or families as I call them. They have over time been re-termed, as not only those, but the term house, and species have been added. But over the time I have been a vampire, I've found this to not be exactly true. I'm not one to really get all technical and stuff, but I have counted at least twenty two different families. Of course this is just in the states, I have heard that there's even more in Europe."

I put my hand to my chin, and thought that, maybe I should share my idea on the subject. With this I went on, "The truth is that every species can literally do whatever another species can do. So I think like the human race has many different kinds of races, I do believe this is where our true differences come from. So like the human race, we are many races, all within one common race. Which if you think about it, makes a lot more sense, then thirteen original vampires. Anyways that's my thoughts on the subject."

Tony nodded his head as Naomi said, "When you meet an elder never mention this. Kitty will teach you what to say, and you can choose from that or this. Vampires really don't like change much, in fact there's a funny joke about that. You walk into a bar and immediately you see a vampire, how could you tell so easily?"

Tony popped right in with, "Because his clothes are twenty to a hundred years out of date."

That got a little giggle or chuckle out almost everyone. I then added, "Anyways Beth. I wanted to tell you the thing about the back, and front door, so your friends that bring us blood don't get in trouble. I'm not saying I couldn't stop myself, but I think its better to be safe then sorry."

Tony then added, "At least he's warning you, in our world they seldom even think of what their fledglings would even think."

Beth then asked, "What has made our world so jaded?"

"Well you've heard John and Naomi say a few times, we aren't nothing if we aren't civilized. This came about, because we have always been look upon with three visions. Some are in awe of us, and have even made societies around the existence of vampires. But for everyone that are in awe, there's one that fears us as well. If that wasn't bad enough, there are those that are just in fear of what they don't know. Take ancient Egypt, and Sumeria, each one loved us on their own account. Everything though has its time, and it is those people that fear us, that seem to make our time bad. I have to say though, that no religion has been exempt from this. Even the Christian belief didn't bother us, when they were young, some this stems from them being ignorant. I don't know about that though, ignorance seems to be every where."

He gave a very heavy sigh as he went on, "I used to be a choir boy in the Catholic Church, and I saw much darker things there then I have ever seen in this un-life. Truth is, I don't think ignorance has a hold on one group of people. I think what is weirder is that there have been very smart people in a body. Oh that's what you call a church congregation, but in truth, I don't think its the ten percent here, or the ten percent there. What I really think is that the most ignorant yell the loudest, because even sounding stupid they want to be heard. Whereas the most intellectual will stop, and try to consider all sides of things. So this last eighty percent that really has no mind on the subject, only hear this loud ten percent. They then side with the louder side, so as to not make to many waves, and this is what society decides from in the end."

He stopped and looked around almost embarrassed, as he asked, "Ah what was the question again?"

I put my arm around his shoulder's, as I replied, "It was what makes our world so jaded? I think you hit upon the right way, even though it may have been the long way around. I maybe wrong here Beth, and Tony correct me if I'm wrong. But the Church in its early existence has very tolerant of us, then I believe before a certain time, some way out there guys said...well I won't get into that. Anyways about six, or seven hundred years after the birth of Christ, things started to change. Rome had already gone into worlds where their beliefs were very dark, then one day the church started to conform to the pagan beliefs. They had a few problems with certain peoples beliefs, so they found it much easier to just call them evil, then to just find out what was similar, or not. With this came the Crusades, the inquisition, with the later came the churches groups of hunters, and finally the Black Pope."

I then looked directly at Beth, and spoke to her, "I'm not a religious man, so I have no idea about the Black Pope, and all that. I have fought some priests that have claimed to have been sent by his holy Eminence, I think that's a reference to the true Pope, and I do know enough to know he's a man of peace. So with this, even I find it much easier to blame it on this guy, our kind calls the Black Pope."

I then came back to everyone, as I said which wouldn't be my last words on this subject. "If you ever, and I mean ever. See a human that looks like he maybe hunting you, come and get an elder. Preferably Naomi or me, no offense Tony, but I think Naomi and I have had to handle this more often. Now the reason why I did say Kitty, is like Arty and Joe they're to important right now to this group. Plus it isn't like it will be a true hunter though. I would say for every real hunter, you'll come across three wanna be's."

It was right then I noticed something strange, at was a well light area a few minutes ago. Everyone started to talk among themselves, as I saw it seem to take form. Joe was right next to me, then and asked, "What is that John?"

Well at least I wasn't going insane, and seeing things. With his comment Naomi, and Kitty were by my side, and the room suddenly fell silent. You have to understand this wasn't happening in minutes, this was taking place in seconds. Suddenly a man stepped out of the shadow, at a lack of words for what was going on. What was weird is that the instant he walked out, there seemed to be a tremendous void. It was like everything that had existed, just stopped.

He was a dark complected man, maybe of Spanish decent. His black hair spoke to the same thing, but you couldn't see his eyes through the dark shades he had on. His clothes though could have come straight out of the God Father. He had on a very dark pin stripped suit that had to be Italian. His shirt was a very dark gray with a nice dark red tie, both obviously silk. His shoes even looked like they were hundreds, if not thousands of dollars. It was certain he was from money, even all his jewelry had to be the real things, worth more money then any of us could imagine. I finally thawed out and spoke to him, "May we help you?"

I figured to go with what was simple, after all any guy that could just appear in a room, screamed powerful. He replied, "I'm sorry I have to be so quick about this. But if you'll be quiet, and let me speak, I'll get on with it."

His accent was thick, even though I can tell you it wasn't Spanish. But I can't really tell you what the accent was, I just knew my gut was telling me it was ancient.

So I nodded my head, and he went on, "You have entered a time on the edge of all things. There has been our time, and not our time, but that time has been washed clean. I don't dabble in the affairs of my lessors, but time has told me this is the time. I bought this house many years ago, knowing something great would be happening here soon. I allowed those that don't concern me, to move in waiting for this day to come. I have felt this change coming for many years, but the strength of it didn't come to me, but six days ago. I have also looked to my line, and found a being suitable for me, within this same said line. Now she is ready, and yet it can't happen as of yet, until she passes the tests. I can tell you, I selected all of you for a reason, and there are more to come."

He looked at me and spoke right to me, "I have left you survive on your own, so you could get tough enough for this job. I dare say that most vampires should fear you, almost as much as they should fear me. You think I've chosen you as one of my Enforcer's, but what if your job is far greater then even you've realized."

He looked at Naomi and said, "My sister told me she sent me one of the true Amazon warriors, so don't dally thinking all you can do is hunt. You are more then the sum of your parts, use your real knowledge on how to hunt. Then you will be a formidable warrior."

He looked at Kitty and said, "I have seen her. I've looked into her eyes, and won her over to my side. You aren't just the servant of the Great Harlequin, you are her personified, in this modern time. Your insight can be used to baffle even the most baffling among you."

He then looked at the entire room and said, "You have all been picked for a reason. I know the ribbon of time has already been sown for all of you. As Kitty can tell you only one being can change it. There are three that guide it and guard it, and they're jealous and won't even allow us a look. They can't keep it all from us, and Kitty's kind can pick on it far better then the rest of us. Rest assured though, we can all pick up on it in the end. So I would love to tell you that this will all workout, but in truth even she can't tell you that. A few of you may have your existence ended, but then the end of it is truly your choice, and no one else's. We are after only as civilized, or as barbaric as we allow, and we choose our real path. So you may ask what is the point of our existence? The has far more consequences then you would believe, this is why we leave you ignorant."

I have to say his deep, and ominous tones were even getting to even me. As he went on, "Some would like to think we serve God with a certain purpose, and in truth there is some truth in that. Most say we serve the devil and it is often more obvious in that assumption then not. But the truth is, that we serve neither, and yet we serve both, that is because our true master serves none and both. He also serves the neutrality that is his to give to the world. In many ways, he's just like us, he lives, yet he's dead, he has life, and yet serves death, he can be seen as good, but is always considered evil. In the creation that is, he made it where it was of an original creation, and within this creation there is the mark of their original state. So as I said we are what we are, and can be what we will be. Even in time, everything becomes to a evening, and this only comes when the balance is off."

At this he stopped and looked up, as he said the next words, "It has been allowed to go to long, and the balance is off."

He stood there for a few seconds, and I was about to say something, when he finally added, "My time is short ,so let me continue."

Then he surprised all of us, by turning to Caty and saying, "You knew your fate, before it came, they chose to just destroy the best among them. I saw you different then they did, so I chose you. I now give a gift that is from my heart, to your breast if you freely except it."

With this he bowed deeply, and Caty just looked at him wide eyed, I then said, "Caty, I know your new at this, but he's waiting for a yes or no."

She then said, "I got that John, I just don't know what to say."

He then said, "Just do what your heart is telling you, my Princess."

I could see the instant change in her face, when he used the term princess. So even though you can never be sure in these cases, I kind of knew her answer well before she said it. "Y-Yes. I think."

He then fished in his pocket, and brought out a necklace that was large. Like maybe hundreds of thousands of dollars large, and one overwhelming stone in it. Rubies, huge rubies, it had some smaller sapphires and diamonds, but even they were overwhelmed by all the rubies. He then place it around her neck as he said, "You have made me a very happy man."

Then he moved to the front, and finally said, "My time is up, if I don't leave, they will know where to find you."

And with that, he just phased out again. It was easy to tell he was gone, as everything seemed to turn back to normal. To say we were all dumb founded is putting it lightly. We all just sat ,and kind of blinked at one another. What had just happened? Later when any of us except for Caty tried to describe what he looked like, we were at a lose. I knew he wasn't God or Satan, well simply because he told he was neither. Then again, I think by the way he talked, he wasn't exactly the number one guy to us. The way he described him as being alive, and yet being dead, and he use this to describe us in general. He was right, it was as confusing as it was thrilling.

Finally Caty thawed out enough to ask, "What just happened?"

I can't actually say I had a clue, but I knew I had to go with my gut. So as I spoke, I knew what I was saying had a certain truth to it. "Correct me if I'm wrong Naomi, and Kitty, but I think we just met one of the primes. But beyond that, I think it maybe best to have a wait and see attitude here."

Naomi then asked, "John have you ever seen the symbols on Caty's new necklace?"

I moved to look at it along with Kitty, and Tony, but none of us had ever seen anything like that before. It was Joe who clued us in, "Oh I've seen that. I don't know how to read it, and the book I'm reading has it already translated into English. In the really old books, I'm reading all have it in them. I'm just glad they've already been translated, I wouldn't be as far as I am now."

Naomi then looked closer and then said, "He's right John. This is ancient vampire script."

I looked at Naomi and just simply said, "Well hell."

Chapter 23

Day 7

The next day John woke up early which was normal for me. I was careful as to do things in the way I was comfortable with. I remembered quite well the events of last night even though I still made sure everyone did train. I went through the clothes that I would normally wear and wish I had time to do some wash. I decided to try the closet and try one a shirt, it fit very well. Then I decided to try the chest of drawers. In there I found one of those sweat shirts and threw it on. I wasn't sure of the jeans, but I tried then on and they fit. This modern generation thought clothes should fit tightly, I found I preferred a looser fit, but not that baggy look some of the real young kids were wearing. I decided though to go with his boots, even though I did put on a pair of white socks. I wasn't use to them, but I loved the fit of these tube socks.

I then put my pistol in the draw of the dresser, not because I did like it. The 50 caliber was a cannon in comparison to most guns, but more fitting was his 9mm, which I had to get back. I always felt nude without some kind of weapon, so I put my Kukri knife on. It was set up to be behind my back, but on an angle so it was easy to pull. I did have to learn how to drive a car with it there, and to readjust it when you got out of same said car. I was then feeling more like myself, and left my room probably far before anyone else was up. I had promised everyone that they would go back to feeding at the end of the day, so I didn't worry about pulling out thirteen bags of blood. Thirteen, what an odd number for a brood. Well now I think we're well past a brood and close enough to call ourselves a house. Better yet I think these kids are becoming part of a family as a whole.

In the end, just before I was joined by someone, I did set out thirteen bags of blood in the refrigerator. I was glad when I saw that Naomi was the first to join me. Naomi sat down, and I could tell she wanted to talk about last night. She confirmed what I thought, as she spoke, "So have you thought about the ramifications that guy told us last night?"

I replied, "Yeah kind of, but its really hard hitting that he chose Caty for something, and we haven't a clue what for. So I guess the bigger question is, do we expend more defending her, or go on with what we are doing?"

"John you heard him, he didn't just choose Caty. In away, he has directly, or indirectly, chosen everyone of us. Plus what is this new thing he was talking about, because I do have an idea where that might start, and it isn't with Caty."

"I know, I was thinking of that also, and I know we've been around long enough to know that it probably isn't the three of us."

"John I think you can include Tony in that. He maybe young, but I truly don't think he's part of this new thing. Well maybe not directly, but maybe indirectly. You see I can only see three there as well. We have Mary, Cheryl, and then Beth. I think he was talking about one of those three, or maybe even all three." She shook her head and added, "We just don't know."

I had to think about this, of course I knew she was right, but what could we really do, we weren't already doing. Then I caught onto something that he said, "You know he said that everything kind of hinged on fate. Maybe that's what we have to go with, I've always been one that has said, we make our own fate, and he was forced to tell us for some reason. You know like one of Kitty's warnings. I can't be sure, but maybe he was technically telling us to change things up. We both knew we would eventually, but with the advent of Beth, we've had to slow down."

I could see her thinking, and I wanted to wait on her, then she said, "I don't know. You know our kind has always had a rule never leave anyone behind, plus he did say he was sending us more. If we did that with Beth, we would have to do that with these too. John you know as well as I do, ignorance in our world usually equates death. Do you, or would you, want to sign the death warrants, for so many young vampires?"

"I guess you're right there."

"But I do think we have to change things up too, I'm not thinking of changing their training, but I think they need a day just for themselves. I don't know what to do yet, but I think we have to play a game that everyone can enjoy."

"Board games are fun."

"John these are kids, how long do you think you can get them to sit long enough to play a good game of cards?"

"Baseball's always been fun. Well except seeing the ball at night, but there is a little park right down the street."

Kitty then came in, and she was playing with a green thing, as Naomi said, "The parks a good idea, but baseball? Really?"

"Well whatever we do, we need some colorful thing, like whatever Kitty is playing with."

At that Kitty held it up, and let it fall on the table. We both got wide eyed as we saw it, was one of those glow in the dark Nerf footballs. I then stated the obvious, "I think our minds have just been made up. Football it is then."

With this Arty poked his head in the door and asked, "Did I just hear right?"

Naomi then replied, "Go tell everyone to put on something they don't mind getting torn, we are off to play the American game of touch football."

He then let out a huge, "YEEHAW!" And after that he went running through the saying, "Get ready, we're going to go play football! Yay!"

I couldn't believe how excited he was, I couldn't even believe how excited all the other guys were. I guess what really surprised me, was how excited all the girls were too. The guys were ready before the girls, so Tony and I led them to the small park. All the boys toast the football around, as we walked down the street, even Tony joined in. The Girls cheated though, and took Naomi's Jeep to the park, so they technically beat us. Everyone was happy, even though I don't think that mattered to any of the boys. The girls had decided, that since there was one more girl, that Kitty would be the ref. I still saw one problem, so I told them I thought it was a good idea for Mary and Caty to be team captains. Then Naomi added that the girls should be pick before one boy was picked.

So Kitty then did the entire pick a number thing, and Caty won. This meant that Mary would pick first, it was surprising how they drew teams. Mary picked Naomi, Cheryl, me, Tony, and lastly Joe. On Caty's team, she picked Pepper, Beth, Billy, Arty, and was left with Paul. This did make me think that maybe they weren't as much as a cohesive group that I had thought earlier, but for right now the plan was to have fun, I did want to take this time to do a little teaching. So as we set up the rules, I said to Caty, when she has time, to take Beth aside for extra training. The two of them, were very happy to do that, which made me think I may have been wrong. One of the rules we made, was that if any of us hurt anyone else, that we would have to sit out the game, until the person hurt felt well enough to reenter the game. Sadly I would be the first one to have to sit out the game.

So the first thing that happened, was that Kitty wouldn't go onto the field. When asked why, she folder her arms, and in her own way, told us no weapons on the football field. It was not very surprising to see whom had to put weapons on the side line. Me of course and my girls made me proud, as both Mary and Caty had to lay down weapons as well. Arty did as Kitty said, she would keep her Mr. Sharpie. Paul and Cheryl laid down, basically empty pistols, along with Tony's two pistols. Of course I didn't expect any from Beth, Naomi, and Billy, and rarely does Joe's type carry weapons. What wasn't as surprising, and was at the same time was the fact Pepper didn't have a weapon. The reason why, wasn't surprising, is she wore an outfit that...well she had to literally pour herself into. Most of her kind usually tried to conceal something, its not part of her normal wear though.

Anyways with this, we were finally able to start the game, and we were having a lot of fun, I can't really tell you who won the game though. At a certain point in the game Pepper found out she could egg me on, of course this wasn't a good thing, because when we get angry, we tend to really get angry. Even a warning from Naomi didn't stop her, she kept continuing on taunting me. So at one point she had finally gotten to me, so she tried to do her dodge thing, and I made the mistake of turning my juice on. I grabbed her around her thin waist, and threw her into the ground, with all my force. As she hit hard, I heard a ripping sound, and I immediately thought that I had ripped my pants. I reached around, and felt to see if there was an open space, I was glad to find no open space. I looked down, and saw how slowly Pepper was moving, and feared I had done the worse. I had broken Pepper.

I then with a little panic in my voice started to say, "Oh God Pepper are you ok. I didn't hurt you to badly, did I?"

She then replied, "Damn Chuck, could you throw me down any harder." Oh no, I did worse, I scrambled her brains, she started to turn around, and I helped her up. She then added, "Don't worry Chuck, I just got the wind knocked out of me."

Naomi was right there, but she was standing oddly behind her as she said, "Pepper you may want to change into your skirt and blouse."

She looked at Naomi and said, "I just need some blood Naomi, then I'll be fine."

"It's not you health I'm worried about Pepper, It's your wardrobe that has me concerned."

Then she whispered to her, and her hands when right to her bottom, as she ran to Naomi's Jeep. I then said loud voice, so everyone could hear me, "That was my bad, I'm out. Everyone go ahead and play on."

I then made it to the side line as I heard Joe say, "Tony are you going to join us anytime soon?"

My head came around, till I found Tony. He was frozen in place, and he was looking into a very dense dark location on the field. I picked up my weapon, and with an almost after thought, got Tony's two pistols. Then I used my speed, and was at his side in a blink. As I reached him, I whispered to him, "Reach around your back, and take your two pistols, and tell me what you see."

He did as I told him, as he whispered back, "I see two out lines for sure, I think there maybe a third, but I'm having a hard time making that one out. I think they are just watching, but I can't be sure. What do you want to do?"

After I was sure he had both his pistols, I whispered back, "We're going to act like you just found the ball, then I'll send Naomi off for something from the house. Once we hear her howl, then we can confront them."

Arty then asked, "What's taking so long you guys?"

Tony then replied, "Nothing, I just found the ball is all, it was kind of hard to find in the darkness."

"What are you talking about, Billy's got the ball. Plus its glow in the dark, its never hard to find."

Well shoot, as I wheeled, and Tony nodded his head, but along with that Beth said, "Hey, I didn't notice those three guys till now."

I then yelled, "BILLY AND NAOMI AFTER THEM, NOW! EVERYONE ELSE SADDLE UP, AND GET READY TO MOVE OUT!"

With this everyone ran to weapons, Kitty ran to the cab of the jeep, and started to hurry up Pepper. Tony and I started our way toward where we last saw Naomi and Billy run off, I knew that Tony and I could catch them, but we really had to give the kids the time to catch up to us. It didn't surprise me that Mary and Caty were the first two to catch us, Beth was the last one, as she was trying to help everyone get ready as well. I had to wonder though, if we would come up on Naomi or Billy disemboweling one of them. I had wished that I had given better instructions, as we really didn't know if they were vampire or human. I was happy when I saw Billy just standing in the middle of the street, Naomi would never make a mistake like that, unless she wanted me to find him.

So I put my hand up, and whispered to the kids, "Watch Tony, If he points to a spot come up only to that spot. If he pumps his arm that means, come running. Like what I did, and that means stop. A wave means move up carefully. Everyone got that?" After everyone nodded I said, "Tony lets go."

Then we walked up to Billy, and as soon as we got near he spoke. "Naomi went that way, she told me to wait for you. Once you got here, to go the other way, and meet you from the other direction, like she is. We caught them, but stayed away to find out somethings, then they went into there."

He pointed at what looked like a typical neighborhood bar. I then whispered back, "You did good, so go ahead and do what she told you to do."

With this he left us, and I saw Tony point to the ground to his side. He then asked, "What are we going to do? We still don't know if they're human or not."

Well there was really only one thing to do, even though I really didn't like it at all. As the others joined us I turned and said, "We have a problem here. We don't know if they were just humans, or if they were Shovelhead's. Worse thing we could do is go in, and break up just a group of humans. We have to know first, so this is something better left to Tony then me. Tony pick who goes with you, and find out."

"Ok we have to do this right, and even though I don't want to, I think I have to use you Beth. Ok Beth, you'll play the part of my wife, and our car broke down the street. Pepper I think you can get away as our kid. Now I know I'm not as good at this, then the two of you are. Beth and Pepper look around, and try and see who's human, and who's vampire. Now I want to be in and out of there, so I don't have to know what you seen until we get back to John." They nodded to him, and he went on with, "John buddy, I really don't want to take Beth with me. So if something goes wrong, I need you to be johnny on the spot. And I don't mean that as a pun."

I nodded my head and said, "Don't worry my girls and I have your back." With this He walked off , so I said to Kitty, "You might want to go off, and see what you can Hun."

She nodded her head and said, "Boy Toy you come with great harlequin too."

I then looked at Paul and Cheryl and asked, "You guys have any bullets in those guns?"

Cheryl replied, "Tony gave me the last twenty rounds. Between the two of us we were able to scrounge three a piece. So both of our guns have the lucky number of thirteen."

"Good I hope that's enough if you have to use them. Lets hope we don't though."

But right then, Tony assured me that we would have to use them, as he came flying out the door. All I could say was, "Shit!" I then moved at speed, and put myself in between Tony, and the big guy that was coming after Tony. I knew I surprised him, as he took a step back. I then allowed my head to come up slowly, and asked, "Where are my girls?"

The big guy then said, "Who the hell are you?"

From one side of him came from Caty, "Your worst nightmare, if you don't answer him."

He jerked away from her to run into the solid wall of Mary. She then said to me, "Daddy can we have fun with this guy? I so want to pull off his arms, and see if he can fly."

I had to smiled at him, as he said with a haunting sound, "Who the hell are you guys?"

Caty replied, "He's the Demon Lord, and we're his demon bitches. Now are you ready to answer him?"

He went to say something, and Mary said as she took his head off, "Oops wrong answer."

Paul came up with Cheryl, with weapons drawn, Tony shook himself off, as he pulled his Walther. I could see Naomi and Billy coming from the other direction. I knew we didn't have time to wait on Kitty and Arty. Tony then said, "That was a really bad idea. It really stinks in there, and I'm not talking about the usual piss and old beer."

I then said, "Naomi and Billy take the lead, Caty and Mary on either side of them. Hit those doors with everything you have, Billy you go one way, Naomi I don't have to tell you. I'm coming up the middle so be ready, everyone then follow up and hit them hard and fast. Ok lets do this!"

With that Naomi and Billy went running for the door, Caty and Mary balled up their fists, and knock the doors off their hinges. I had my knife out, and as Naomi and Billy cleared the door I was in. I started to take heads off, as I started to hear our three guns going off. This was a far to enclosed space for our style of fighting, but we were going to get to those girls, no matter what. Just about the time, I thought we would get overwhelmed, I heard a shotgun blast, and saw Arty behind the bar. He had snuck back there, and was now using it on vamps. Well I knew right then, it would just be seconds before I saw Kitty. And with that thought, I saw a head hit the floor, and another guy that looked like he was dancing. It was obvious he had a little harlequin on his back, and she was digging in her teeth. With this they started to collapse, and we got the upper hand on them.

One good thing about killing vampires, even new ones, is they don't bleed much. Right at this point, they showed that real well, as there was only one sniveling vampire on his knee's. Of course he was asking for mercy, and I had him by his hair. I then carefully listened for Beth and Pepper, but I figured they must have been gagged. So I looked at him and asked, "Would you like me not to kill you?" He nodded his head, "Then tell me where they took those girls?"

He then spoke, "In the back cooler, there's a trap door, you go down there to a short hall way. At the end there's a door, I bet they took them into there for Nicholas. Normally he would just let us drink them, but something…"

I cut him off with, "Girls take care of this scum."

"But you said you weren't going to kill me?"

Caty then replied, "He's not killing you. We are!"

He barely had time to scream, as Caty pulled his arms out, and Mary took off his head.

Naomi then said, "Move kids, same order as before."

And we were down the steps in mere seconds, the small hall way was a lot smaller, but we were able to do the same door thing. This time though they shattered the door, but that did deter us as we entered.

There were only seven of them, and they were very surprised at our entrance. We did are work even quicker then upstairs, I saw Pepper on an operating table, and saw a couple of strips of skin missing. I immediately directed Tony toward her, as we finished the fight. As the last one fell, I saw Beth strapped to a chair, so I directed Cheryl toward her and said, "Get them out of here."

Chapter 24

Then a voice came from the darkness, and it sounded of eastern European decent. "Why bother? I'll taste all of you soon enough."

I knew I couldn't win a fight with this guy, well without my special weapons. I knew I had to try and stop him from attacking the kids, so I moved fast, and that's when I first got a look at this horror. As I watched my blade dig deeply, his eyes widen as he spoke again, "You are much older then you smell, but no bother, I have killed, and used your type before."

Then I remembered something, I had nearly forgotten about. So I said as I swung at him, and he fended me off, "Just get them out of here now! I have a plan." With that I saw Tony start to push the kids out, Naomi then thawed out, and did the same. Kitty tried to join my fight and I said, "No!" I calmed my voice, and said, "Kitty I have fought these guys before, I know what I'm doing."

He then said, "I know your type, you'll battle me until you make a mistake, and your neonates will be mine. You don't have a chance."

I did have to admit his skin was far harder then I remembered, but as I fought I watched the kids, and as the last one cleared the room, I spoke. "All your kinds problem is, when a low life actually kills you, you're to stupid to realize it."

He made his first attempt to strike me, as I then used my speed to get around him. I saw what I was looking for, so I grabbed it, and came around him again. I made it to the door, as he wheeled on me, and saw what I had in my hand. With that I threw it with all the force I had in my arm, the oil lamp lite him up like a Christmas tree. He made a screeching sound as he tried to put it out, I then turned around and ran out of the cellar, as I cleared the door I heard a loud explosion. Then the shock wave hit me, and I slid across the ground. I got up, and knew the scrapes would be taken care of by some blood. I moved to rejoin the group, and they were doing a lot of the same. Pepper was fully nude and Beth had on Tony's jacket already to cover her bare breasts. He was going to offer his shirt, but I stopped him. I then pulled off my sweat shirt, and it fit her like a dress. Well like a very short dress, which probably made Pepper very happy.

I saw Joe staring off, and I was sure it was that Nicholas guy coming after us. It was then that I saw two things, first the bar was fully involved in flame. Second was the very skinny vampire walking toward us. He had on a nice suit, with one of those Panama hats on. I knew the type of vampire he was, and the hat was a clear sign I was right. He walked with his head down, but as soon as he got close, he lifted his head, and everyone could see his eyes. He had the eyes that had been mistaken as a demon many a times in our history, I knew they didn't usually smile much, because their teeth showed this as well as they were abnormally demon like. They had two other signs, one was their ears, but I figured he had his ears done, as they didn't look abnormally demon like. He tipped his hat, and everyone could see his bald head now.

He then asked, "I am talking to the leaders of the kids that have taken over the safe house here?"

I knew what he meant when he said that, but I was sure the kids didn't. I didn't actually answer his question, as I didn't want to trap Caty in this situation. "I am one of the elders of the house, yes."

"We were seeking information about one of our lost ones, when your attack stopped us in our tracks. I do believe you owe us a favor."

"I don't think so? You knew of us, so you could of told us of you attack, which left us in ignorance. This means that we did what we needed to do to get two of our own back. If anything by getting rid of a group of Shovelhead's, you owe us."

He then gave that terrible guttural chuckle, his kind are known for, "Very well, but my employer will want to meet you before we settle such a thing. Can we come to you on the morrow, and discuss this with you?"

I sighed, I knew it was wrong, but it was the break we were looking for. I then put one finger up as I turned to Naomi and Tony and asked, "What do you think?"

Naomi then replied, "It means dealing with capes."

"I know."

Tony then said, "It couldn't be good for the kids also."

"Well I don't see any other way to get what we need. Got any ideas about that?"

Naomi shook her head as Tony replied, "Sadly no."

I then turned back him and said, "We will see you on the morrow. Can you make it early though, I need to train these kids?"

The guy then replied, "I will try, but you know how these elders can be. My name is William, and I will present him to you. I thank you for my lord." He then tilted his head and said, "We must leave, your handy work has drawn attention of the local authorities."

He then turned and walked off, as I could now hear the sirens too. I directed the kids to leave, as I saw two others leave the wood, as William passed. I didn't know if this was a good thing, or a bad thing, I just knew we, and the kids needed what we could get from them. So we left, and walked carefully back to the park.

When we got back to the football field, Naomi took the girls home so they could help Beth, and especially Pepper. I know you don't have two strips of skin removed from you, and don't have problems. So I was good with it, I then walked with the boys home, as I felt with all the police, it wasn't safe for us right then. The four other boys, played as Tony and I walked together. He then asked, "What did you do to that thing?"

I replied, "Well I couldn't kill it with my normal means, so I had to find a way to burn it."

"That was your plan then?"

"Well it was made easier that I saw an oil lamp, I had no other way to beat him if that didn't work. Well short of running all the way home, and getting my special sword."

"Good thing there were all those oil casks down there, but what would of you done if he had been able to put himself out."

"Truthfully, I don't know, my next idea was that hanging down electric socket. I was sure that would have been a fight in a half."

"If you had to, do you think you could of taken him down?"

"I have before, I've just always been prepared. I wasn't even close this time." Then I realized what he was saying, "Big mistake on my behalf. Next time we need to keep extra stuff in the car, oh and bring a car with us."

He sighed and added, "I guess number one on our agenda with this cape will be ammo."

"I'm hoping to take him for a lot more. I wonder who this person they lost is though? Must be pretty important to send out a yes man like William."

One of the boys came up excitedly and said, "There's music booming from the house."

With that we all hurried up, and as we approached, I could tell it was some like that new music. In fact I think I recognized the voice of the woman singing, Britney something or other was her name. It was rather refreshing then what we had been through, so when the boys asked if they could go ahead, I had no problem with that. I was the last one threw the back door, even though I was surprised that Tony hung back with me. I came into the kitchen, and saw Naomi was sitting there, so I sat too.

I then asked, "Hows Pepper and Beth doing?"

She replied, "I gave them both a bag of blood, and told them to go get washed and changed."

"Good, good. Where did the music come from?"

She sighed and looked at me, "It's mine. I haven't used it in so long, I forgot I had it. Kitty found it, and she was all over me to listen to her music."

Well I had a clue that this wasn't Kitty's music so I asked, "This is Kitty's music?"

"No actually this is Caty's music, but she said her and Pepper listen to the same type, so shes playing it for her."

"I thought about waiting there for you guys, but after the third police car, I decided it was better to come home."

"I thought it a good idea to stay here as well, but I thought you would get it eventually. I also told her as soon as we came into the room, she could start her music. Apparently this is a very important piece of music she's been wanting to share with all of us."

"Well this might be a first."

"What's that?"

"We get done with a situation, and have nothing really to share with the kids."

"I think that's a good thing."

"I think that's a very good thing."

With that the two of us got up, and walked into the room. In truth it might have been smart not to let Kitty play her music, I mean she thought it was Important for us to listen to it, should of clued me in that something was up. Entering the room was a comedy all in itself. Here were two groups of vampires, that I would call at least good. One group all boys, the other group all girls, on opposite sides of the room. The only two separate from the groups were Tony and Kitty, I thought of grabbing Caty or Mary and just start dancing. Then something told me that wouldn't work either way, I looked at the six girls and knew there was only one option.

So I walked straight over to her, and asked, "Beth would you like to dance with me?"

She shyly replied, "What?"

"Madam, would you like to trip the life fantastic with me?"

She kind of grimaced a little, as she admitted, "I'm not a very good dancer. To tell the truth, except in my bedroom, I've never really tried."

"I'll tell you what, I'll try not to step on your feet to much, if you promise to do the same with me."

"Well, I would love to kind sir."

I put my hand out, as I bowed to her, and just as we started, "Now don't all of you laugh, because I only know the waltz."

I watched as I saw first Naomi, follow my lead with Billy. I think they were dancing one of those new dances. Tony look at me with a look that told me he was surprised, I was dancing with Beth. He took it in stride, and then ask Caty to dance with him as well. Kitty had stomped over, and grabbed Arty's hand, and pulled him to the boom box. With three boys, and four girls left, I was happy to see Paul take the initiative, and and asked Pepper to dance. This must of broken the ice though, because the Joe walked over and asked Mary to dance. Then happily added, "Cheryl if you would like, I'll dance the next dance with you."

She agreed, so I was happy that things were going very well. Kitty waited until the song was done, then she replaced Caty's tape with her own. I thought it was funny how everyone had tapes, because I could see this boom box was an old one. It had a slot for an 8 track and two cassette decks, with an AM/FM radio. I was sure that only the oldest of us, might have an 8 track or two. Cassettes had lasted longer then the old 8 tracks, but they still went their route with CD's. I had heard about these new things called DVD's, and more recently something called blue ray. Whatever that is. Well at least I knew it, I wasn't like the older generation, which thought the light bulb was a keen invention. And they wonder why we call them capes.

The minute Kitty's music started, I knew it was different then anything I had ever heard. It was very melodic, and almost hypnotic in its sounds. The first weird thing was how easy it was for us to all move to its tones, not to mention that everyone seemed to be moving alike. I knew almost the second when Beth started grinding up against me, this isn't something she would generally do. My mind was screaming stop this, but my body just kept moving along with Beth's. Somewhere about now is when I lost all sense, and only really know the end product of what happened.

As the music changed to a new song, I did two things. First I set down Beth's limp body, then I moved to the boom box, and pulled the plug. Once I got my head around what may have happened, I ran to the fridge in the kitchen, and yanked out one of the new coolers of blood. I then ran, hoping there was enough blood in this thing, as I didn't really check it. I also knew the only fair way to do this, since I knew I had emptied Beth. I lifted up her head, and place my arm at the edge of her mouth, then I sliced my arm, and allowed my blood to run into her. I did this three time, and saw her color start to return. When she latched onto my arm, and used her tongue to keep my wound open, I knew she was out of the woods.

With horror I now saw that there were six two person groups, where one partner was latched onto another. I then grabbed a bag of blood, and threw it at Kitty's head. With that, she wheeled letting Arty hit the ground. She had just enough time to barely let out a hiss, then she heard the thud, and realized what had happened. I repeated the act with Naomi and her reaction was slightly different, but close to the same. I looked for Tony, and was surprised that it was Caty that was latched onto him. I then looked for Joe, and he had Cheryl latched onto his mouth. I repeated the act quickly with both of them, I then saw Paul latched onto Pepper, which to me looked really weird. I made the decision to throw at him, and Mary in quick succession.

At that very moment, it didn't dawn on me, how wrong that was, it just dawned on me, how wrong what everyone else had done. I then started to suck on my very own bag of blood, and said in between sips. "Don't worry if you feel a little faint while you do this, you have to get everyone's blood level up. It shouldn't take long though, because they're young." I took another sip and then added, "We'll all get a bag of blood and meet in the meeting room."

Naomi added also, "To you that haven't heard that before, it's also the ballroom."

I looked down as her and asked, "How do you feel Beth?"

She let go of my arm and asked, "Are you ok? Are you feeling light headed?"

I smiled at her as I answered, "No, I said that for the younger vampires. Even though I will need blood after this, and older vampire could do this with two or three young vampires. I'm not sure if Tony and Naomi could do that, but I'm sure Kitty and I could."

She took a little more and said, "I think I can stand up, if you help me."

I kept my arm there and said, "Ok, but this is your wound, so you need to stop the bleeding."

I knew I didn't need her help, and I knew right away what I said was far deeper then what it seemed. Her tongue snaked out of her mouth as she did exactly as I told her to do, just in case. As I got hold of myself, I said, "We need to help the others, but if you feel faint just go to the kitchen."

I then helped her up, and we started to move around the room. I directed her to Naomi, as I went to Kitty. With that we then moved onto the next two, and I said, "Kitty and Naomi get the kids moving to the ballroom."

Once we had, I had Tony and Caty moving, I heard the low almost weeping sound. I directed Beth to move to the other two, as I moved to Mary. I looked down in horror to see her feeding her blood to, what I assumed was a bum. She looked up at my face, as she said, "I'm sorry John, I didn't mean for this to happen. He just happened in, and that music. Well I killed him that's for sure."

I was upset, but not at her, at me. If I had taken half a second, and counted, I would have known something was wrong. I took him by the arm, and turned him over, as I said, "Ok, lets see who we have her. Don't worry Mary, that tape did a number on all of us. Man he smells, and why does he look so familiar to me?"

From next to me a sharp intake of breath, told me Beth knew who he had been. I looked at her, and asked as I smiled at her, "Do you have any idea who this is Beth?"

She looked as if she was going to cry, as she replied, "It's Sammy. He must of come back."

"Are you sure, I mean he does kind of look like Sammy. But how old is this guy compared to Sammy? Twenty or thirty, Sammy had to be in his fifties."

Then when she said the next words, it hit me she was right. "I saw his wedding picture, back when he was married, that's how he looked in his picture."

Well shoot she was right, because what had happened to her, had just happened to Sammy too. The only problem was, I thought it was because Beth had been a nun. Now I was sure it wasn't the reason, but exactly what the reason was it, I was at a lose. I looked at Mary, and said, "Mary if I'm right, he's changing then, and that means we both really made bad mistakes. You accidentally killed Sammy, but me not taking the time to count, forced you to make a new vampire. So take him to your room, and stay with him till the change is complete. After the meeting, I'll send as many of the girls that are willing to help you out. I willing to bet you aren't willing to sleep, even in the same room with how he smells. I really have to explain to everyone what just happened though."

She picked him up, and I was sure she was surprised how light he was. I had explained to her about her strength, but this was the first incident that put it into context. As she walked away, Beth said to her, "I'll be there as soon as the meeting is over Mary."

This all happened in the living room, that was on the first floor, the ballroom was on the second. Beth and I made a detour to the kitchen as we got our own bags of blood, Kitty was already sitting in a chair up front. I moved to stand next to her, Naomi joined us on the other side of her. I didn't want to be side tracked, but I knew I had to tell everyone what I had done. I cleared my throat as I started, "I would like to apologize to the entire group, Mary had inadvertently killed a human. Through my fervor to help all of you, and not knowing she didn't have to do what I ordered. She did as I said, and made a new vampire. So without wanting too, I added another mouth to our house. Again I apologize to you all."

Tony looked at me and asked, "Isn't that almost the same as making another vampire yourself?"

"Yes it is, Why?"

Naomi cut him off with, "It's because he knows that inadvertently, you did the same crime that he had caused with Beth. But ask yourself Tony? With all John knows, and can do, do you really want to follow the path you started?"

Paul then said, "I know, I don't want to, but if you think about it, fair is fair after all. Joe you have been studying the laws as you can, have you ever found a law that covers this one?"

Joe replied even though I already knew the answer, "No. I'm not done, and it's going to be awhile before I really get done. The laws are a lot of that I, me, my stuff, so I'm willing to bet, because he didn't actually do the act, he's free and clear. I think that maybe we have to vote on this too, John I can't ask you, so what do the other elders think?"

I then replied even though he basically said I couldn't, "Both Paul and Tony have a valid point here, and yes I know I'm not supposed to reply, but I think a vote should be held. Before that there is a bit of something that has become a paramount issue, so lets have the vote after what Naomi and I have to tell you. Is that agreeable to all of you?"

Everyone said yes or nodded their heads. So I looked at Naomi and asked, "You want to handle this, or should I?"

She smiled and replied, "You start, and I'll add as you go along."

Chapter 25

"Ok. Except for our newest vampire, and Mary we all might have a problem. When someone drinks from a vampires blood, a bonding happens." I looked around as I allowed that to sink in. Then I added, "Now in a few days it may fade away, but seventy five percent really never do. In away its like what a maker, and a child will always feel for one another. With everything that happens, when you first change, it weakens within three days. This is a problem, because of what that means to the person you're bonded to. If by any means, if the bond broken, or the person you're with, gets killed there's a pain that can't be described."

I let that sink in as well, and Naomi went on with, "You have to understand that most bonds go one way, most vampires will allow another to feed from them, and then that vampire is almost his or her slave. There is a good thing as in only one being can be bonded at a time, but no vampire will do this lightly, I mean drink another vampires blood. Also to us it is a very intimate thing, so most won't share this part of them with another unless they're in love. In the human world sex is it, because you can have a baby, and that bonds you with the man that I hope is your husband. This is how we feel about the bonding process, as it's almost like sharing part of you. John saw where we had left the rest of you, and knew there was only one way of bring you back."

She looked at me, and I continued, "If you didn't have the blood of the one that had taken your blood, as that meant they were stronger. Well I didn't hold much hope of any of you making it back to us, I think the music that Kitty had put on had taken us over, and we drank from our lessors, or weaker partner. Now you could say I may have been wrong, but we just don't know enough, and that might take Joe at a later date. So I made a snap judgment, and had you all drink from those that cause this. Since we all had drank from the other, that meant that we may have been bonded to the first said vampire. Then with the first vampire having to drink from the second, this completed the partner bonding."

"And here lies the problem that John, and I are talking about. We are all know bonded, as if we were in love with each other. Now I think that means that older vampires could separate from their loved ones for awhile, but I think you younger ones will find it hard to go the night without finding your partner, and making sure they are safe. John knew how young all of you were, and I think didn't want to start this early on. I see no way around it now, so it would be very good for you to sleep with your partner. I know this will be inconvenient, but I think we have to go the full way with this."

I put my hand up to stop her, and said, "Maybe we should make it volunteer at first, and compulsory over time Naomi."

Tony then said, "Well hell. Ok guys lets vote. Who wants to sleep totally nude, and who doesn't?"

I knew how the vote would go as soon as I heard almost every girl gasp, I didn't stop the vote though, and was surprised that only three voted no. So I spoke up, "Good going Tony. If we keep going this way, you'll be trampling one the rights of three of the ladies of the house. Is that what you set out to do?"

"No. I just wanted to get this over and done with though."

"Wow, they say my kind are the inpatient ones."

Naomi then asked, "Are you two done bumping chests yet?"

Tony replied, "We're not butting chests, its just John has this way of beating around the bush. I think he's cool, it just really long winded though."

I then replied, "I'm not long winded. Thank you anyways. I think for your type you're cool as well."

And I think that was it, that is what made Tony and me friends finally. Naomi went on with, "Ok John has a point here, so I agree if we make it mandatory after a time. Caty and Joe that will be on you to discuss, and give the time line. You can ask us question, but it really is on you two. Now I think the next part is on you Joe?"

Joe then stood up, and held my trial because of what happened. I know my defense would have been a weak one, if these had been normal vampires. I knew it was kind of weak though, and decided to go where the dice rolled. I will say though, the way the votes have been going, I kind of knew they would vote to not allow me to be destroyed. After a lot of thought on it though, I sort of knew that I had been saved, and with farther thought it was really a simple thing with their decision though. They all being so young, I knew they were going on what I could add to the group, and I'm pretty sure none of them wanted to hurt Beth either. So in hind sight, it was kind of a given, that they would have voted that way.

There was more of a pressing thing to attend to though after that, I told them more of our new member, and how he really needed a bath. Except for Beth, no one wanted to volunteer. So I put my hands on my hips and said, "Really!"

Everyone looked at me like I just pulled out a whip and whipped all of them. I looked at Caty, then to Pepper, and added, "Joe's worth saving, but we have a new member, and he isn't! I know if I asked Tony, Naomi, or Kitty, they would jump at the chance to help this poor new neonate. Have you became like those that would rule you, and feel that you are better then them even?"

Naomi cleared her throat and said, "John you didn't exactly tell them about that part."

"Oh. I guess I passed over that so as to protect all of you."

Caty then asked, "Protect us from what?"

"Ok you all know. we are nothing like this, but in the vampire world there are those that only seek the power that this life brings with it. As a young vampire. it seems ok, until you are one the creatures they want to possess. I can tell you that Mary, you and me are lucky, because most vampires see us as a problem to possess. But to find young vampires not only possessed, but sometimes to be barely less then slaves, in the possession of another vampire. You would think that in all worlds slavery was dead, but in the vampire world it is very much alive. You've heard us call them capes, but that term is for more then just their thoughts on progress. It also has to do with how backwards thinking they happen to be also, they say we are nothing if not civilized, but if a human comes in their presence, they think nothing of bearing their teeth."

Joe then spoke, "But John we have been taught over and over again, not to allow our presence to be known?"

"I know, and they're the ones that made that rule. Think about it, if you wanted something, like a persons blood? Just break your own rules, and make it look like it was a mistake, and then you did the right thing. Then all the elders slap you on the back for doing the right thing. I said this un-life is a hard life, but in truth you don't know the half of it. I guess what is worse is that most of our kind hide all this through fake platitudes, and false kindness, to tell you the truth, it's enough to make you sick, but if you want or need anything, its best to just play along with them."

Naomi then said, "That's why Tony, John and I had words about that guy William. It isn't that we want to deal with him, it's that we see no other way then to deal with him. So even though we are meeting with him, don't think we're friends. We're only talking to get as much as we can from them, but in the same sense, they're doing the same with us too. I do have something to say though John, do you think its smart having the girls deal with this new child? I mean he is a guy, and he may get embarrassed if they do what is needed to be done."

I hadn't even thought about that. So I nodded my head, as I replied, "Yes. I guess I'm getting used to just throwing out orders. Ok, that was my mistake, so I guess I can help whomever help clean this new guy. So which one of you guys will give me a helping hand?"

Tony then spoke up with, "I think this is going to be disgusting, but to show the willingness of the elder's, what they don't want to do, I'll help you. I do think Pepper needs to be there at least, to get his correct size, so she can get him clothes."

"That might be a good idea. Pepper do you think you can do this without getting embarrassed?" Pepper nodded her head, so I then added, "Ok, lets get this done with. Arty get my soap from my room so we can do this the right way."

Then we all moved off, Beth still wanted to help. I told her she could help us with Mary, I knew as we did, what needed to be done, she may feel anxiety in being apart from her first child. Tony and I carefully undressed him, and Pepper left just as soon as we did this. Arty came in with the soap, so I told him to take his clothes, and burn them. Most bodies that die go through the death process, do the same thing. So we washed every part of his body, and then Arty came back in with new clothes for him. Then we moved him back to Mary's room, I allowed her to sit on her bed as the both of us carefully set his wet head on her lap. We then talked, to try and figure when he would most likely wake up, that is if he did. Well anyways, we figured out about and hour and a half there abouts. So I told the kids to keep an eye out on Mary, and for Cheryl to bring her blood in the same said hour and a half.

After all of that, I walked around, since everyone just went back to dancing. I did dance a bit, but I wasn't into it, after everything that happened. Plus I wasn't that much into the new dances, give me a waltz any day. Even though there was this one kind of music I did kind of like, but all the girls got mad when Billy tried to put in on the boom box. I can't say that I heard enough to be sure though, I did hear this one line. It's 6 AM Christmas morning, the shadows but no reflection here. I'm not sure, but to me that sounded like a vampire wrote that. Probably one of Tony's kind. Later I would find that I like this guys music, and he looked more like Kitty's kind.

I looked in on Mary a few times, I could tell the guy was just a hair darker complected then Cheryl. He was also kind of handsome, with a sort of greasy look to him. I figured since I was no judge of how a man looked, he was probably well past handsome. I thought Pepper had done well, as he laid there in what you could almost call dungarees. As I didn't really look like our kind, he most definitely did. More like he would be at home as a warehouse worker, or such. A guy that was really used to using his hands, more then I had been. With that it kind of brought me back to my days as a human, I had thirty five years as a human before I was brought into this life.

I had lived a life of just above the poverty level. My Dad though was set that, we would do better then him, so he made sure we live a more comfortable life, then we should of. He apprenticed me out to a very good local cobbler, and I thought that's what my occupation would be. The cobbler was very old, and died one day. I tried to take over his business, but I had two major problems. To be a good cobbler, you had to be able to read, and I really wasn't that good of a businessman. I lost his business, and with that, I had to go to work in a warehouse. I had never worked so hard in my life, and thought if I kept working there, I was going to die soon.

Little did I know, that there was this vampire that was trying to escape justice, and had found me at the shipping warehouse. The night he made me into a vampire, was all wrong, but in the end it brought me into this life. We stowed away on a ship that was leaving the very next day, it's bad enough to have a single vampire on a ship, let alone two of them. When we made it into Boston harbor, they thought it was a plague ship. So we escaped, and got out of the city, so we could set things up between us. I learned far more from other vampires then I ever learned from him, he was truly a fugitive, and we were on the run from the most powerful vampires in the vampire world.

I remembered that day that they took him, the only reason I had escaped them was a river. You see I was a very strong swimmer, and he wasn't. So we were attempting to cross a very wide river then, I made it to the other side. He was forced to turn around, and literally walk straight back into their hands. It would take them almost a hundred years for them to find out he had made me, in that time I had entered my office, and no one was willing to really destroy me. Plus along the way, I learned to read and write in four languages, and if you counted the few Indian dialects I spoke, I think I was up to ten spoken languages. My kind are kind of known at one time to be intellectuals, but hadn't been that way for a very long time. So in a sense I was an oddity in this also.

It is weird that for many years, those in my office were known to use what some others called blind justice. To me I was just doing the right thing, I mean I'm sure I broke every rule in the books, three maybe four times over again. It was in a sense to me, not just justice as much as it was just doing the right thing. Yeah I do have to admit that over time you do get a bit jaded, I put my hand to my chin as I thought about that. Then I knew for sure I was right on this part. I think this group has moved me from just being just another jaded vampire to being more then I had been. Well at least I wasn't one of those brooding vampires, I just think way to much. Then I saw Billy in the hall as I was getting to know this house.

"There you are," he said. He continued with, "Mary's ready, and Joe's called a general house meeting."

I answered him with, "Ok, I'm coming. I wouldn't want to miss my child's first child."

So I walked to the room we used for this kind of stuff, the ballroom. Cheryl met me immediately and asked, "Where were you?"

"I was just walking the house, getting to know it better. I did check in on Mary four times."

"Well Mary's been ready for like ten minutes, and Naomi was saying you may have left."

I looked at her and said, "Well she was right in suspecting that of my kind, but I gave all of you my word, and I never break my word. If I had told her that, she wouldn't of suspected me of just getting up and leaving. Plus I bet after she thought that, she realized that Mary was still here."

Naomi interject then, "I did, and I knew I was wrong, and I told them that your kind is never known to leave their children behind. Once it was out there though, everyone just ran with that."

I nodded my head as I sat next to her, I added, "Beth I'm an elder, so I have the privilege to sit up front. As we are bonded, you have the privilege to sit next to me, if you wish."

Caty then asked as Beth moved up next to me, "Does that go with everyone that has an office John?"

"Not usually, age has its privileges, but then again, an office isn't usually awarded to a young vampire. Most of the time only someone of one hundred and fifty years are give an office, and to be a prince or princess of a city or province, you have to be around three hundred. Now I know a house isn't a city, but I wanted you to know why we didn't name you princess of the city."

"So that means because of that only you and Kitty could actually lead the house? And with everything I know only you could lead the city?"

"Technically yes, even though a vampire can't take away what's already yours. So if you owned the house from your old life, a vampire can't take it away from you. You'll never be considered the princess of that house until you are of age, you do have to know though, that our kind are known to have leaderless broods all the time. So when everyone else sees our house they'll think it's just more of the same for our kind, but it is rare to have a brood, haven, or house with such a diverse collection of vampires. Most of the time vampires prefer to stay with like minded vampires, so most houses are of the same family. If there are more then one family it's two, possibly three family types."

Naomi then added, "Plus, most of the time, they only seek out John's or my kind, because of our special abilities. That's why when you find a house, that is protesting against the capes, it's our two families. My kind will join together for a common cause, but no family joins together for a common cause like John's family does. Most vampires will say if you have a common cause, never piss off John's kind, unless you have my kind to help out. So even though John, and my kind respects each other, we have commonly found ourselves on the opposite side of a vampire war. So this is why most of our kind, knows the others kinds, of peace ritual."

I smiled and said, "Even though this has nothing to do with our house's newest member. Joe we'll stop talking as soon as you are ready."

He then poked his head in and answered, "We're ready I was just waiting for everyone to be quiet."

Chapter 26

Everyone then got quiet, and he walked in, he then said, "There is no way to formally bring this meeting to order, so let's just start this then. As judge of the order there in this house, I call us all to be present, and ready to receive Mary's new child." He then turned to Caty and said, "With your permission I shall proceed?" Caty then nodded her head, so he went on, "I present to you our follow house mate, and loved like our very own mother Mary."

She walked in, I was always so surprised at just how normal she really looked, but be on the wrong side of those claws, and you were pretty much done for it. She then said, "I don't know about mother, but maybe older sister Joe." Everyone had a good chuckle at that, "I didn't know Sammy when I turned him into what we are, but I had a wonderful father that gave me insight of how to start a new vampire out. So he woke up about a half hour ago, and I talked to him about what had just happened to him. He also related a few things to me, and I think he should be allowed to talk other then the typical hello. So without any farther a due, let me introduce you to my new child, which we had a laugh about. I think he wants to tell you that story though. Here is my new child Samual Nasatir."

Well if I hadn't before actually known, when he came into the room, I was sure by how all the ladies sat up and took notice. He moved to the front and said, "That was what they called my father. You all can call me just plain old Sammy. I have lived a long time, and had a life. I won't say it was a great one, because I had a wife and two beautiful kids. A drunk drive drove into a building. My wife and two kids never saw it coming, so I have to be thankful that they never saw what he did to them. Even though I have no idea if their deaths were quick, all I knew was what I loved the most in the world, had been just killed. So my life went down the tubes fast from there, and I live forty five years in the gutter. I was twenty eight when that all happened, so you can do the math."

He then sighed and went on, "The one day, I met a woman, that changed my life. Now I will tell you that it's hard to get off the bottle, but she helped me almost kick the habit, and I think I would of if the church hadn't messed things up. I'm not a religious man, so I don't know anything about why they did such a thing. Then again what was I going to do really though. so I was looking forward to death with this last slap in my face. Well so you can say I loved this sister, even though wasn't nothing I could do about it, plus I don't think they're allowed to marry guys like me."

Everyone chuckled at that comment, and he continued, "So when she called me to help her, I jumped at the chance. So I did everything she asked me to do, save except for one thing. I walked out front with her, and saw that huge gun under John's jacket, and knew I had to find away to protect Beth. Before anyone tells me, I will say that Mary has told me why you carry that cannon all the time. Well anyways, I heard that strange music, and decided to see what was going on. I didn't get much of a chance, because Mary had found me first. I know even at my age I'm a strong guy, but there was no way to fight off Mary. She explained that too. Well after it all happened, I know I didn't have to drink, even though in my own defense, having such a hot lady offer you her blood. Well, I'm just saying, no sane man would ever refuse that."

He turned to Beth and added, "This isn't your fault. When you told me to stay away, after I brought the blood, I knew I should of listened, but instead I thought I would be johnny on the spot, and come and rescue you. I knew I wasn't a kid anymore, and it was a really stupid thing to do. So I guess that's it, except hi I'm Sammy and nice to meet you."

It wasn't what any of use had really expected at all, so there's no wonder that there were a few seconds of silence. Then almost at the same time, Naomi and I jumped to our feet, and moved toward Sammy. Naomi grabbed his hand, and then into a hug, and I patted him on the back. We were both saying, "Welcome to the house."

I moved right over to Mary, and gave her a hug as well and said, "My darling daughter, you have brought what I think will be a very good additive to this great house."

She then gave me the biggest smile, I had only seen once. With that, it was like the ice melted, and every kid went up, and hugged or shook his hand, and welcomed him into the house. The girls all even gave Mary hugs, I sure it didn't mean anything, but none of the boys did that. Joe then asked, "John should I give time to see if anyone else wants to share like Sammy?"

I replied, "I think that's a good idea Joe, but don't make it mandatory though."

So he stood up and said, "Anyone that wishes to share a personal story, may now if they wish."

Beth stood up and moved to the front, "Sammy, I never knew. I can tell you, I always looked at you as a father figure. One I never had. You see I don't want to share much of my story, I just want to share why I've done what I've done. When I turned of age at my home, it got worse then it had been before I had been a teenager. I don't know what's worse having a father that abused you, or a mother that didn't listen to you. You see in the physical sense he loved me, but in the real sense he never really did. So when you, and Johnny showed me all that attention, I thought I was doing some good for once. I became a nun on false pretenses, I don't think when they asked you if you're a virgin, you're not supposed to lie and say yes."

She looked off like she was looking into the past, "I always felt I was being placed into these bad positions, because of that lie. How could you tell the Lord whom you loved so much, that you lied? Then again it says in the good book, he knows your heart, so I thought I was being punished for what I had done. I thought I was finally doing something with you and Johnny though, when they pulled me out of there, though that was it. I knew I had to do something, or go some place to make my life right. I do have to tell all of you though, it was a very hard choice, and threw a lot of prayer and fasting I made my decision. I knew that once I made it though, even if it lead to my death, I had to do it. So when I was asked if I wanted this life or not, it was an almost given conclusion to what my answer would be. Since I made that choice, I've had no regrets."

I then asked, "Even if you're forced to destroy another being?"

She smiled at me and replied, "I don't care to take a life, but the good book says there's a time for all things. A time to plant, and a time to sow. But what is farther poof is it reads a time to give life and a time to take it away. I hope that answers your question John?"

I smiled back at her as I honestly replied, "Not exactly, but as they say, 'Close enough for government work,'"

She then sat next to me again, Joe then asked, "Anyone else?"

A few more talked, but no one really said anything we didn't already know. When Joe finally brought everything to a close, I added, "If you want to share, but not in public. All of the elders will be available to listen to you, even though it would be best to talk to your sire first. Then they can refer you to an elder. I think that's it then, Joe go for it."

Then he finished up, and we had a new family member. The next thing was for all the new couples, even though Naomi and I assured them that was a necessarily truth. I mean I knew that it was probably a lie, but I had to give them as much hope, just in case they were paired with the wrong person. Since Beth was with Tony we had a short talk about that, and it was decided that our bond was probably better then what he had anyways. Now I can tell you, none of us were sure about that, we just knew that the personal bond always seemed to be strong. So Beth set out to move her stuff into my room, which led to a terrible fact. I walked to my room, and realized that the single bed I had was much to small for two people.

I turned and said in a loud voice, "I need help. My room is far to small, and my bed is truly to small. Can someone direct me to a larger room with a larger bed?"

Pepper leaned out her door and said, "There's a room on the third floor that's big. I know the person in it has moved out, you might want to see if anyone else has moved in there?"

"Thank you Pepper."

Then I moved up the steps quickly to see if I could claim the room, in the hallway I saw Beth on the steps for the forth floor struggling to get down to the second floor. As I moved I said, "Beth my room was to small, so I want to see a room Pepper directed me to. Follow me, and I bet it'll be a shorter trip."

I would of stopped to help her, except I knew the way kids are. So I almost ran to the room, and flung open the door. I was surprised at the size of the room, and the size of the bed. I moved to the opposite side of the room, where another door was. It was a large empty walk-in closet. Since it was empty that was one sign of good luck, I then moved to what looked like another closet. I flung that door open to see a bathroom, it wasn't huge, but I could see that it was comfortable. Lastly I moved to the chest of drawers, and every drawer I opened was now empty. With this I now moved to Beth, and helped her the rest of the way. Once that was done, I left her there without realizing exactly how many clothes she had now.

I was coming out of my room, and Pepper met me, and said, "You may want to just take the chest of drawers up, when you get ready to move that. I have three more outfits I found, and I'll give them to Beth to put up."

I nodded to her as I moved everything that was in my closet, and my bedroll this time. When I got back, I saw that Mary and Sammy were now helping Beth. I think Sammy had even brought another load of clothes, well either that, or Beth was carrying a heck of a lot clothes. I put the few hangers of clothes, I did carry in on the opposite side of Beth's clothes. I could see that Beth was carefully sorting threw the clothes, as she did her best to place them evenly. I turned to Sammy and asked, "Sammy do you think you can help me with my dresser downstairs? I think that would be best, so Beth has that whole chest of drawers."

He replied, "Sure I can do that. Hey is it true that Pepper girl gets all of our clothes?"

As we moved down to my room I replied, "She tries, and she does seem to be good at it. Just give her a little while, and she'll have you an entire wardrobe."

We pasted her as she said, "I heard that, and what's wrong with a good wardrobe?"

"Nothing, even though you may have gone a little over board on Beth. Even though I maybe wrong, maybe an ex-nun is a fashionista?"

Sammy had to hide his laughter with a snort, and Pepper came back with, "I heard that."

He then added, "Jesus that girl has good ears."

I then had to cover a chuckle with a cough, as I replied, "Yep." As we moved to the room, I asked, "Do you think the word Jesus would still be offensive to her, now shes not a nun?"

"Not really sure. You could ask her, but it's probably better to just watch your P's and Q's."

It didn't take much thinking to actually say, "Yeah, probably a better idea, then the first one. I guess its a good thing, I don't like to swear anyways."

We then grabbed the dresser, and we moved it quickly upstairs. I mean it really didn't have much in it yet. Well then you have the fact that it was Sammy, and me moving this thing. If it had been a safe we may have had to struggle just a bit, I guess the real reason I needed his help, was the fact that it was big and bulky. When we got into the room, Pepper said it really didn't go with the décor, and had us move it in the closet. Truthfully I couldn't believe the amount of clothes that Pepper had already gotten Beth. I would find out she had a little help from Tony as well. I had always thought their kind had this automatic knack for fashion, but it would truly show itself, when Beth even started to show an knack for it.

Before my entire room seemed to be filled with people helping out, she had chests of stuff and Billy, Sammy, Joe and I had all been drafted to carry it from her room to our new room. Once this was done, the four of us did what the ladies basically told us to do. It did take awhile, but not all night. I did have to wonder how all the kids passed up this room though, they all then gave Beth a hug, and one and two at a time left. Then the two of us were alone in our room now. I had been with a few women before, but it is surprising how crowded a room can be, with just two in the room. She had a six drawer chest of drawers with a mirror, I think that's called a vanity. There was a small chair near that, and an oriental rug that seemed to cover the entire floor. The bed had to be one of those king size ones, it had a night stand on either side. I had to wonder if at one time it had a canopy over it. We were both sitting at a table that had two equally nice chairs, queen Anne I think. With a real old lamp on it, I had to wonder if it had been oil at one time. It also had two of those really nice floor lamps off set in each corner, well not exactly in the corners. But they lite the room very well though.

As I was looking around the room for the real first time, I hadn't noticed that Beth didn't say a word. It was right then, I noticed how deafening the silence was. So as my gaze came around, and I looked at her, she seemed to be only glancing at me. I then asked, "Beth is there something wrong?"

She looked at me with a more complete look, and sighed, "I'm just scared is all?"

"Of what?"

"Well you for one thing."

"Of me? Beth I would never ever hurt you."

"But this is all so fast, I mean we're bonded, and everything. Not to mention that I am a new vampire and all. John how would you like to be a normal human one day, and the next day you were a blood thirsty vampire?"

"Beth that's exactly how I was made. One day I was just a dock worker, the next day my sire was forcing to get him aboard a ship, so he could escape the vampire authorities. In a way I can tell you, your sire is far better then mine, but if you survive till tomorrow, that's one more day, we live day to day."

"Well there's a lot more then that, I also had a life changing religious experience. Then I get bonded to a guy I barely know, and worse I haven't had sex since I was sixteen. John I'm not sure I'm ready to even have sex now. How do you do it? I mean you seem to be able to turn it on and off just like that."

I knew what she was saying, but truthfully it was all an act from being a vampire for so long. Well they always said confession is good for your soul, so I decided to try that. "Beth it isn't that easy. Sure I make it look simple, but I even second guess myself all the time. I guess the best way to put it is, something my father said to me before I disappeared. He said, 'Son a parent does the best he can, but in truth there's no guide book to direct you. All you can do, is put one foot in front of the other, and hope all your decisions were the right ones.' So I could say that I'm doing the best I can, and I hope they're the right decisions in the end." I almost left it there, then I added. "Oh and the thing about sex, don't worry about that."

"But you expect us to one day, to sleep fully in the nude."

"Beth nudity doesn't equate sex. Ok, let me tell you why I made that rule. You, your sire Tony, and Pepper come from a family that after awhile, feel the human body is a beautiful work of art. Not that it isn't, but they feel this must be shown off. You know like a great work of art in a museum. So they make houses dedicated to the beauty of the human body, now I will tell you that there are other families just as bad as your family of vampires. If I did nothing, and just allowed you to sleep with your clothes on, I would be amiss. So in truth, this is as much a learning tool, as it is an act. Now about the sex part, your body is your body, and never let anyone tell you different. So when it comes to sex its your choice, not mine or anyone else's. I will defend that privilege for all of you girls, till the day I'm no more."

I can't tell you if that was it, but with all I said she said, "Good, and I thank you for all the rest of the girls. I think I can do this now."

And just like that, Beth undressed, and I did the same, and we slept together for the first time. For all you guys that may read into that, I mean we just slept together. Keep reading if you want to find out why I made a point to say that.

~Fin~

Next; The Anvil and the Cross

Printed in Great Britain
by Amazon